DEAD

A DETECTIVE LUCY GAUTHIER THRILLER

WEIGHT

NIAGARA NOIR SERIES BOOK 5

LIZA DROZDOV

BOOKS BY LIZA DROZDOV

Blood Relative

Dark Water

The One That Got Away

In The Weeds

A Life Spent Looking

Dead Weight

ACKNOWLEDGEMENTS

Thanks to my dear friend Gail Logan—who I've known since middle school, which is basically forever—for her help with proofreading and her enthusiastic support of the series. And thank you to Rob Hill, whose knowledge of boats and silent electric motors was invaluable. Thanks also to the Damonza team for their fabulous cover design and formatting and to Dr. Sammy Barakat for his pharmaceutical and medical advice.

As always, thanks to my friend Martha Mason for introducing me to PoCo and her beautiful family cottage, which provided the inspiration for Niagara Noir. And I'm very grateful to my cats. Seriously, they did a lot of work on this and my previous books and I've been remiss in not acknowledging them sooner.

The characters and situations in this novel are my own invention and any mistakes in the book are my own.

Most of all, I'm grateful to my mother for inspiring me with a love of reading and of books, and to my children for their love and support.

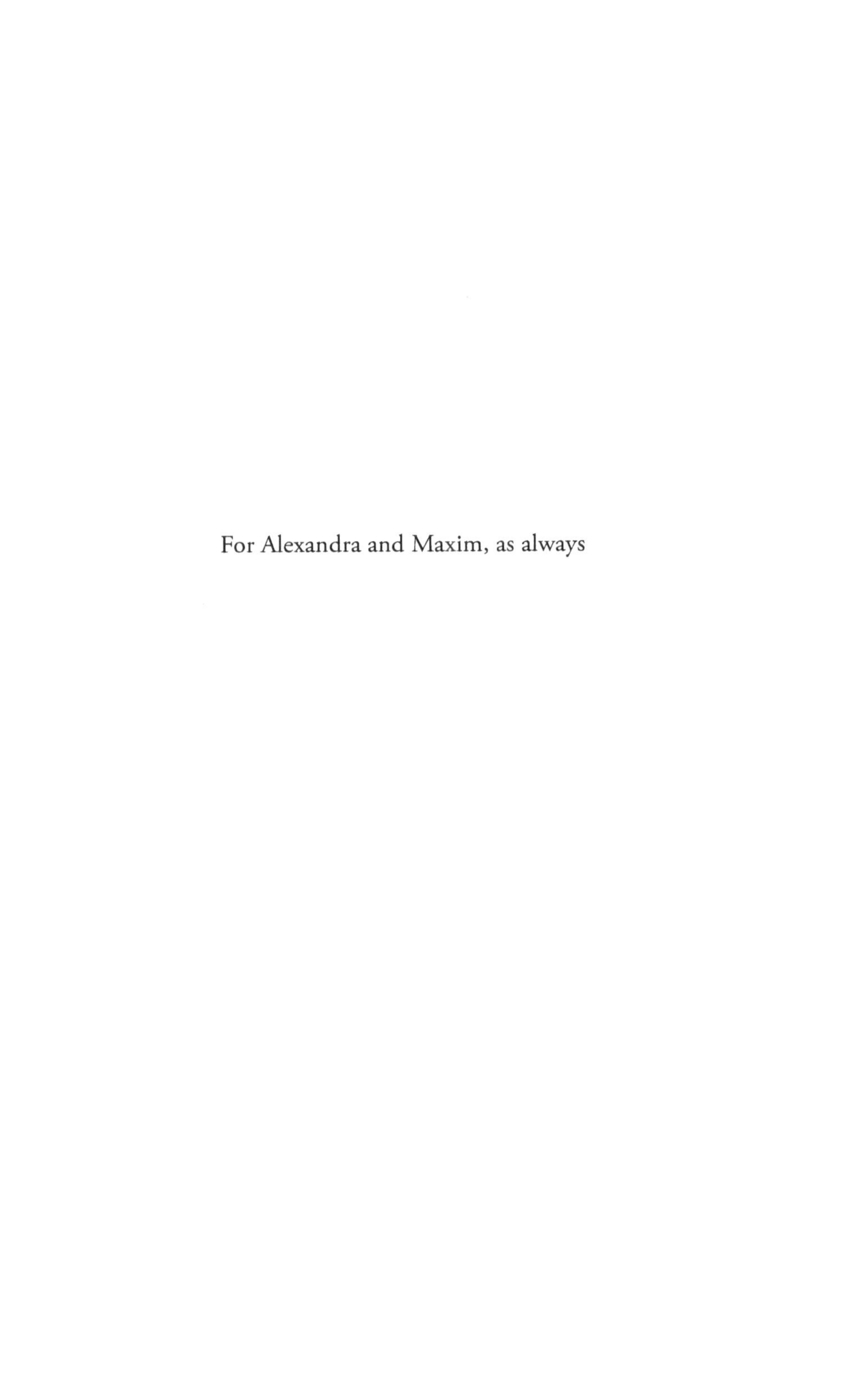

For Alexandra and Maxim, as always

DEAD WEIGHT

ONE

She made me do it. Stupid bloody cow. Always fussing around, watching me. Who asked her?

He wipes the last of the mess from the floor and struggles to his feet.

What did she expect me to do? I warned her. Snooping into things that aren't her business. Spying. Now look what she made me do.

Tossing the filthy towel into the open trunk he slumps against the back of the car, breathing hard and struggling to catch his breath.

This is where that gets you. Stupid cow. It's not my fault.

He slams the trunk shut and makes his way back into the house then slumps into his chair as darkness falls.

TWO

Tuesday

"Body parts before breakfast isn't how I was hoping to start my day," Vogel grumbles as he climbs in the car. He looks like death warmed over. Probably hungover.

"I'll buy you pancakes after, as a consolation prize."

"Waffles, please." Vogel groans then pops a couple of painkillers as I pull out into traffic. "Late night." He leans his head against the headrest and closes his eyes and his self-satisfied expression says he'd really like me to ask how his date went, but I don't bite. I have no interest and know he'll tell me soon enough, whether I want him to or not.

"Where are we going?" he mumbles.

"Just the other side of Gravelly Bay. You could probably have seen it from your balcony, if you were paying attention."

"What is *it*, exactly?"

"An arm." Vogel looks relieved. I get it; an arm's not so bad, given the options. "Found by a guy who was out kayaking. Just floated by as he was launching off the beach by that little point near the Yacht Club."

Within a few minutes we're at the crime scene. The severed arm is now up on the beach, thanks to the work of one of the uniformed constables, who is now soaking wet wet from the waist down. They're both now keeping a close eye on it, as if they're afraid it might crawl away.

The constables fall back to allow Vogel and I a better look, but I'm not in any rush to get closer. From where I'm standing I can see the arm is decomposed and bloated, the skin slimy and yellowish. I'm sure if Vogel gets any closer he'll puke.

"It doesn't really look like a human body part at all," one of them says. "Not at first glance. I'm surprised the kayaker even noticed it."

"He thought it was a dead carp," the other chimes in.

"Where is he now—the guy who found the arm?"

"Just over there," the constable indicates a figure sitting on a bench in the parking lot. "He's not feeling so great." The kayaker is wearing a wetsuit and has his back determinedly to the arm. He's not risking another look.

"You've taken his statement and contact information?" The constable nods. "Then let him go home. There's no need for him to hang around any longer."

I take a deep breath and walk over to the arm, with Vogel and one of the constables following behind.

"Where do you suppose it's from?" I have to force myself to look more closely at it. I think it's male, given its size, but maybe that's from being in the water. Not sure if the bloating would make it seem bigger. "No distinguishing features that I can see—no tattoos, no watch or jewellery. It's just an arm, torn off somewhere above the elbow."

"Torn off?"

"Yeah I'd say so. It definitely doesn't look like a clean cut."

"Where do you suppose it's from?" Vogel looks out across Lake Erie. He's doing his best to not actually look at the severed arm. "A boat out there, maybe a body dump?"

"Or just some poor drowned guy whose arm got torn off by a passing propeller." There's nothing more to see, so we head back to the parking lot to wait for the Forensic Services Unit.

"We need to contact Missing Persons… see if anyone's been reported."

"Wonder where he went in," Vogel says, still scanning the shoreline. "There's not a lot of current here on the bay."

"From the canal, maybe?" one of the Constables interjects. "The Welland Canal locks move about twenty million gallons of water in ten minutes. Maybe when the lock opened the water just… flushed the arm out?"

"It's a thought…" Vogel begins, looking intrigued at the idea.

"… Doubtful," a voice interrupts. It's Jun Song, a Special Constable with FSU, who has just arrived. "Generally speaking," she continues, "water flows downhill—that is, from Lake Erie toward Lake Ontario. The lock doesn't discharge that huge volume of water in this direction—it's going the other way." She gives the Constable a look to make sure he understands. I see his forehead is wrinkled in thought. Nope, he doesn't.

"So," Vogel says. "It seems unlikely the arm came from someone passing through the canal."

Jun holds up her hand. "I'm not the expert here," she says. "We'll have to wait for Todor." I can't suppress a groan. Todor is a dick and I know from bitter experience he's not going to give us anything. Vogel and Jun grin.

"Is there any chance we'll find fingerprints," I ask with a glance at the rotting arm.

"Maybe," Jun says with a shrug. "It depends on the amount of decomposition. There is technology to lift fingerprints from severely decomposed bodies."

"Really?"

"Not here, of course," Jun says, her brow furrowed in thought as she studies the arm. "We'd need to send it into CFS." The Center of Forensic Sciences in Toronto is the leading forensic scientific lab in North America, with facilities far beyond anything we've got in the Niagara Region.

"It depends on how long it's been submerged, how many predators might have had a nibble…" Jun continues, as she inspects the arm. "Water's been cold, which helps reduce bacteria. But sure, the technology exists. They inject the artery with formaldehyde and various agents—basically embalming it to stop decomp. Then they reconstruct the flesh volume of the finger pads so they can get a print. I understand the quality is pretty good," she says. "All things considered…"

An SUV pulls into the parking lot. It's Todor, the Coroner on duty. I immediately head for my car, leaving the chat to Vogel. I am not in the mood to deal with Todor today.

Even though Vogel had three cups of coffee to wash down his waffles he's still barely awake when we leave the restaurant, but at least he doesn't look green. He tosses me the car keys and climbs into the passenger seat, which irritates me. Our understanding is that he drives whenever we work together—because he enjoys it and I don't, and now I'm going to have to reverse out of a tight spot.

"So who is this guy again?" Vogel rubs his eyes and looks pathetic.

"Seriously? Did you sleep through the briefing yesterday?" My irritation grows when I check the rearview mirror. Damn. Some jerk has blocked the car in, probably in a rush to get the breakfast special. I try to back out of the narrow parking spot and fail.

I reverse and take another try at it. Fail.

"Shaun Pearson." I put the car into drive and take another shot, turning the wheel and creeping forward. "He's on day parole, residing at the halfway house on Main Street. Last seen before he went to visit the family home on Sunday morning. Father's Day."

"What's his family say?"

"They wouldn't open the door to him, so he left a card in the mailbox. They say they last saw him walk away, down the street."

"Happy families, eh?" Vogel shakes his head. "Wait a minute," his eyes snap open. "Father's Day was two days ago. Why didn't the halfway house report it when he was first in breach of parole?"

"You tell me."

I tense as the car bumper scrapes against the brick wall. *Damn. Damn. Damn.* Vogel wipes the smile off his face, but not before I see it. He knows to keep his mouth shut. I'd kill him if he tried to tell me how to drive.

"Probably some bureaucrat was hoping to avoid paperwork."

"Did they put a shot of cynicism in your coffee?" Vogel laughs. "Or are you just pissed off about scratching the car?"

"Why would I be pissed off? It's your car Vogel—mine's in the shop so I borrowed yours. Remember?"

As we drive past City Hall we have to slow down to get past a media scrum. There are satellite news trucks and reporters blocking the street out front. Margaret Lawrence, one of our local Councillors, is standing on the top step behind a podium covered in microphones. She's flanked by the Co-Councillor from her Ward and the Mayor, showing their support.

"Asking the media to respect her family's privacy *at this difficult time?*"

Nude photos of Councillor Lawrence were leaked online last week, creating a media sensation across the province. She'd told us—the police—that she was being blackmailed. But she'd called his bluff and refused to pay him what he demanded. This is the result—embarrassment all around and local government doing frantic damage control.

"Doubt it. She's lost her privacy and her dignity. Now she's losing her job."

We cross the bridge over the canal and drive along the island, heading for downtown. I can see the sparkling water of Lake Erie, glistening in the brilliant summer sun. It's going to be hot later today, but since it's a weekday there aren't many boats out on the water yet.

"Didn't we just do this last month?" Vogel says. "Seriously. It feels like these guys are being released on parole and end up just walking away. I've never returned one yet."

"Eight have gone missing in the past two years," I say. "Which you'd know if you'd been paying attention during the briefing."

Vogel gets no argument from me. Offenders like Shaun Pearson may be released to halfway houses on day parole to serve out their sentences in the community. But they're under strict conditions—or they're supposed to be, and one of those is to return nightly to the halfway house. Eight of them didn't comply, nine if you count Shaun Pearson.

There'd been a lot of resistance to the residential facility opening in the first place. The general public disapproved and several people were very vocal about it. *Put that shit in Niagara Falls. Not here.* There was a Letter to the Editor in the paper just last week criticizing the halfway house and its negative impact on the community. Another prisoner breaking parole and going on the run isn't going to look good if word gets out.

Heated debates had gone on for weeks in Council, and legal wrangling for months before that, around the zoning change required to turn a private home into a multiple residence. Once the zoning was changed it would allow for any kind of future development, including condominiums and hotels—and they felt that kind of precedent spelled the end of the heritage district of downtown.

But really, the biggest concern was having these ex-cons and addicts in town at all. Even though there were only going to be a couple of dozen living at Kerr Residence at any one time, nobody felt reassured.

"The locals didn't want these guys living in their neighbourhood in the first place," Vogel says. "They sure won't want to hear another one is at large. Can't say I blame them."

"Look on the bright side Vogel. He might be dead."

THREE

KERR RESIDENCE IS housed in one of the Town's designated heritage properties in the heart of downtown, in the oldest residential area in town.

"It's a beautiful home," Vogel says, standing back to admire the three-story building. "Italianate style. Look at those elaborate eaves and ornate cornices." I try not to roll my eyes as he shows off, but I can't deny the house is beautiful.

There's an historical plaque out front and I pause to read it while Vogel goes on about the architecture. The original house was built in 1865 for a local merchant and at one time the property included stables, a smokehouse, and a carriage house. For the past hundred and fifty years it has been occupied by several generations of the Kerr family, until it was donated to the Town and recently turned into a halfway house.

We need to pass the security entrance to get inside, then we take a seat in the lounge area and wait for our meeting with Joan Morton, the social worker who's run the facility since it opened two years ago.

I feel the dark cloud of resentment forming over my head the minute we're inside, so heavy that I'm surprised Vogel can't see it. Of course, he's caught up in whatever text conversation he's now having on his phone, oblivious to my mood. Probably with whoever kept him up late last night, which leaves me free to look around the room and not have to engage in chatter.

This must have been the front parlour of the original home and it doesn't seem to have been too badly damaged by the conversion from heritage family home to a residential facility for parolees. The original leaded glass windows and carved wood trim are all still in good shape, as is the hardwood floor. But then, I'm only seeing the main room. I expect the upper floors would tell a different story, as they'd have been made into some kind of dormitory for the group home.

Group home. Nothing like the one I'd lived in, for over a year after I'd been released from hospital. I can still remember how it smelled, even though I've worked hard all these years trying to put it all out of my mind, but never able to since it keeps coming up in my nightmares.

On a stand in the corner there's a television, playing with the sound off. Below it on some shelves are stacks of board games, books and magazines. There are two men playing cards at a table in the corner and a couple of younger guys on a couch by the picture window. They're just sitting in silence, amiably looking out at the world passing by. I still remember the endless days and empty hours I spent at the group home, staring out the window, wondering what would happen to me. Not belonging anywhere. Not wanted anywhere. I feel a rush of emotion so strong I don't know if I want to burst into tears or smash something to pieces. I hate it here.

One of the guys on the couch suddenly turns his head and looks at me, his expression intense. It's as if he can hear what I'm thinking. He comes over to sit next to me, too close for comfort. He's wearing a huge shapeless grey hoodie, big enough to hide inside, baggy jeans and new trainers.

"I heard you calling me," he whispers. He's nervous, keeps his head down, face averted. "I'm here now."

"Pardon?"

"You called. I heard the voices calling, over and over. It was your voice." He looks at me. "I know it was your voice. It had to be."

He reaches his hand out toward me and touches my wrist. I instinctively recoil and he gives me a sad smile.

"I love days like this. The trees are so… so green. And the sky. It's blue. Right?" He looks at me for approval. "Not red."

Vogel puts his phone away. I can feel him tense as he overhears the conversation.

"Blue, definitely." That earns me another smile.

"Can I ask you a question?"

I shrug. "Sure."

"Are you real?"

"I am real, yes. Definitely."

He takes a deep breath and closes his eyes in relief.

Joan Morton enters the lounge and waves us into her office. She looks like a typical social services stooge; another pencil pusher, paper shuffler, and bureaucrat mouthing platitudes. I had my fill of those before I was thirteen years old. I hate her on sight and drag my feet behind Vogel, dreading this interview.

"I expect you're here about Shaun Pearson," Morton says as the door closes behind us. The sound it makes as it locks is so loud I flinch and it brings on a memory rush that I work hard to suppress. I work to control the panic rising in my chest and have to clutch at the back of a chair to steady myself for a moment.

"We understand he didn't report in last Sunday?" Vogel says, taking a seat across from her. I prefer to stand, as far away from her as possible.

I wonder if Vogel's noticed my momentary lapse, but decide I can't worry about it. I've worked with him long enough that he's seen it before and to his credit he doesn't push. Mostly.

Morton looks distracted and she shuffles papers on her desk and checks her computer screen, for so long I think she's avoiding meeting our eyes, that she's hiding something. Then I realize she's hiding the fact that she has absolutely no idea what's going on in the facility, and she doesn't care why we're here, not really. My temper flares, but I take a deep breath and count to ten, intensely annoyed with Morton and trying to control myself. It doesn't work.

"Hardly a trivial thing," I snap and Vogel turns in his seat to give me a warning look. I ignore him. "Why didn't you report it immediately?"

Starting out in an openly aggressive and adversarial way isn't going to help anything, but I can't help myself. Morton handles it better than I would.

"It was believed Shaun would be back the next day," she says. "It was thought he'd just had an argument with his father and was taking some time to cool off." Her use of the passive voice just irritates me more. "It was decided we'd give him some time."

"Why do…" Vogel begins.

"By whom?" I demand, interrupting him. "Who made that decision, exactly?" I hear Vogel sigh then he leans back in his chair. He knows there's nothing he can do to stop me now. "I think we need to speak with the staff who work directly with Shaun."

Morton gives me a look, her eyebrow arched. "I take full responsibility for that," she says. "It was my decision." This is all about damage control. She's not about to let us talk to the counsellors who might have something to tell us. Morton works in the office and I bet she's never even met these parolees. They're just names on a piece of paper to her.

"I expect you just didn't want to have it on record that another parolee violated," I say.

Morton glares at me. "That's not the reason," she says. "I was being kind."

I doubt she's got a kind bone in her body. "It wouldn't look good on you. What number does this make it? Nine? Seems very high…"

"Eight. The numbers here at Kerr Residence are completely within average norms," she says. "There is no concern."

I'm stunned. "No concern? No wonder there was such resistance from the community at your being here. If it's *completely average* that eight parolees violate probation."

Morton glares and me, her lips pinched tight in anger. I realize I've gone too far, but it's too late now.

"Why did you think Shaun Pearson had an argument with his father?" Vogel takes over the interview, giving me a look that I know is intended to make me back off. I step back and Morton looks visibly relieved to be dealing with the good cop—not the crazy, angry cop.

"He'd signed out to visit him… it was Father's Day, as you know— a particularly difficult day for most of our residents. When Shaun said he was going to see his father, we had an idea what might happen…"

"You know his father?" I interrupt, and Vogel shoots me a look.

"No, not exactly. We only know whatever Shaun has shared with the team in group sessions or in passing conversation." Again her gaze drifts off to her computer. God, this woman.

"So you guessed how it would go?" Vogel asks.

She nods, reading from the screen. "And I was right. Our first call when a resident doesn't sign in is always to the family—or to wherever the resident has signed out to go visit. His father was… not pleasant."

"So, what did you do then?" Vogel says.

Nothing, I expect. Morton's a typical pencil pusher. Just like the ones at the group home, the ones who did nothing, and so nothing happened except I got beaten up, again. All they cared about then was covering their asses, which I'm sure is the only concern Morton has now.

Morton's tone is conciliatory as she pastes on a diplomatic smile. "Despite what you may have heard about this facility, none of our residents are dangerous criminals or violent offenders. No sexual predators or pedophiles here. Most are young offenders."

"What kind of crimes are we talking about then?"

"Drugs, mostly trafficking. Robbery, extortion, fraud, firearms…"

"Sounds dangerous enough to me…" I mutter under my breath but they both hear me.

Morton looks at me. "You never made a mistake when you were young, detective?"

I have to take a deep breath to stop myself speaking. She has no idea. If I told her half the mistakes I'd made in my life her head would explode. I'm about to make this the worst meeting of her life when Vogel interrupts.

"What do you suppose Shaun Pearson did after he left his father's home?"

"It's difficult to guess," she says. Morton directs her answers to Vogel and even turns slightly in her chair to screen me. Not a good idea. "He might have met a familiar face and gone off with them."

"So you don't think he broke parole?"

"No, I do not. Shaun was a first offender. He did well while in prison and he was definitely on track for full parole." She shuffles some papers around on her desk and shrugs. "He just… disappeared."

"What do you mean, he *just disappeared*?!?!?" I start, but again Vogel cuts me off.

"Any substance abuse issues? Addictions?"

She shakes her head. "Many of our residents are in some kind of rehab, but not Shaun. He's clean." She looks thoughtful for a moment. "I had thought that maybe he'd gone on a bender."

"He drinks?"

"Well, no… certainly not here. Residents are required to abstain from alcohol and drugs as a condition of their release—and to refrain from associations with people involved in criminal activity."

Morton sees me roll my eyes and she gets defensive.

"We're very proud of our security here, detective. We conduct random breathalyzer and urinalysis tests to ensure its integrity. We do physical checks, we have video surveillance, and we carefully document all the residents' movements."

"And yet Shaun Pearson is missing." I'm not letting her off the hook.

"I thought that maybe after being rejected by his father he might have found one of his old buddies and had a few drinks."

"And then he what, he missed the bus, didn't make curfew, and he figured *Screw it, I'll just stay away?*" I hear Vogel take a deep breath.

"Something like that," she says. "It was thought he'd just come back the next day."

"Look—we're like a family here." What a crock of bullshit. I doubt any of the residents buy into it and have to wonder if she thinks we do. "We try very hard to make the residents feel safe, feel part of our community." I have to fight to keep my eyes from rolling.

"What about Shaun Pearson's mental health?" Vogel asks. "Could he have killed himself?" Not that any bodies have been reported, but it could take a few days for someone to wash up on the beach. I try not to think about the arm found floating in the bay.

"I doubt that very much. Jay—who you met in the lounge? He's schizophrenic and not doing so well with his meds. But Shaun had no mental health issues, no depression. He was… fine."

"Is Jay also a parolee?"

Morton shakes her head. "He attends our adult mental health day program.

"{In addition to providing transitional support to those leaving prison, we also work with community support networks and provide them a space to meet clients and offer counselling, as well as mental health support, crisis intervention and controlled medication distribution."

"For addicts?"

"For those withdrawing from dependency." She glares at me, then turns and addresses Vogel, again cutting me out of the conversation.

"Tell us about Kerr Residence," Vogel says. "You seem to do good work." He's good at talking with people, with gaining their trust, and I'm sure nothing will make Morton happier than blowing her own horn.

"This facility was very controversial when it opened," she continues. "There were fierce battles fought over it and they are still going on, two years later. But when the last owner died, the building was left to the community specifically for charitable purposes.

"It sat vacant for a long time," she says. "Too long, while the Trustees dealt with the options for its use. All sorts of people had to weigh in——or got to weigh in, shall I say—pitching their case for why they should have it. Local groups, regional groups. It should have been dealt with much faster, much sooner. Anyway, the social services won the tender. They had the funding available to renovate it as needed."

"Renovate?"

"Whatever group the building went to would have to make interior adjustments to it, allowing for public washrooms, disabled access, offices, whatever they needed to make the space functional. In our case, they also made a big kitchen, ten single bedrooms and six double, most with ensuite bathrooms."

"And security?"

"Of course. That was a priority. This residence is staffed twenty-four hours a day. All exterior doors are locked and alarmed after midnight, until six am. And security cameras monitor all exterior doors as well as the property around the building."

"And yet eight of your residents have gone missing from the facility since it opened," I say. I can't help myself from sniping. "That seems like a lot."

"The national average rate of failure is around thirty-five percent. So maybe *slightly* higher than average." I'd love to argue with her but there's no way I can do the math in my head.

I don't understand how eight men going missing from Kerr Residence over the past two years hasn't made the media. Did the Ministry of Correctional Services suppress it? Certainly Joan Morton wouldn't have wanted that information out in public, but how hadn't anyone in the police force flagged it as a trend, or at least questioned the security of the facility?

"And of these men who've gone missing… I assume many of them have been re-arrested? Are they back in prison?"

"Not that I'm aware," she says after a moment. "But, if they were found out of province I wouldn't necessarily even know about it. The information isn't always shared as it should be."

"Or, they could be living their lives out in the world," Vogel says. "Free as birds."

Or maybe they aren't living at all, anywhere. They could all be dead. Maybe someone's been killing them, undetected and unsuspected, for the last two years.

FOUR

THE MINUTE WE'RE back outside Vogel is back on his phone again. Now it's well past irritating.

"Vogel," I hold my hand over the screen so he can't see his texts. "What the actual fuck are you doing? You've been on the phone all morning—except when you were about to throw up."

His embarrassed expression makes me forgive him, a little. "Sorry. It's just… last night…"

"What about last night? Your *hot date*? The one that clearly kept you up all night?" Vogel's history with women is long, unrewarding and exhausting to hear about. He meets someone he likes, falls deeply in lust for a few days or a few weeks, then she's gone, never to be spoken of again. Based on his behaviour this morning, we're in the first phase.

"C'mon Gauthier." He's getting irritated, but I don't care. "Give me a break."

"No! I won't *give you a break*. You're always on your damn phone. It's annoying and rude."

"I'm not *always* on my phone," he snaps. "But speaking of a*nnoying*—look in the mirror. And while you're at it, try angry. If I hadn't taken over in that meeting you'd have blown a fuse with Morton. You went way past *rude* into belligerent, provoking her like that. What's your issue? You've been nothing but pissy and unpleasant for ages. I understand Maja's leaving, but…"

"Mind your own damn business," I cut him off. "If I'm angry I've got my reasons." Vogel immediately looks so regretful I melt slightly. "Let's get a coffee. You drive, I'll buy."

Vogel starts the car without another word and heads into traffic, leaving me with my thoughts. He's right. I'm always angry, and it's got nothing to do with Maja. Well, almost nothing.

After the time in the group home I was placed with a foster family for over a year, where I worked very hard to be the model child: obedient, polite, helpful and perfect in every way. It worked. They'd adopted me and changed my name to Lucy Gauthier. I'd worked so hard to become someone new I'd almost forgotten that little girl. With any luck one day she'll be gone forever and I won't have to hide behind the mask, afraid to show myself to the world.

But I can't help showing myself. Every time I unleash my anger, I know the real me comes out— if only for a little while, for just long enough to remind me I'm still there.

We're sitting in Gateway Park near Bridge 19 over the Welland Canal, enjoying the morning sun. I'm trying to enjoy my coffee but Vogel is explaining the heritage value of Bridge 19 to me in excruciating detail. His interest in architecture is exhausting.

"It's a classic old bascule bridge, Gauthier. The engineering on those is phenomenal. It's like a drawbridge, open at the top. See?" He's pointing out the features while I make appropriately interested noises. "It's a rolling bridge—do you see that huge counterweight? And the rollers? The counterweight rolls back and the bridge swings up out of the way so the ships can pass along the canal. You wouldn't want to get stuck under one of those rollers while the bridge is in motion."

All I see is a grey metal bridge, one of the several in town I've driven over for years. Some lift up, like the Clarence Street bridge, and some swing up, like the one on Main Street, but apart from that they only time I notice them is when I've got to wait to cross the canal. This bridge is currently closed for repair, and now that Vogel has pointed them out to me, I can clearly see the enormous twin roller tracks on either side of the platform. He's right. I wouldn't want to be crushed under one as it rolls.

Vogel points out the windows on the bridge tender house. They're boarded up and have been for decades now. "All of the Canal bridges are remotely operated now. Shame, really. They could have kept those original windows in place, for the heritage value."

We watch as two men wearing high-visibility vests and hard hats walk near the bridge. They look like a survey crew or maybe civil engineers. There's a white van parked next to the bridge, its back doors open.

Suddenly a couple of cruisers with their flashers going pull up to near side of the bridge, just a few hundred yards from us. Vogel and I dump our coffees and run over, arriving just behind the uniformed constables.

The two men are staring at a computer monitor, with horrified expressions at what they're seeing. Suddenly a diver pops up out of the water, pulling off his mask and regulator.

"Oh my god," he's gasping. "I just puked in my regulator!" He's swearing and rinsing his mask and mouthpiece in the water then he swims over to the ladder they've suspended from the side of the canal and climbs up.

"Jesus! What the hell is that?!?!" He's pale and looks like he might pass out so one of the constables leads him over to the van and sits him down.

Vogel and I approach the two men at the monitor. "What's happening here, Sir?"

"I just called it in," one of them says. "I called 911." The other keeps looking down into the water, a disgusted expression on his face.

"Sir?" I repeat. "What is it? Is someone still in the water?"

He looks up at me, wild eyed, and steps away from the monitor. "Look!" he says. "Look at them!"

I step forward and look into the black and white monitor he has set up on a worktable and see nothing, except some murky water and shadows passing in front of the light cast by the underwater camera connected to the monitor.

"What am I supposed to see?"

The guy looks at me like I'm stupid or crazy. "Dead people!" Then he bursts into hysterical laughter. "I see dead people…" I hear the diver in the van vomit again.

Vogel and I exchange a look. Is this guy okay?

"There are bodies down there," the second man says, as he steps forward and takes charge. "Lots of them." He stands at the monitor and takes control of the remote camera. "Look. Now."

Vogel and I lean in for a closer look then immediately recoil as the camera swims past the decaying face of a corpse. Then the camera pulls back and I can see a full body, standing vertical and swaying gently in the current. The camera moves again and bumps up against another body, this time almost skeletonized, its remaining clothes hanging off bare shoulder bones.

"How many are there?" I hear Vogel ask as I get on the radio and call it in.

FIVE

Within an hour FSU has arrived and a screen has been set up to shield the scene from the public view. At least the bridge is already closed so we won't need to deal with irate citizens unable to cross the canal via their usual route onto the island. With luck anyone driving past will assume the extra activity is just part of the ongoing bridge restoration. The media isn't yet aware of the discovery and we mean to keep it that way for as long as possible. Lucky for us they're busy with the Councillor's nude photo scandal.

Vogel and I are interviewing the civil engineers and diver who discovered the bodies when I notice DS Agu has come out to the scene. Detective Sergeant Quinn Agu is my boss, and he's probably the most impressive police officer I've known.

"Uh oh. Dad's here," Vogel says when I nudge him. "He knows this is going to be a high profile shit show."

I'm actually relieved Agu is here. It takes the pressure off us. He can run the investigation and own the big decisions, which will probably end up biting him at some point when this does become a *high profile shit show*. How could it not? It'll also allow Vogel and I to get on with the preliminary questioning.

"Sorry, who is your employer again?" I turn back to ask one of the inspectors.

"The St. Lawrence Seaway Management Corporation," he

says, glancing at my notebook to make sure I'm writing it down correctly. "We're independent consultants, hired to do inspections for them."

"What are you inspecting? The bridge?"

He nods. "The footings, as part of the bridge rehabilitation. We're also inspecting the canal floor and the gates at Lock 8."

"Is there a structural problem with the bridge?" Vogel asks.

"Not that we've noticed yet. We're always inspecting, looking for wear or corrosion, or maybe damage if a vessel might have struck something on its way through the canal."

"And you use this monitor and remote camera? Why the diver then?"

"The camera doesn't always have great resolution in murky water, or if there's debris. So the diver will go down and do a visual inspection if needed. He's like a back up."

I look over at the diver, still sitting miserably in the back of the van. He'll never forget swimming right into a forest of dead bodies. Poor guy.

"The camera streams a black and white live feed," he continues. "But it records in high resolution. In colour." I see him shudder.

"We're going to need that footage," I say as DS Agu joins us.

"It's of no use to me. Believe me, I never want to see it again."

I take a deep breath, dreading what I need to do now. "Can you please let us take a look at the footage now? Best quality you've got."

Within a minute he has set up the video and pressed play, before turning his back on the monitor. He clearly does not want to see those images again.

This time the high-resolution footage is eerily clear and distinct, and in colour. And, even though it's still shadowy, the light cast by the camera is bright. We can clearly see the tea-brown water flowing through the underwater vegetation. The camera tracks smoothly, swimming through flecks of underwater debris.

It's peaceful, almost serene, until it turns left and reveals what was once a human face, its flesh now bloated and pure white in the camera's light. The eye sockets are empty. The camera keeps moving past the face, tracking further left until a minute or so later it reveals another body. Mercifully this time it's a back view and we can see longish hair flowing like grass above a spinal cord protruding from what remains of a torso. Then the camera cuts off and the monitor screen goes black.

DS Agu joins Vogel and I and we review the footage a second time.

"I don't need to see that again," Vogel mutters as he returns to interview the witnesses. "Guess it's no mystery where that arm came from now, is it?"

Agu watches in silence, then gets on his phone. He orders in police divers and an underwater rescue unit, and additional forensic support from Toronto. I have no doubt he'll get exactly what he asks for, at lightning speed. When Agu says jump the only question is *how high*? He may be just a Detective Sergeant in the Niagara Regional Police Homicide Unit, but his bearing and his deep, resonant voice command respect. And fear, in me at least.

There's nothing much for Vogel and I to do once we've finished the preliminary interviews with the diver and two inspectors. But there's no way I'm leaving the scene; I'm staying for as long as it takes us to fully investigate and retrieve the bodies from the canal.

We've had no choice but to stop all ship traffic, both downstream from Lake Erie and upstream from Lake Ontario, with the full cooperation of the St. Lawrence Seaway Corporation. The huge freighters and assorted pleasure boats will have to hold their positions out in the water until we've cleared the canal. And as soon as we do that we know there's no hope of containing the story. Word will spread and we'll have a crowd to contain and media to feed.

I call Maja to let her know I'll be late but have to leave a message when she doesn't pick up. I'm ashamed of myself, but my first thought is that she's avoiding my call. I can't help it. As the time for her to leave gets closer I get more anxious that she's never coming back to me. A refugee camp in Bangladesh working with Doctors Without Borders is a lifetime away from what we have together here.

It seems like all we do is argue lately, which is the last thing I want to do. She's going away for at least six months and I want our last days together to be happy ones, ones that we'll both remember, and ones that she'll be eager to come home to. But despite everything our conversations end up in a spat, and the romantic evenings we've planned end up as quarrels. No wonder she's avoiding my calls.

Daylight is fading as I walk over to the end of the bridge. They're already setting up work lights and that'll bring a crowd in no time, like moths to a flame. I brief the constables on duty and suggest they call for reinforcements; they're going to need them. There's already a small crowd forming, just of dog walkers and cyclists—people normally passing through the park. But that'll grow exponentially over the next few hours.

"You there," an older man in a fishing hat calls me over. His tone is belligerent and angry, which is guaranteed to piss me off. I may be a public *servant*, but I don't like being summoned.

"Someone jumped off the bridge, right?" A woman says, looking excited at the prospect. "Damn kids are always…"

"I demand to know what's going on," the man in the fishing hat talks over her. "We have a right to know." He looks around for agreement from the rest of the crowd that's forming. I hear some murmurs of agreement and take a deep breath to calm myself. There's always one like this in every crowd, and it's usually some old white guy, a nosy parker disguising himself as a concerned citizen.

"There's been an incident, Sir." I try to maintain an appropriate tone. God forbid we trample on his *rights*. "Please Sir," I continue before ask another question, working hard to keep the irritation out of my voice. "We need everyone to stay clear of the area. Please move back, now."

He glares at me as I wave over one of the constables to better manage the group of rubberneckers and to deal with entitled fishing hat guy.

I'm not the person who should be dealing with the public. It's not something I'm any good at or that I have any interest in. I'm not diplomatic or sensitive or even aware of how I come across—at least that's what I've been told, on several occasions. Apparently even my *No Comment* has attitude, if you believe some people.

Public Information Officers are specially trained in dealing with the public and especially the media. PIOs are adept at handling media questions as well—and as I see a satellite news truck pull up I wish we had one present and in the meantime, media need to be barred from the crime scene. I advise the constables and then beat a hasty retreat. Let someone else deal with them.

When I get back to the bridge the emergency lights are all on. Ten thousand lumens of LED light makes it feel as bright as the surface of the sun. There are several Nomads on tripods, all powered by a generator in one of the police vans.

This intense lighting definitely helps us see what we're doing topside but the real action is all below the water's surface. Down there, police divers are investigating the crime scene.

The divers need to use special underwater lights. Visibility is very poor, thanks to the combination of sediment and silt they're stirring up, let alone the pollution. Because of the particulates and debris in the water it's difficult to see—let alone photograph, the crime scene. When I lean over the bridge I can see the divers and their underwater lights moving like ghosts through the water of the canal, eight meters below the surface.

They're looking for more bodies, and doing both a visual and fingertip inspection, feeling their way along the canal bottom, sifting through the muck and picking up anything potentially relevant, like bones or items of clothing and personal effects that the victims may have lost.

Whenever they find a body the divers set a float to mark the spot. I count eleven, and as I walk back to the bridge one more float appears. Twelve: I wonder if one of them is Shaun Pearson.

We've set up a tent on the bridge to shield the video monitor connected to the diver's camera. But apart from that, there's nothing to see up here. An underwater crime scene has two distinct areas that need investigation: the surface and whatever is submerged. Vogel and I would normally be looking for the point of entry into the canal, tire tracks or the point of entry into the water. None of that applies to this situation given the length of time the bodies have been in the canal, as well as the fact that it's a public bridge next to a busy skateboard park. Any potential evidence that might be on the surface is already contaminated.

Police boats are parked on the canal, screening the divers from view—the crowd is several hundred yards away and the surface of the water is ten feet below, but still. Five media vans are parked at a safe distance and crowds of people have been attracted by the noise, or by social media notices that came across their feeds. It's not every day we get this kind of excitement in our small town and they've got a front row seat.

Vogel and I maintain a safe distance from the horror the video monitor revealed for most of the night. I already know that bloated eyeless corpses will return to haunt me in my sleep. I don't need to see any more and Vogel feels the same. But we can clearly hear the audio feed from the divers' communicators. For the most part it's a catalogue of discoveries, mixed with banter and the black humour anyone would need to do that job. Then Vogel and I stare at each other in shock as the divers report a discovery.

"Their feet are in buckets of *cement*?" We both say at the same time.

"Isn't that a mob thing—concrete boots?"

"Sure, in the movies. It's easier to just shoot someone. Dump the body overboard, out in the middle of the lake."

"This is definitely something else."

We've been listening as DS Agu has been leading the investigation, viewing the monitor and talking with the divers as they inspect the underwater graves. Dr. Lewis Yun, the duty Coroner, is in there with him doing his best to analyze the onscreen evidence. He has already pronounced and he definitely won't be doing the autopsy, but he's stayed with DS Agu for hours now. These bodies are all heading straight to Toronto for forensic examination. It's way past Dr. Yun's level of responsibility and I know he'll be relieved. Maja would have been all over this, if she'd been on duty today. But, since she's heading off to Bangladesh, she's taken leave from her Coroner duties. That's another disappointment—if her leaving wasn't enough; now I won't have her helping me with her medical expertise and insights into homicide cases.

Finally when the grey dawn light begins to break on the horizon DS Agu comes out of the tent and joins Vogel and I on the bridge.

"The bodies are a mix of ages and levels of degradation," he says. "It looks like some have been down there for over a year, though most are more recent. One looks like it's only about a week old. All of them have their feet encased in buckets of concrete."

"I count twelve, Sir. Is that correct?" Agu nods. "There are eight men missing from the halfway house. Do you think there's a connection?"

He thinks for a moment before answering. "It would be a hell of a coincidence if it wasn't." He rubs his eyes in frustration. "Damn. As if this could get any worse."

"How much longer will they be down there?" The divers have been working most of the night, taking shifts underwater. "They must be exhausted."

Agu sighs deeply. "Yes, they're tired. But at least there's not much of a current to fight." Often police divers have to struggle against strong rivers and need to be weighted down and tied together to keep them from being swept away.

"We're bringing the bodies up now, what's left of them," Agu continues. "Not much more we can find."

"How is that being done, Sir?" Vogel asks, scanning the police boats and their equipment. "Won't you need a winch? They'll be heavy." Two large containers are being handed down to the officers on the boat, and Vogel looks at Agu, eyebrows raised.

"Reciprocating saws," Agu says. "We've decided to cut off the feet and bring the bodies up separately from the buckets. It'll be impossible to keep them in one piece anyway. Most aren't fully intact anyway."

I take a deep breath to control my nausea, grateful for the deep water so I won't be able to hear the noise of the saws. Then a horrible idea rises in my mind, like the dark murky water at the bottom of the canal.

"I just hope they were dead when they went in."

SIX

Wednesday

I DIDN'T GET home until six o'clock in the morning and was still too wired to fall asleep, so I had a hot bath to wash off the imagined stink of death before I slipped into bed next to Maja. She was quietly snoring as I spooned her and tried not to cry. I miss her already and she isn't even gone yet.

When I woke up the house was empty. Maja had left for the clinic and the silence felt heavy. *Better get used to it. Maja is leaving in a week.*

After I get dressed I stay in the kitchen, nursing a cup of coffee before I head into the station. When Maja first announced she wanted to volunteer with Doctors Without Borders I fought against it. I tried everything I could to convince her to change her mind about going to Africa. *It's dangerous*, I told her. *There are Civil Wars and child soldiers and famine and militia everywhere. It's a war zone!* The one thing I didn't do was try to understand why she needed to do it.

The Universe must have heard me because Doctors Without Borders have deployed her to Kutupalong refugee camp in Bangladesh, the biggest Rohinga refugee camp in the world. Rohingas speak Urdu, and so does Maja, which is helpful. At least there's no war going on, but the area is prone to floods and mudslides—I've Googled it of course—and monsoon season is coming. I'll never sleep again.

I'm about to leave for the station when my phone rings. I see Doreen's name light up on my phone and feel a rush of adrenaline.

"What's wrong?" I answer.

Her familiar voice rumbles down the line. It grinds like the brakes on my car and reminds me I need to get it in for service. "Why the hell would anything be wrong?"

"You never call me."

"First time for everything," she says. "When are you coming around?"

"I'm guessing soon…" I know when I'm being summoned. "Is an hour okay?"

"I'm not going anywhere."

Doreen lives at Pelham Woods retirement residence up on the escarpment and she's my best source of information about everything in town—and in my personal life. To my constant surprise, she knows me better than I know myself, and she's always reminding me of that fact. I visit her once a week or so and bring her a coffee and cinnamon bun from our favourite coffee shop—the spot we first met, just before I joined the Homicide Investigation team.

I drive up to Pelham Woods and find her in the usual spot, chain smoking with her cronies. As soon as they see me, they all get up and move to another table. Looks like Doreen's instructed them.

"What's up?" I ask, handing her the usual coffee and cinnamon bun.

"You look tired," she evades my question. "Somebody dead?"

Doreen loves hearing about any homicide investigations I'm working on. I think she gets a sense of personal satisfaction whenever someone dies—and it isn't her.

"Yeah. I've been up most of the night…"

"I saw the news," she interrupts me. "Kerr Killer!" She cackles.

I'm stunned. "What are you talking about Doreen?"

She rolls her eyes and takes a deep drag on her cigarette. "Seriously? Dead bodies in the canal? Missing men from the halfway house? Sound familiar?"

Shit. The media has jumped the gun. "We haven't made that connection yet… officially."

"Uh huh. But it's true, right?" I slump into my chair and take a sip of coffee. Doreen's right, as usual.

"Still… it should have come from us," I mumble, not entirely sure why I care. She's going to find out soon enough. Doreen has better sources than the Niagara Police, thanks to her network of elderly friends at the retirement residence. Each one of them is linked to dozens of people and all of them report back to Doreen.

So I spill it all to her: I describe the rotting corpses in the canal, the cement buckets, and the possible connection to the missing men from the halfway house.

After a few minutes I realize Doreen doesn't seem to be enjoying the grisly story with her usual relish. Then she lights another cigarette when she's already got one burning and I feel the bottom of my stomach drop out. Something's on her mind and it's not the dead bodies in the canal.

"What's going on?" I ask, hoping I'm wrong.

"Not sure how to tell you this." She takes her time taking a sip of coffee. "And I doubt you're going to like it."

"What is it?"

"You know you had two uncles," Doreen begins. I suddenly feel sick and there's a rush of blood to my face and neck. I'm breathing quickly and my pulse is racing with anxiety. But I control it, taking deep breaths like my therapist taught me and like I've practiced for years.

"You're right. I don't like it." My mother had two brothers, both addicts and dealers. I've spent years making sure I know as little as possible about either of them. "They're both dead."

Doreen nods. "One of an OD on some junkie friend's couch and the other in jail. Hepatitis C from shared needles."

"You've been keeping track?" I'm not sure why I'm surprised. Doreen always kept up to date with people she knew from the East Village, following rumours, asking around her network of elderly citizens. But I never imagined she'd been looking into my mother's family too. I'd shut that door behind me and was happy to never open it again.

Doreen shrugs. "It passes the time. You probably don't know that Nick had a couple of kids, before he went to prison." My heart starts to beat faster.

"No. I don't."

"With one of the neighbourhood girls. She still works at the discount grocery store—heavy set woman with red hair?" I make a mental note to start shopping elsewhere. My whole life I've made a point of avoiding any contact with my birth family, denying their existence and any connection they have to me.

"How long have you been doing this? Keeping track of my family?"

"Years. Ever since you went away."

"Why?"

"I thought maybe one day, I don't know... Maybe you'd want to know. And if not, no harm done."

"No harm done..." I echo. It doesn't feel like *no harm*... It feels like my world is suddenly tilted to one side and everything I've taken for granted is sliding toward the precipice. "Thanks, I guess."

We sit for a minute in silence, drinking coffee as I process this new information. Doreen lights another cigarette and smokes it defiantly. We're sitting directly under the No Smoking sign and I know there's not one person at Pelham Woods who'd dare challenge her.

"And the kids?" I break the silence. "Are they still around?"

Doreen nods. "The son lives over in Fonthill. He's doing okay, working as a mechanical engineer." *Fonthill. Engineer. I make mental notes. It should be easy enough to keep an eye out for him— and make sure our paths never cross.*

"And the other one?"

"A girl. No idea where she ended up but the road she was on wasn't heading in a good direction." Doreen gives me a look and I know what that means. "Drugs. Haven't heard a thing in a few years now." That tells me the woman has either left town or she's dead.

"So this guy in Fonthill," I'm doing the math in my head. "He's the son of my mother's brother. That makes him my… cousin?" Doreen nods.

I exhale deeply, blowing out my cheeks. In the past couple of years I've gone from being completely alone to having both a grandmother and a half sister. Now this.

"So now I've got a couple of cousins," I shake my head. "I'm not sure what I'm supposed to do with that information."

"Up to you," she shrugs.

"Nothing," I say after a minute. "I'm not going to do a thing. It's worked for years. Unless I need a kidney, what's the point?"

Doreen laughs. "Never much point in turning over rocks, just to see what's underneath. Let them lie. But it's good to know they're there, so you don't go tripping over them."

"Sounds like good life advice."

"It is. *However.*" She pulls on her cigarette and gives me a look. "I think he needs some help." My heart sinks.

"What kind of help?"

"His son is talking about running away."

I have absolutely no idea what this has to do with me. "What do you think I can do? I'm not a social worker."

Doreen laughs. "Honey, you don't have to tell me that. Definitely not your skill set."

"If he ran away from home a file would be opened with missing persons—I'm assuming he's a minor? But until there's a file…" Even still, the last thing I want to do is get involved in a missing person case, when it's my cousin's kid—my cousin I'd rather go back to knowing nothing about. I could just pretend he doesn't exist.

"Oh there's definitely a file," Doreen says with a chuckle. "He's on parole. Living in a halfway house." She raises an eyebrow and meets my eye. "Kerr Residence."

Shit. So that's why she's called me. I'm overcome with panic when I realize the significance of what she's asking me.

"I can't have anything to do with this!" Investigate the disappearance of this guy I want nothing to do with, that I can't dare anyone ever knowing I'm related to?! My entire world, everything I've built, will collapse in on itself if the truth about my past ever comes out.

My heart starts to pound and I feel a panic attack coming on. *Fuck it.* Deep breathing won't control this wave of terror building up inside me. I reach into my pocket, fumbling for my medication. I slip an Ativan under my tongue then start taking deep breaths to try and stay calm.

Doreen just watches me struggle, tears in her eyes.

"I'm sorry," she says. "But I had to ask. Now that this Kerr Killer is out there…"

My head is spinning. "How does he need my help, exactly? He's not missing yet, is he?"

"As far as I know he's still at the halfway house. But I think he's planning on running. He's scared," Doreen says. "And when he hears the news he'll run for sure."

"When did you hear this?"

"Last couple of weeks or so, I'm not sure. It was just some gossip. I wouldn't have said anything except when I heard…"

"Two weeks? Then what's he scared of? We just found the bodies last night."

Doreen shrugs. "Dunno. Maybe he heard some talk? Guys going missing? You'd have to ask him."

I don't want to ask him. I don't even want to talk to him. I'm sorry I even heard he exists, is what I think. But I don't say any of that aloud.

"You do realize I have no influence there, no authority. It's Ministry of Correctional Services. The police only get involved if we're invited—or if something impacts the community outside the facility."

"You're smart," Doreen says. "You'll figure something out."

"C'mon Doreen. Seriously, you really think he'd risk breaking parole—and going back to prison, just because he heard some stories?"

"Maybe not." Doreen shrugs. "But he's just a kid. Not exactly a hardened criminal. Honestly, if he did take off I doubt he'd even know where to run."

"Would his family hide him?"

"Maybe. But he's only got a few months left on his parole. He must be really afraid if he's going to run now."

I try not to let her see my frustration, or my resistance. "Okay, then why are we worrying? Don't borrow trouble, right?"

Doreen gives me an exasperated look. She never asks me for anything, and the first time she does I push back. "Just keep an eye on him, please."

Dammit. It's impossible to withstand the pressure of guilt and I cave.

"What kind of guy is he? What did he get sentenced for?"

"I'm not sure. He was a minor. Trafficking I think."

This makes no sense. "If it's his first offense he wouldn't have been sent to prison, especially if he's so young. There must be more to the story Doreen."

"Maybe," Doreen shrugs. "Maybe he had a gun? I don't have all the details." But she knows enough to drag me into this, and to involve me in my messy family. "Want me to ask around?"

"NO!" That's the last thing I want. God knows where that could lead. I take a deep breath, hating myself, but it's not like I have a choice. "Fine. I'll look into it." I'm already on the canal case. Let's just hope he doesn't end up making it unnecessarily complicated.

"What's his name?'

"Melnyk. Same as yours was," she says. "Nick Melnyk, like his father's." *Melnyk.* My birth name.

It's still early when I leave Doreen's and my heart is racing, despite the Ativan. I'm feeling palpitations, chest tightness and pressure and know I need to do something physical, now, so I head for the gym. An hour of weight training and some bag work might help me work off some of the anxiety and rage I'm feeling. When my anxiety takes hold I'm unable to concentrate or focus on anything, except my repetitive thoughts and my racing pulse. I feel like all of my senses are heightened and on overload and I want to run, blindly, without knowing or even caring where to, and I have to do something physical to burn it off. If I don't do something to release the adrenaline and cortisol flooding my nervous system I'm afraid I'll explode. Or I'll lash out and hurt someone else—maybe even someone who doesn't deserve it.

I know I'm dangerous. It's self-harm, but I'm driven to do it anyway when the anxiety becomes too much. When I can't stand it anymore I have to do something, and this is what it is. I feel the intense impulse building before it erupts. I'm irritable, my thoughts race and I have palpitations and pressure in my head.

My shrink calls it IED—Intermittent Explosive Disorder, not exactly like the bomb. It's caused by childhood trauma. But labelling it and identifying it doesn't make it stop, and if you'd been through what I have you wouldn't judge me too harshly. It's a constant, grinding anxiety I control through meds, and meditation, and exercise, and more meds.

My response is my responsibility, my shrink says. Of course it is—I'm responsible for the disproportionate aggressiveness, for the explosive anger impulses and destructive behaviour. But I can't restrain the violent impulses and aggressive acts that get triggered, and part of me doesn't really want to. Despite the havoc my anger can create, the damage done isn't to myself—it's to someone who deserves it, if I can find them. Believe me when I say that feels empowering. I was a victim for a long time and there's no way I'm ending up like my mother did.

SEVEN

Predictably, media is camped out in front of the station and as close as they can get to the crime scene. DS Agu hasn't issued any public statement, but the witnesses who were on the scene last night have done their part, and the media has done the rest. The story even bumped the nude photos of the Councillor off the front page, so at least someone will be happy.

The headline Kerr Killer is plastered on the front page of the local newspapers and further down, next to photos of the crime scene is the smug face of the man in the fishing hat. The caption identifies him as Warren Kerr, chairman of the local historical society, keen fisherman, and member of one of Town's founding families. I guess that's where his pushy, entitled attitude comes from. No wonder I didn't like him.

DS Agu is standing in front of the white board, with DC Evans recording, as usual. He's always stuck with that job because he's got the best handwriting of anyone on the team. Seriously, it's like he was once a graphic designer or elementary school teacher.

The board is already loaded up with the mug shots of all the missing parolees, their date of disappearance, reason for incarceration and any other potentially relevant data.

"We had no choice but to stop looking just after five-thirty this morning, and we've had to re-open the canal. Over three thousand cargo ships use the canal every season and we're under enormous pressure from local, provincial and federal governments. Not to mention the St. Lawrence Seaway Corporation."

"But, we've got the bodies," Agu continues. "And the buckets."

"Buckets?" "What buckets?" Several voices around the room mutter.

Agu signals for Evans to begin the video. He's certainly got a gift for the dramatic and the room falls silent, apart from the sharp collective intake of breath when the first corpse makes an appearance.

"The victims were all weighed down in five gallon plastic buckets filled with concrete. Both the buckets and concrete appear to be generic, available anywhere, but FSU is checking them for forensic evidence, just in case."

"Our killer will need to have access to a place to mix the concrete, prepare the buckets and possibly to keep the victims until he disposed of them—whether alive or dead. We'll need to look into sales of concrete and see if anyone has been flagged as buying an unusual amount."

"We haven't identified the remains yet," Agu says. "But we can't ignore the coincidence of twelve bodies being found not six blocks from the halfway facility from where eight men have disappeared from over the past two years."

"The media's already done it for us," someone says. *"Kerr Killer."* A muttering goes through the room and Agu holds up his hands for silence.

"The water is between 8 and 10 metres deep in the area, and the bottom is thick with sediment and littered in shopping carts and bicycles and god knows what else, which made it difficult for divers to continue the search.

"We retrieved twelve set of human remains from the canal, not all of them complete. Divers did a fingertip search, but were unable to find all the skeletal fragments. Bodies decompose quickly underwater, and the remains have been skeletonized by whatever fish or turtles or whatever else will eat flesh…"

"*Fish?*"

"Channel catfish and gobies will consume soft tissue from carcasses of larger fish, so it's likely they've eaten our bodies."

"I'm never eating fish again," Vogel blurts amid groans of disgust from around the room. "Not gonna happen."

"We did, however, manage to find all twelve skulls, so identification will likely be possible, based on dental and DNA records." Agu pauses and looks around. "We know the dates the men disappeared from the halfway house—which is not necessarily the same as the day they died. They may have been held somewhere for a time before they were dumped."

"We don't know how long the bodies were in the water or how they were killed. The skeletal remains and badly decomposed bodies aren't going to be able to tell us much, but preliminary evidence taken from the newest cadaver suggests they were breathing when they went into the water."

"*Alive? Wouldn't they make some noise?*" Questions erupt around the room. "*It's a public area! How could it not be witnessed? What about cameras?*"

Agu holds up his hand to restore the room to order. "The St. Lawrence Seaway has IP Video surveillance all over the canal and bridge, and we've put in a request for the footage. Apparently they all have night vision mode, but we'll see what we get when it arrives."

Agu points to the map of downtown. "The bodies were found here, under Bridge 19, just down from Lock 8 in the canal. They were all grouped here, close to the canal wall."

"Across from the skate park?"

"Yes, "Agu says. "Basically, right downtown. Someone managed to get the victims onto the bridge and dump them over the side and into the water, unseen."

Everyone in the room shakes their head in disbelief. How is it possible that twelve men could have been placed in the canal in such an exposed and public place?

"The canal bridges are all remotely operated by controllers who monitor and coordinate vessel traffic from a control center in Thorold. After dark there's no canal personnel around, and in any event it's unlikely we'll find any eyewitnesses at this point.

"The Seaway Corporation has been doing some regular maintenance—stabilizing the banks and anchoring the floor of the canal—which is what the inspectors were doing there yesterday when the discovery was made. They were doing some testing before they proceed with the work."

"Why wouldn't they wait until winter? Isn't the canal drained every year, for maintenance?"

"No… it's not drained between Lock 7 and 8, since there's no operating equipment in that twenty five kilometre stretch. And obviously it can't be drained between Lock 8 and the lake."

"So that's how the Kerr Killer knew to dump the parolees? He knew they'd be there, undiscovered, for years?"

Agu holds up his hand, calling for silence. "First—I don't want to hear anyone of you say *Kerr Killer* again. Second—let's not get ahead of ourselves. We don't have confirmation of the identity of our victims yet. While it seems probable that eight of the victims are the missing parolees, but we have no proof yet.

"As for the other four, we have no idea who they may be. Forensics is working on that now. In the meantime, what we need to do is follow up on the missing parolees, to learn what we can, beyond their criminal records. Most are local, some are from

Toronto and points further east. And, if and when the time comes as I suspect it will, we'll have to deliver notices to their families."

When Agu assigns us parolees to follow up Vogel and I end up with Shaun Pearson. I breathe a sigh of relief I won't have to involve myself in Doreen's investigation, at least for the time being.

EIGHT

VOGEL AND I walk along the canal, looking at the scene of crime in daylight. We've walked all the way up to the skate park, turned around and come back to the public wharf. It's a small tie-up dock on the west side of the inner harbour, just south of the bridge, mostly used for small craft waiting to enter the Welland Canal at Lock 8.

Looking down into the black water of canal I feel a chill. I'm not a big fan of water in general, especially when I can't see the bottom. It's dark and cold, and even if I didn't know for a fact there were bodies down there I'd have assumed as much. And monsters. Definitely monsters.

The bridge alarm sounds and warning lights flash as the barriers descend to block traffic. The bridge starts to lift as a huge freighter glides towards us along the canal, its massive bulk blocking the sun and dwarfing the small craft tied off along the wharf. If the freighter went even slightly off course it could easily obliterate the smaller boats.

"Look at that, eh Gauthier!" Vogel's grinning with excitement. "It's a Laker."

"Laker?" I try to show some interest.

"They stay in the Great Lakes," he says, staring up at the enormous rust coloured ship as it powers its way past us. "Not like a

Salter—they're ocean going vessels. You can tell by the shape of the bow. And the wheelhouse—this one's in front, so definitely not a Saltie." Vogel stares at the ship, shaking his head in admiration.

"My father used to bring me down to the canal all the time when I was a kid," he says. "We'd have ice cream, look at the boats, and he'd explain it all to me."

I try to suppress the rush of irritation at yet another of Vogel's happy childhood memories. We used to come over the few blocks from the East Village to play by the canal when I was a kid, but mostly we just threw rocks at the ships. Sometimes we'd dare each other to jump in, down by the old canal near the Clarence Street bridge. And if we had ice cream we'd have bought it from beer bottle empties we returned for cash or maybe pilfered from our parents' pockets.

"See how low it's sitting in the water? Its cargo is full of coal or grain or steel, heading right up the St. Lawrence to one of the ports on the coast. It's a small one though." He sounds disappointed.

"Looks pretty big to me."

"No," he shakes his head. "The biggest Lakers can't even fit through the canal—too wide and too long to fit the locks. And big Salties can't take a full load because fresh water isn't as buoyant so their draught is too deep for the canal."

An idea starts to take shape. "Vogel, what did you just say?" He looks confused. "About the depth? Or was it the width?…" He repeats himself, but I'm not listening.

"… I think I know why the bodies were found along the side of the canal, not the middle," I interrupt him. "It's not because it was more convenient—he wanted to keep the bodies intact!"

"I don't follow."

"The killer knew if they were dropped in the middle of the canal they'd be cut up by passing ships. They'd never be found, or they'd be in bits scattered all over the place, buried under silt."

"You think he wanted them to be found?"

"He knew they'd be discovered eventually. And he wanted us to know who they were, to be able to identify them."

"Why would he want us to know he's killed parolees from Kerr Residence?"

"Maybe making a point?"

The freighter has passed and now the bridge alarm sounds and the bridge lowers again. The barrier goes back up, allowing traffic to flow and Vogel and I make our way along the pedestrian walkway to the center of the bridge.

"I really don't see how anyone could bring a body up here, heave it over the railing into the water without being seen. Cars go by all the time…"

"Not much traffic at night."

"Yeah, but still. It's a big risk to take."

"The bridge is wide open," I say. "And there's no way he'd have been able to do it from the side of the canal," I say. "It's all fenced off. How'd he even get to it?" The entire canal is secured on both sides with eight-foot tall fence, topped with barbed wire. Behind the fence several sets of concrete steps with rusty handrails lead down to the water. It looks like they haven't been used in decades.

"There are access gates for staff, but they're all secured with padlocks," Vogel says. "Someone must have a key." Vogel says. "We definitely need look into their staff, see if anyone is worth investigating."

"It's easy enough to cut wire fence," I say, speaking from childhood experience. "Let's see if there's been any vandalism reported that fits the time frame of the body dumps." I turn to watch the freighter disappearing in the distance as it enters the lock and idea takes shape in my mind. One so obvious I can't believe it hasn't occurred to me earlier.

"What if he used a boat?" Vogel nods as he considers it.

"Sure. You'd need to come up from harbour to the opening of the canal, under the Clarence Street bridge, all the way up to this spot…"

"Exactly," I interrupt. "Carefully choosing your time so you aren't observed, you just drop the body over the side. Right here, off to the side and away from the big ships' hulls, where you know it'll be found one day."

"No fence to cut, no heaving a body over the bridge railings, no risk of being seen from the skatepark." We start back along the canal, heading back toward the harbour.

"So, what kind of boat are we talking about? Something smaller than a Laker I'm guessing. Any way we can trace who has access to the canal?"

Vogel takes a deep breath and thinks it over before he replies. "Yes and no. If you're actually going through the canal—all the way through from Lake Erie to Lake Ontario or the other way around—you'd need to book it and pay for it. So, yes, there's a record of those boats. But if you're only coming up as far as the first lock, then, no."

"Nothing? Really?"

"Boats aren't supposed to be this far up the canal, unless they're passing through the Lock. I'm sure they'd be seen—and sent packing."

"If you were noticed." Vogel nods. "So maybe he did it at night? Seriously, who's even going to see anything? The bridges and locks are all remotely operated, right? Nobody keeping watch."

"I'd hate to bring a boat up here at night, Vogel says. "Look at the scale of everything! It's designed and built for commercial shipping. The bollards and mooring points are huge. Your fenders would be covered with creosote in a minute."

"What's that?"

"It's a preservative they paint on dock pilings. It's black and oily and really hard to get off your hull."

"Something tells me whoever used his boat to dump bodies isn't going to be that fastidious about it."

"So, not likely a luxury yacht?" Vogel smirks. "What about a fisherman?"

"They're up early, right? Before the rest of the world is even awake."

"Can't just leave it at fishermen," Vogel shrugs. "Lots of people have boats."

I recognize that tone. I've heard it from Vogel before, whenever I find out things like that he went to Ridley College, or that his parents have a place in the Caribbean, or that he's gone duck hunting with the Chief of Police. The tone people who were raised with money have, but don't want anyone to know it.

"You've got a boat." He looks away and attempts a casual shrug. "I bet it's a big, fancy, expensive speedboat. Right?"

"It's not a big deal Gauthier. It's just an old Chriscraft cabin cruiser. You know I like fishing."

"I do?" Honestly I have no idea. Vogel does go on… and I admit I often just tune out.

"You can't fish without a boat," he continues." It's moored right here—at Sugarloaf Marina. There's great fishing along here—anywhere along the shore out of Fort Erie. It's shallow and rocky, but the water's pretty clear and there's lots of bass. You can usually see down fifteen or twenty feet."

Vogel doesn't even care that I'm not listening. I sometimes think he talks to soothe himself. Maybe I should suggest he try anxiety medication. It works for me.

While Vogel's droning on about fish I see a figure out at the breakwall in the harbour.

"Over there, on the pier on the east side of the harbour," Vogel is pointing out past the lighthouse. "It's great for perch and small mouth bass. You'll always lots of boats here…"

"What about there," I interrupt. "Out on the breakwall?" Vogel sees the man, who's climbing in and out of a boat, carrying something.

"He's definitely not fishing," Vogel says, eyes narrowed.

"How about showing me that boat of yours?"

NINE

Vogel's boat is docked in a slip at Sugarloaf Marina and within a few minutes he's piloting it out into Gravelly Bay, heading for the breakwall. As we leave the marina we pass a huge boat moored right at the end of the outermost slip.

"Is that a yacht?"

Vogel grins. "That's a Carver C52 Command Bridge, Gauthier! It's got two luxury staterooms, a washer and dryer, and a chef's kitchen. You could live on it. It's so trim, so sharp…"

I can't help roll my eyes. "And it's even carrying a mini-boat on its back…"

"That's a *dinghy*, and it's on the *swim deck*," Vogel corrects me.

"So, definitely a yacht then," I stand corrected. "What's it worth?"

"About one and a half million dollars. Ish."

"*Ish*? For a boat?"

"A *yacht*, Gauthier. A yacht."

I realize we aren't moving very fast and decide it's so Vogel can take a good long look at the yacht. I'd really prefer to get over to that breakwall, and out of the lake, as quickly as possible. I'm starting to perspire and my breathing is becoming shallow and rapid.

"Can't you go any faster?

"There's no wake," Vogel says, pointing to a sign. "Can't go faster than 10kph within 100 meters of shore. "

He glances down at my hands, white knuckles gripping the rail. "Relax Gauthier. He's not going anywhere." I'm not tense because I'm afraid he'll get away. I'm just scared of the water, but Vogel doesn't need to know that.

It's only a couple of hundred meters out and I keep my eye on the guy out there the entire time. Not just to see what he's up to, but to avoid looking down at the water below me. It's dark and deep and despite what Vogel said about it being clear and great for bass, all I can think is how it looks bottomless. I don't like it and I have to consciously practice my deep breathing the entire time. Luckily the engine noise is too loud for Vogel to keep up his usual small talk and I can focus exclusively on not having a panic attack.

But Vogel's not stupid. "You don't like boats?" I shake my head. "You can swim though, right?" For a minute I think he's going to insist I put on a lifejacket.

"Yes I can swim," I snap. "I just don't like deep water." I can't even bring myself to look over the side into the dark, cold blue depths.

Vogel laughs. "You like to see the bottom, right? Like in a pool?"

"Or a Caribbean beach, yes."

"Look, Gauthier," Vogel takes my arm. "It's just like driving a car. Easier really, since there's not much out on the water to run into." He places my hands on the wheel and steps back, letting me take control.

I feel a momentary rush of fear then once I understand I'm in charge it's instantly gone. My anxiety is always about things I can't manage, things being out of my control. I can manage this boat and that is empowering. I feel my breathing return to normal as I turn the wheel back and forth, feeling the boat respond.

"How do I make it go faster?" I ask.

Vogel laughs. "You've just learned to walk, let's not run, okay?" I roll my eyes and he shows me the throttle and how to pull it back to slow down or push it forward to speed up, which I do.

"It's not a speedboat! Take it easy." He takes the wheel and pushes me aside. "That's your first lesson."

Vogel speeds up enough that I can feel the spray on my face, and within a few minutes we're pulling up alongside the east-west breakwall, at the point where it joins the south arm. At the intersection is a pile of limestone boulders and gravel and the figure of a man.

As we get closer I can see he's working on something, but he's not wearing a uniform that would indicate he's on legitimate business. He looks up when he hears our boat approach, his expression more irritated than curious.

Then he waves his arms and starts to run toward us, shouting something I can't quite hear but that's clear enough from his gestures.

"Stay off! You can't tie off here!"

Vogel cuts the engine and waits until the guy gets nearer. "We're with Niagara Regional Police," he says, showing his ID. "We'd like to speak with you."

"Please leave, now." The guy looks desperate. "You're disturbing the nesting sites." I look around and can't see anything but piles of rocks. Is he kidding?

"What if we pull in down there?" Vogel points to the far end of the breakwall, about four hundred meters away, closer to the lighthouse and helipad. "Will that be better?"

He grudgingly agrees and Vogel pilots the boat to the far end, where he stops next to another small boat and we wait as the guy makes his way down the breakwall to meet us. His hair is long and he's got a beard, but it's not styled so he looks more homeless than hipster. He's really twitchy and agitated and his eyes keep flitting back and forth. My first thought is that he's hiding something. Or maybe he's high.

As we approach the lighthouse, hundreds of large black and white birds with long necks take off, making grunting and croaking sounds like frogs or flying pigs. I'm liking this breakwall less by the minute.

Vogel hops out of his boat with amazing agility for such a big guy, ties off the line and then helps me climb out onto the rocks. I practically kiss the ground I'm so relieved to be on solid land—even though a narrow breakwall held up with a pile of rocks doesn't seem all that solid to me.

"You can't be here!" The guy actually seems like he's losing control and could possibly get violent. "There are signs!" the shouts at Vogel and points down the breakwall.

I hold up my hands, trying to calm him down. "Okay, how about we stay in the boat?" I suggest. His eyes narrow as he considers my suggestion. Then he nods and I climb back into the boat. Vogel doesn't want to give in.

"Vogel," I hiss. "Get back in the boat!" Once we're off the breakwall the guy seems less hysterical, but he's still clearly resentful of our presence.

"We need to ask you a few questions." Vogel repeats, holding up his ID again to reassure him, but I'm not sure it makes any difference.

"What about?" he asks.

"Let's start with who you are," I say. "And what you're doing here."

"I'm Andrew Croft. I'm doing research on shorebirds and their nesting sites." Vogel and I clearly look confused. He shakes his head and starts to speak very slowly. "I'm a student? From Brock University?"

"Nesting sites?" I look around the barren concrete and piles of stone. "Here?"

"Yes, *here*. We're looking at Common Tern and Ring-Billed Gulls colonies. It's part of a long-term research study."

"*You're serious?*" Why would any self-respecting bird nest here? Even the strange grunting black birds infesting the lighthouse must have some standards.

I've clearly pissed him off, so he starts addressing his replies to Vogel, but he never raises his head to actually look at us. In fact, Croft never makes eye contact with either of us and he's constantly twitching, pulling at his sleeves and collar of his worn shirt or brushing his hair off his face. His tics and peculiar mannerisms tell me Croft is either an addict or is dealing with some mental health issues.

"There are large numbers of Terns and Ring-bills nesting here," Croft points down the breakwall. "And at another colony on a landfill just over there." He gestures across the water to the east side of the mouth of the canal. "These colonies represent globally significant numbers of Ring billed Gulls. Both species are under threat, from human disturbance and destruction of their nesting sites."

"*Under threat?* There must be hundreds of birds here," I say.

"Those are cormorants," Croft says, his voice full of disdain. "They're a threat to the tern nesting sites."

"Oh?" Vogel acts interested, using his superpower of making people comfortable and willing to talk with him, in a way I'll never master. "In what way?"

"They've destroyed trees by stripping off the bark to make their nests. And their guano is very acidic—it kills any plants and vegetation." There's certainly lots of guano all over the place and I can't see a single tree out here, so it looks like the cormorants are very good at what they do. Still, I'm not sure why the terns just don't move to a more hospitable spot, with nicer neighbours.

"So, what are you doing here today?" Vogel asks.

"Monitoring. I'm helping keep watch until the breeding season is over. To protect the fledglings," Croft says. "Any disturbance at the tern colony at this time of year can have disastrous consequences. Gulls will eat the eggs and chicks if the parents are frightened away from the nesting site. And if the juveniles attempt to fly away in a panic they'll end up in the lake and drown."

"You aren't allowed here," he repeats, pointing to a sign that says trespassing or disturbing the birds is prohibited by law. "The colonies are protected by law. You should know that."

"Actually, we weren't sure what *you* were doing here," Vogel lies. "Which is why we came out to investigate."

Croft looks chastened. "We've had vandalism to some of our equipment in the past," he mumbles. "Destroyed our blinds too."

I spot several bags of commercial concrete mix lying in the bottom of Croft's boat. I nudge Vogel.

"What are you doing with this?" I ask, pointing to the concrete.

"We use it to fortify and build their nesting sites. We have to artificially manipulate the substrate to improve nest-site selection—which of course contributes to successful breeding."

"You're building them nests?" I blurt. "Out of concrete?" I've never heard anything so ridiculous.

"Yes," Croft looks at me like I'm the one who's nuts. "On rafts, covered with sand and gravel. And we also build some here on the stones."

"Doesn't seem like a very comfortable nest," I mutter and Croft shoots me a dirty look. But Vogel nods and acts interested, which seems to get Croft excited. He probably thinks he's found a fellow bird fanatic.

"Many seabirds require open areas of sparse vegetation to nest," he says. "So we create those by creating artificial rafts—islands, if you will. Some have driftwood and sedums and even decoy birds. Last year, we had terns successfully nesting on these floating rafts we installed. Over 150 fledglings were counted!"

"You do a count?" I ask, but he replies to Vogel.

"Every year, the third week of May. This year there are also pair of Herring Gulls and a few years ago a pair of Great Black-backed Gulls nested here, for the first time!"

"Decades ago, when the study first began, a major storm washed all of the nesting material into the lake, leaving just these bare concrete slabs. So we redistributed rock and gravel from the rock pile to make the site more attractive for nesting. We have to do it every year. By hand."

"That's a big job," Vogel says. "You're clearly very committed to the study."

"Oh yes…" Croft smiles. "We also built some control rafts of just bare concrete and gravel—similar to the breakwall. But they had much lower success rate of nesting. So, I'm creating some new ones, on a concrete base, planted with a thin layer of grasses and sedums. We'll also provide a variety of nesting material, early in the spring—some small sticks and pebbles, driftwood and feathers. They can select whatever they'd like to use…"

"Fascinating," I interrupt. If I let him I'm sure he'd happily go on all day, and Vogel would let him. "I wonder if you can tell us anything about who else you might have noticed out here. Anything… unusual?"

"You mean, like, birds?"

"No, like people."

"Well there are lots of people who come by here, in boats. Fishing, mostly. I don't really pay attention." He shakes his head. "It's unbelievable really. These guys are out here every day, all day, *fishing*! Obsessive." I have to bite my lip to keep from laughing. Pot meet kettle.

The cormorants we scared off have returned, and are now

alighting all over the lighthouse and breakwall. Croft glares at them, pure hatred on his face.

"Do they disturb your birds?" I ask.

He shrugs. "Not as much as gulls since they don't prey on the chicks or eggs. But they destroy the habitat."

"Anything you can do about them?"

"Shoot them," he says. I'm sure from his tone he thinks of it often.

"Is that legal?"

"They're now considered a game bird," Vogel answers for him. Figures he'd know. "But they're inedible. Tough, taste like fish and full of PCB."

"Hunting season doesn't start until September though," Croft adds, glaring at the birds. "Bag limit of fifteen a day." That seems like a lot to me. It wouldn't take a cormorant hater more than a season to kill every bird on this breakwall. Sounds like a recipe for extinction.

"You sound disappointed," I say. "I thought you liked birds."

"Not all of them."

We climb back into Vogel's boat and slowly leave the breakwall under Croft's watchful eye, doing our best to not disturb the birds.

"That's one very peculiar man," I say. "Who happens to have a boat full of concrete bags."

"Doesn't mean he's our guy," Vogel says as he casts off. "Could be legitimate. I mean, the guy obviously is building bird nests out there. I'd say he's harmless."

"Still. Let's do a background check on him. Make sure that's all he's doing."

TEN

Vogel docks his boat and ties it off then we walk along the floating docks heading for the marina.

"Hello! You there!," a voice booms out. We turn and see a portly older man shouting at us from his boat. It's the guy with the fishing hat, docked at a slip near us. I brace myself for another encounter.

"Hello, Sir…" I hesitate. I've forgotten his name, but I remember him announcing it that night, as if I should know him.

"Warren," he says, with a big smile. "Warren Kerr. We met the other night… at the bridge? I was there when they first discovered those bodies in the canal."

"Of course. I remember you, Sir." How could I forget? He was the entitled pushy guy demanding information. I wonder how long he'd stood behind the police barricade that night, watching the investigation.

"*Sir?!*" He laughs. "Call me Warren. Everybody does."

I'm instantly on my guard. I've seen guys like this too many times to fall for it. These old guys, acting all jolly and friendly when they're just trying to get some information and get close to investigations. They try to offer help and advice, as if they know something useful, when they never do.

Anyway, this guy certainly wasn't jovial at the bridge. If I was a nicer person I could say maybe he'd been having a bad night—he wasn't alone in that. Then Warren's demeanor abruptly changes. He looks nervous and I think he's afraid of Vogel and me, but then I realize he's looking over my shoulder at someone behind me. When I turn all I see is Jay, from the halfway house, shuffling toward us.

But when I turn back to Warren and he's smiling again, raising his hand in greeting and I think I must have imagined it. "I'll just be a minute Jay," he says as he turns back to his boat. "I'm just finishing up, then I'll get the fishing tackle ready."

Jay waits patiently, keeping a safe distance from Vogel and me. I have no idea if he remembers meeting me and I can't think of any good reason to mention it, so I remain silent.

"Nice boat," Vogel says, heading along the slip and peering into Kerr's boat. "Looks brand new. A Bayliner!" He looks very impressed.

Warren has disappeared from sight but I hear his voice coming from somewhere onboard. "Thanks. New to me anyway. I just bought it last month."

"Beautiful," Vogel waves me over. "Gauthier, come look at this! Nice downriggers!" I have no interest in the damn boat, but can't exactly refuse to admire it, so I stand next Vogel and pretend to be interested. It's big, mostly white with blue stripes and I can't help but notice some smears of black tar along the boat's sides.

"A Helix fish finder! Sweet!" Vogel's getting excited. "You must know the best spots."

"You bet!" Warren pops back up into view. "I know this lake like the back of my hand."

"Diesel?"

"Yes. Engine's a bit loud, but it's got new mufflers so that helps. I don't hear so well anyway." Warren looks around his boat, nodding in satisfaction. "It's a good small boat, perfect size for me."

"*Small?!*" I say. "Looks like a yacht!"

"It's thirty-five feet long, thirteen foot beam." He beams with pride.

"What's the draft?" Vogel asks.

"Only three feet. Perfect for getting in close to the rock shelves along the shore here. That's where the Walleye hide, especially early in the season. But I've also got a dinghy," he motions toward the back of the boat where I can see it's tied off. "With a small outboard on back, just in case I need to get in real close to shore."

He looks around his boat, nodding in satisfaction. "This boat is great," he says. "It's stable, easy to pilot and manoeuvre here in the marina. Perfect for me, since I'm usually out alone."

"Is that safe?" Vogel asks. "Storms can blow up pretty fast out on the lake. Good idea to have someone with you." Warren isn't a young man, maybe he shouldn't be out on the water by himself.

"I keep an eye on the forecast," Kerr says as he ducks back down, out of sight again. "Believe me, I'm too old to fight the weather... if a storm's coming, I'll run."

When I get closer I see that Warren is crouching in his boat, pulling dead fish out of a bucket and tossing them into a black garbage bag. One of them isn't dead. It slips out of his hands and starts to flip around on deck. He picks it up, sticks a finger in one of the fish's gills, pulls its head up and snaps its neck. Then he tosses the dead fish in with the rest. He has a fishing knife next to him, one I'm guessing he'll use to gut and filet his catch. It has a curved and polished six-inch blade and looks dangerously sharp.

"Damn gobies," Warren says, when he sees me. "Invasive species." He points at the bag of dead fish. "They came into our lake and are wiping out the native fish. If you find an invader you've got to kill it."

"Can't even use them as bait," he grumbles. "If the Ministry of Natural Resources catches you they'll fine you. But I've heard they're great for catching pike." He breaks into a grin and winks at Vogel. "Not that I'd know, you understand."

Warren ties up the garbage bag and drops it onto the wooden slip.

"Mind carrying that for me?" he asks Vogel. "Just toss it into the garbage bin over there." Vogel hoists the bag and heads off into the marina parking lot to dump it. Warren climbs out of the boat and, carrying his fishing tackle and two rods, walks over to where Jay has been waiting patiently. The three of us stroll over to meet Vogel, who's waiting next to the garbage bin.

"Do you live nearby Warren?"

He nods. "In a condo apartment, just over there, on Sugarloaf Street," he points to a low-rise complex overlooking the marina. "It's a big change from my last home."

"You downsized?"

"You could say that," he laughs.

When I see Vogel and Jay are far enough ahead I turn to Warren. "Is Jay a friend of yours? Or family?"

"No!" he looks horrified. "I'm just taking him fishing."

"Okay… you're a supporter of Kerr Residence?" I remember seeing Warren Kerr's photo in the paper, protesting the halfway house, so I can't quite make the pieces fit.

Warren sighs deeply. "I didn't like it, at first. I won't lie," he says. "I went out to all the protests against it, even led some of them. But then I prayed on it, and I decided to get to know some of the parolees and hear their stories. So now I offer what help I can."

"That's generous of you."

"I sold my business and I'm retired now." He brushes off my compliment. "Got a lot of time on my hands, so why not?"

"So you volunteer at the home now to fill some time?"

"Sure do. Fishing seemed like an easy way to help out."

"You take them out in your boat?"

"No, never! We just fish from the pier here." He points to a small dock jutting out into the bay. There are a couple of young kids out there already. "I supply the tackle," Warren continues. "We just have a few hours in the fresh air. It's good for them."

Vogel joins us, leaving Jay at the dock waiting for Kerr. "Only so far you'll go with the ex-cons?"

Warren looks over his shoulder to check if Jay can hear him. "Yes, to be honest. I don't feel safe… don't like to judge, but there it is. And it's not just parolees. There are quite a few clients from the mental health drop-in center. Schizophrenics, depressives, addicts. I'm an old man now. I do what I can, but I can only do so much."

"It's generous of you to donate your time," Vogel says. "And your expertise."

"Expertise?" He laughs. "Fishing's not great here, but it's close to my apartment. I don't have a car so we can't drive out to any-place else. And I'm too old to walk much further."

"You look pretty fit to me," Vogel says. I agree. He looks strong enough, no matter what he said. He's tall and broad shouldered, and seems energetic. But maybe he's got some health issues I don't know about.

He winks. "I may be old, but I'm not done yet. Lots still to do in this life."

He and Vogel stroll down the dock and start organizing the fishing gear. I don't really need to hear any more fishing talk and the water in the bay looks like it smells bad. There's thick green algae floating on the surface, and I can see dozens of empty plastic water bottles and beer cans stuck in the cattails that line the shore. This little cove off Gravelly Bay seems to gather all the floating debris and garbage in Lake Erie, including the arm that drifted in on the opposite shore yesterday.

Jay is hanging back as well. It's almost as if he doesn't really want to go fishing. Or maybe his mental health is so poor he's just barely hanging on.

"Hi Jay," I say.

"I wasn't sure I recognized you," he says after a moment. "I'm back on my medication now," he offers.

"Feeling better?" I have no idea what I'm supposed to say to him.

"I guess so, yes." He shrugs. "But to be honest, I feel good when I'm off them too. Which makes it…"

"Difficult."

"I remember everything that happens, all of it. But I can't tell you now—or then—what's true or what was my delusion. It's all real to me."

"That sounds hard to navigate."

"Speaking rationally, I can say that it's not possible that you were an angel, with a gleaming halo while we were chatting the day we met. Your eyes, they shone with light like the sun… and I heard voices. I know it was angels singing," he steals a glance at me, checking to see if I'm listening. "That's the crazy talking. But at the time… it's all very real to me."

"Halo?" I'm glad Vogel didn't hear that; I'd never hear the end of it.

"Like I said, I wasn't sure I recognized you."

ELEVEN

WHEN WE GET back to the station there's a delivery for me waiting at the front desk—a bankers box. My heart sinks.

"Anything interesting?" Vogel asks.

"No." I know what it is. I've been expecting it for a couple of weeks now. Dreading it would be more accurate. Vogel looks disappointed, but knows me well enough by now to not push.

A few weeks ago I got a call from one of my siblings—my adopted siblings. They don't have my home address and I don't want to give it to them, so they've sent the parcel to my attention at the station.

My foster mother died last month. I'd only just found out from one of her children—one of her *real* children, that she'd had a stroke and had been in hospital for months. No one had told me.

I'd called her home a few times and left voicemails but never had a reply. But I was busy with work and preoccupied with Maja leaving, so I'd let it slide. Then it was too late. I never had a chance to say goodbye.

When I'd returned from the funeral I couldn't even tell Maja the truth about what had happened there. I'd have to explain too much. It doesn't really matter anyway; not even Maja can help.

After the funeral I'd gone up to see my adopted sister and brother, both of whom I barely know. My two elder siblings—the *real* children, are much older than me. By the time I was fostered and then later adopted, they'd already moved out of the house. They'd moved on and had their own lives. I suspect that's what inspired my parents to take in foster kids, to fill their empty nest. But I was the one that stayed the longest and I was the only one they adopted.

"Why wouldn't you tell me she was ill? I don't understand." She'd given me a pitying look.

"It's not as if you were their real child," she'd said. "You're just one of the kids they'd fostered over the years."

"*Just one of the kids*?! *They adopted* me. Legally." She'd averted her eyes.

"Don't feel bad about it," she'd continued as if I hadn't spoken. "None of them came to visit her in hospital either. Just shows you... ."

"Nobody even told me she was sick!..."

She gave me a simpering smile. "At least you came to the funeral."

"How could they? I bet you never told any of the other *kids they'd fostered* about it either."

My blood was boiling. I was so enraged I thought I might hit her. And if I started I wouldn't be able to stop. I took a deep breath and got hold of myself.

"It was the same when mom first went into the retirement home," I'd said, trying to keep my voice down. "You sold her house and divided up all their stuff."

A sly look came into her eyes. "Their *stuff*? So you think you're entitled to something?"

"*Fuck you both!* You never gave me a thought!" Tears were streaming down my face and I didn't care. "I never even knew about it until it was a *fait accompli*."

"Do you want some token?" she'd asked, maybe taken aback

by my emotion. "Something to remember them by? I'm sure we could…"

"You're not in the Will," my brother had interrupted and it felt like a punch to my gut. They thought that was all I cared about.

"I don't need their money, thanks."

Money is never what I needed from my parents.

I get it. I'm not a blood relative. Still, they fostered me and then adopted me. I took their name. But it turns out my adopted parents weren't really mine. Not to keep.

I tuck the box under my arm and take it home. When I get out to the car I quickly open it and glance inside, half afraid to open it at all. It feels like Pandora's box. If I open it, who knows what pain and suffering I'll unleash into my world. I take a deep breath and tear it open.

There's a random assortment of photographs, trinkets, and mementos that they decided I might like to have. Based on what, I have no idea. They don't know me at all. More likely it's what was left over when they've taken what they wanted.

"What's in the box?" Maja asks when I walk in the door, but I don't reply. I need a drink not a conversation.

TWELVE

Thursday

Before I even got a chance to get inside the station in the morning I collide with Vogel, who's on his way out.

"C'mon Gauthier," he says, spinning my around. "We've got a call. It might even put a smile on your face."

"What are you talking about?"

"You'll see," he winks.

He drives out of town, heading along Highway 3 toward Fort Erie while I sip my coffee.

"You're pretty chipper this morning," I manage to say. "Good night?"

"I'll never tell," he laughs. Which is a lie, because one fact about Vogel is he will always tell, and always more than you ever want to know. But I don't bite. If he's going to overshare his personal life, it won't be at my invitation.

Just past the Speedway he turns left and heads north toward Humberstone Marsh Conservation area. I can see a police cruiser pulled over on the side of the road, next to what's left of a large four-door sedan. The car is burnt out; I can't even tell what colour it used to be.

The constable greets Vogel and me with a big grin. He looks

familiar, even with my morning brain fog. It's Peebles—long-term constable, no career aspirations beyond his occasional stand up routines at open mic nights in the area. He also has a YouTube channel and keeps busy on social media, posting satirical videos.

"Nice way to start the day," he says. "I love the smell of burning rubber in the morning." Peebles isn't as funny as he thinks he is, but it doesn't stop him from trying.

I'm still not quite awake, but I get the Apocalypse Now reference. Still doesn't mean I'm going to laugh. "Why are we here?"

With a theatrical flourish the constable bows, sweeping his arm toward the open car trunk. "Be my guest."

Inside the trunk is a human cadaver, blackened and charred from the fire. It's small, possibly a woman or a young adult. I can't tell anything else and I don't especially want to get a closer look.

Vogel calls it in and we wait with Peebles until the Coroner and FSU show up.

"It wasn't here last night," Peebles says. "I just live up the road over there." He waves his arm in the general northeasterly direction. "I got home around midnight and the road here was empty."

So whoever dumped the body did it sometime between midnight and…"

"Seven-thirty," he interrupts. "That's when I called it in."

I note Peebles is in a cruiser and in uniform, which means he had already been into the station this morning. "What route did you take in this morning? You didn't notice it then?"

"I dropped my wife off at work on the way. She works up on the Third Concession, so I went that way and came down into town along the canal."

"Car's still hot," Vogel says, looking around. "Must have been quite the fire."

"Think someone might have noticed it burning?"

"Nobody lives around here," Peebles chimes in. "This road

basically cuts right through the Humberstone Marsh Conservation Area. Closest farm is a kilometer south of here."

Peebles looks excitedly at us. "Definitely looks like murder, don't you think?"

"I don't imagine he or she crawled inside the trunk and set fire to it from the inside, by accident." I say, then take Vogel by the arm and guide him away. I can't deal with Peebles being so helpful.

"It's at least 10K back to town," I say to Vogel once we're out of earshot. "Whoever dumped it would have had a long walk back."

"Unless they live nearby. Or they had a ride back, from an accomplice."

"What kind of car was it?" I walk around and try to take photos of the license plate and VIN. All I can tell is it's a big old style sedan, but Vogel might have some insight; he's interested in most things with engines.

"Definitely a Cadillac," he says. "An older model, early 90's I think. Maybe a Fleetwood or Coupe de Ville, based on the squared off back end. Lots of trunk space." I can't tell if he's making a joke.

"Came in handy," I smile. "Can't be many of those around."

FSU arrives and Vogel goes over to intercept them while I put in a call to the station to trace the vehicle. As I suspected it doesn't take long. It belongs Mr. Clive Deeping, of Coronation Drive.

THIRTEEN

Clive Deeping's home is a well-maintained side split near the mall with an attached garage, a freshly mowed lawn, and a For Sale Sign on the lawn. Vogel and I pull up in front and watch as a middle-aged man carries moving boxes out the front door, loads them into a rented van parked in the driveway, then returns to the house.

"Looks like Mr. Deeping is moving," Vogel says as we make our way up the front path. "He could have saved himself a rental fee and used the Cadillac. Lots of room in the trunk."

The door is open, so we walk in "Mr. Deeping?" I call out. "Niagara Police. May we speak with you?"

The man rushes to the door. "Police!? What's happened? What's going on?"

"Mr. Deeping?" Vogel asks and the man nods, clearly alarmed. "Mr. Clive Deeping?"

"Yes. I mean, no." He shakes his head. "I'm Lionel Deeping. Clive was my father." Lionel Deeping is a tall, thin man with bad posture and dark hair in a comb over. He's wearing glasses and the overall impression is of the guy on the beach who'd get sand kicked into his face by the bullies. He's twitchy and so tense I wonder at first if he has a neurological condition or needs medication.

"*Was* your father? Is he…"

"Dead? Yes. We just had the funeral yesterday."

"We're inquiring about his car," Vogel says. "It was found early this morning, out on Neff Road." I wonder if someone knew Deeping wouldn't report the theft of his car, given that he was dead.

"His *car*? What do you mean his car *was found*? It's *missing*?"

"Were you not aware it was gone?" Lionel Deeping pushes past us and heads for the garage. He yanks on the handle and the double door rolls up, revealing an empty space.

"Where is it?" Deeping says, his voice high and verging on hysterical. He walks inside and looks around. Suddenly he starts giggling in a strange way, as if it's all some kind of a joke and he doesn't quite get it. "It's always right here. He kept it in mint condition."

"Do you happen to know when he last drove it?"

"No, I have no idea. He didn't go out much… he was old… not well…" He leans against the wall and it looks like he's about to pass out but Vogel rushes over to support him. Deeping's head slumps forward and his glasses slide down his nose, but he manages to push them back up before they fall off. Whatever Lionel Deeping's condition might be it's clear he's reacting very badly to the news about his father's car and I can't help but wonder why.

"Sir, let's go inside," I suggest. "You can sit down. Maybe have a glass of water?"

He allows himself to be led through the connecting door into the kitchen, where he slumps into a chair. Vogel gets him a glass of water.

"I just can't believe it," he says, giggling again. "We just never thought to look. There's been so much going on, what with the funeral and everything."

I wonder if we need to call for medical help. Deeping's behaviour is so odd I wonder if he has some condition. He's alternating between hysteria and complete lack of affect. Is he having some kind of breakdown?

"The car's always in the garage," he says, shaking his head in bewilderment.

"Did your father live here alone?"

He nods. "Our mother died years ago. He had some home help come in a few days a week. My sister and I both live in town so one of us would pop in most days, to see how he was doing, help him with groceries and all that."

"Was he unwell?"

"He was old, and cranky. Always in a miserable mood, but in pretty good health for his age, though he did die of a heart attack. I found him in his favourite chair, dead." He points to a recliner in the corner of the living room.

"That's a nice set up," Vogel says, pointing to a big new computer sitting on the dining room table. "Looks brand new."

Deeping frowns and pushes his glasses back up his nose again. He starts to get twitchy again and he stutters when he replies. "Just got himself that. Cost a fortune." He clearly disapproves of his father's hobby, or maybe the expense of the new computer meant Clive Deeping was spending his kids' inheritance. "He spent all of his time online."

"Really? What did he do?"

He shrugs and turns away, leading us away from the computer. "The usual old person stuff I guess. Facebook groups about politics, conspiracy theories, cat videos…"

"Did your father have many friends?"

Deeping starts to laugh so hard he ends up choking and has to take a sip of water to calm himself.

"*Friends*?" Deeping is still giggling. "My father didn't have any friends. He was a very unpleasant man. If he once knew people who'd tolerated him in the past they're likely already dead. As I said, he was old."

"Unpleasant." Vogel echoes, eyebrows raised as he makes notes.

"Mean and crazy works too," Deeping says. "He was abusive, insulting, rude to the help. We couldn't keep anyone here."

"Abusive to his care workers?"

"He'd call them names, make ignorant, racist remarks—even lash out with his cane if they irritated them. You name it."

"So not a lot of people at his funeral I take it?"

"Nope. Just my sister and me—and her two kids. Mine refused to come. They hated him and rightly so, if I'm honest. He was a miserable old Tory bastard, who hated immigrants, gays, women, brown people… and Italians."

"*Italians?*"

"I don't even know…" he shakes his head in exasperation. "Something to do with the war? Or the mafia?"

"I had hoped that maybe the funeral announcement would have brought out a few people, but no such luck. It was sad, but maybe not in the way you'd expect. Nobody mourning your death? That's a terrible way to go. "

FOURTEEN

WE'RE JUST COMING through the front doors of the station when I notice a man in a fishing hat leaning on the desk, chatting with the duty clerk. It's Warren Kerr. I nudge Vogel to get moving so we can duck through the security doors before he spots us.

"Nosy old coot," I mutter. "Nothing better to do with his time."

"He's just bored," Vogel says. "Looking for information about the case."

"Wasting our time, you mean. Let him read it in the newspaper like everyone else."

We get into the packed briefing room and manage to find seats just as DS Agu joins us, standing in his usual spot in front of the white board. It's been updated to include all the photos of the missing parolees and the dates they went missing.

"The twelve sets of remains," DS Agu begins. "Or what we could find, have all been sent to the Center of Forensic Sciences in Toronto. They've given us a preliminary report, which confirms a few things.

"Eight of the victims are the missing parolees from the Kerr Residence halfway facility on King Street. We got lucky there, since all of their dental records are on file with the Ministry of Correctional Services. The other four are as yet unidentified. We're working with Missing Persons to see if there's anyone that might fit the profile."

I'm not hopeful. Approximately ten thousand people go missing from the province every year, so odds are several hundred of them are from the Niagara region—and that's just those who've been reported as missing, or if they're even from the area. Who knows who these bodies are? Homeless? Addicts? The only thing they may have in common with the parolees is the manner of their death.

"They're still working on cause of death, in as far as they'll be able to determine it, given what they are working with. Four of the skulls have clear depressed fractures, indicating they suffered a head injury at some point. Three also have broken hyoid bones, indicating strangulation or hanging, which probably caused unconsciousness or possibly even death, before they were placed in the water. As for the rest, there is so far no obvious injury, so it's possible they were poisoned, sedated or smothered somehow to either kill them or allow the killer to deal with them.

"As you know, all twelve bodies were sunk in buckets of cement. And the autopsy of the most recent victim—Shaun Pearson—confirms he was definitely alive when he was dropped in the water. So, that makes me think that's likely the case for all the men.

"Were the victims clothed, Sir?" someone asks.

"It's difficult to say," Agu replies. "Not all of them were, no. But that could have been a result of being in the water rather than how they went into the canal."

"Any evidence of sexual abuse? Torture?"

Agu shakes his head. "Not as far as we can determine. No indication the killer is a sexual sadist. We don't have any clear insight into the deaths or what the satisfaction might be for the killer."

"Whoever killed these men was in a position to get close to them, somehow. He had access to, or the ability to purchase, buckets and concrete, and to mix it up in private, as well as to put the bodies into the buckets and transport them to the drop site in the canal. So," he counts off the list as DC Evans notes them on the board. "One: someone with a vehicle. Two: someone with enough physical strength to manage the transportation and disposal. Three: someone who had contact with the parolees, and the opportunity to abduct and kill them."

"They may have come willingly, Sir," I say. "If they knew him. Or trusted him. These men, the victims, were all vulnerable. They were unwelcome here in town—which I suspect they were well aware of. They didn't have friends and many were estranged from their families. If someone could gain their trust, they might have gone willingly with him. He could have easily drugged them and subdued them…"

I can't help but think of the McArthur, the serial murderer in Toronto. He lured vulnerable gay and homeless men, then murdered and dismembered them and hid their bodies in various gardens he worked in as a landscaper. He was able to approach these men and make them comfortable enough to go with him to their deaths. He got them to trust him, somehow.

"Who are you thinking of? A social worker? A parole officer?"

"Maybe. Something like that. A counsellor at the halfway house?"

"Or there might be more than one killer. If there were two… then strength isn't such an issue."

Vogel and I are parked in the East Village, next to a fixer upper that someone's working on, trying to spruce up. Two men who look like father and son are on the roof, stripping off the old shingles and tossing them into a dumpster parked on the lawn. The small house has new siding, new windows and trim and the front door has been freshly painted a cheerful periwinkle blue.

Shame about their neighbour's house though. It has a torn

tarp lying over the swayback roof, the front porch is sinking and the fence between the two properties is sagging. Replacing that fence would be next on my list if I were the DIY people next door, so I didn't have to look at it every time I came home.

Some properties one the street are fenced off completely, the houses either condemned or the subject of a police investigation into criminal activity. Others are abandoned, either because the owner is dead or maybe in jail, or they can't be sold and remortgaged because nobody will lend on the property. It's common in the area, either because the house is full of toxic mould or more likely the land it's built on is contaminated by the residual heavy metals from the refinery that shut down years ago. The refinery was the biggest employer in the area for decades and when it shut down it marked the beginning of the neighbourhood's decline.

The East Village never changes. I lived here as a child and I've been out here countless times on calls when I worked patrol: domestics, drunk and disorderly, car thefts—arresting someone who'd done it, not because a car was ever stolen from here. Not a lot of property crime, since nobody who lives here owns much of anything. But for all its faults, there's a strange sense of community here. All through the area there are flyers up on telephone poles, looking for the missing men. Many of them are weathered and faded, clearly having been posted months ago. Some of the missing parolees were brothers and sons and husbands that someone did care about—but I can't help but notice none of the flyers are for Shaun Pearson.

We're waiting outside Pearson's family home for his father to return. When we'd knocked there'd been no reply before a neighbour had called over from his front porch.

"Just left for the beer store," he said with a drunken grin, holding up a bottle of Labatt Blue and giving it a shake. "He'll be back any minute."

"It's been ten minutes already," Vogel grumbles.

"Are you surprised? I doubt that guy even knows what day it is." It's just a typical summer day in the East Village. The neighbour's drunk before noon and probably Pearson's father is driving drunk to the beer store. Nothing ever changes.

Vogel starts the car. "Let's just leave and come back later."

"No, wait. Look." I point up the street, to just in front of the Youth Drop-in Centre. Vogel turns off the ignition and together we watch a crime being committed.

A young man on a mountain bike is leaning on a car, speaking with the driver. He's wearing a huge shapeless grey hoodie, baggy jeans and new trainers. I clearly see money and a packet change hands. No question someone's dealing.

"Isn't that the kid you talked to at Kerr Residence?"

"Jay," I nod. "And who was going fishing with Warren Kerr. He's got… problems."

"I'll say," Vogel says. "He's about to have a lot more." He turns to me and grins. "What do you think? Something to pass the time?" Before I can say anything he's out of the car, running toward the dealer and Jay. I've got not choice but to follow him, but it's not how I would have played it.

As soon as Vogel shouts Jay takes off on his bike and Vogel gives chase.

The driver is starting his car when I slip into the passenger seat and pull the keys out of his ignition. "No. I don't think so."

He takes his hands off the wheel and laughs. "What's the problem officer?"

I inform him of his rights as I cuff him to the steering wheel.

"Do you understand?" I ask. He shrugs. "Do you understand?" I repeat as I pull out my radio and call it in. He finally nods and I take off after Vogel.

Listening in on the radio communications I hear Vogel say

he's pursuing the suspect along Nickel Street, then south on Fares. Of course he's on foot and Jay's on a bike, so odds aren't good he'll catch up. I take a shortcut down Davis then through some backyards on Mitchell and along the alley behind Rodney Street. My daily 10K runs make this a breeze and at least I won't have to workout tonight after work. I catch a glimpse of Jay through a gap in the houses and see he's doubling back, going back the way he just came up a side street. I run out in front of him by the variety store on the corner of Nixon and he spins out on some loose gravel then falls off his bike. I grab him by the arm and pull him to his feet, giving him a hard shake on the way up.

"Where are you going in such a hurry?"

The door to the variety store opens and one of the customers steps out, dragging a little dog on a lead. She's a scrawny older woman with a deep tan, wearing sunglasses and a sunhat. She smells strongly of coconut and pineapple suntan lotion.

"What are you doing with him?" she demands. "Leave him alone or I'll call the cops on you."

"I am the cops, Ma'am."

"What do you want with him?"

"I'm taking him into custody." I'm careful not so say too much. Jay's a minor with mental illness and I need to tread carefully.

"I don't think so," she says, taking hold of his arm. "I don't know who you think you've got here, but Jay's been inside this store for the past hour playing arcade games. I'll testify to it in court."

The woman is lying, that's clear, but Jay gives her a big grin and nods. "It's true," he says.

The little shit. He may be schizophrenic, but he's smart enough to avoid arrest. Typical East Village BS. I glare at the suntanned woman and let go of Jay's arm. He stares down at his feet and I wonder if he even remembers me and my halo. Or maybe it fell off in the chase.

I get on the radio and let Dispatch know where I am, and that I've apprehended the suspect as Vogel arrives, sweating and out of breath.

"Is that so?" I say, knowing we've lost this round. "We'll just get him home safely then." I look at Jay. "Where do you live?"

He looks nervous for a brief moment, then gives us his home address, a place just up around the corner. I guess he knows he's got nothing to fear there.

The three of us walk in silence to the address Jay gave us, then Jay breaks free and runs in ahead of us, no doubt alerting whoever's home to the fact that two police officers are on their way in. We walk into a scene that could have been my childhood home and I almost stumble in recognition.

Six guys are sitting around the kitchen table littered with beer bottles and Tim Horton's cups. They're playing cards and the room stinks of cigarette smoke and weed. I guess the workday is done and it's time to drink and gamble away the pay packet.

They all look so familiar my heart skips a beat. I know them. I couldn't tell you their names, or where they live, but I know they spent time hanging around my house. They must be friends of my uncles, which definitely makes them losers and druggies.

Instinctively I duck my head, trying to hide my face. It's completely unlikely they'd ever recognize me, and my name was changed when I was a child, but I still have a visceral fear of being drawn back into the past, into that time, whenever I feel its breath on my neck. It's the monster under my bed. It's the thing in the closet and it's haunted me for years.

One of the men is huge and hairy and is unfortunately wearing just a muscle shirt so I can't miss that fact. Two others look like brothers—both with long dark hair, wearing old t-shirts and work pants covered with paint. One is painfully skinny and the other is covered in homemade stick and poke tattoos. The last one looks completely unremarkable until he opens his mouth to smile, revealing a gold incisor.

"No man, I can't do the drop off," Tooth says as we linger in the hallway. "I already said I can only pick up."

"Don't look at me!" says Hairy. "I don't have wheels."

"When's this going down?"

"What are they planning?" Vogel whispers to me. "A robbery?"

"More likely a family picnic," I say. "They know we're here."

"I don't have a license, remember?"

Skinny laughs. "Since when do you care about driving without a license?"

"C'mon! I'm on probation," Ink whines. "Give me a break."

"Then let Junior drive."

"No way I'm lending him my car! He's not right in the head."

Vogel and I step into the kitchen and they all turn as one to look at us. I put on my game face, the mask I always wear whenever I'm in the East Village. It's a shield and I defy anyone to see through it.

"What's going on?" Vogel asks.

"Just planning a birthday dinner—who's going to get grandma out of the care home and bring her for the party."

Vogel scoffs but it's entirely plausible. They look like hardened criminals and lowlifes and they definitely act like it. It's just the life they lead. Probably one of them just got out of jail, and one's in rehab—again. And they're planning a birthday party for their grandmother. Everyone's got family, even guys like this.

"Where's the kid?" Vogel asks and every one of them looks dumb—not that it's a challenge.

"Who?"

"He just came in ahead of us. Jay?"

They exchange a look, not doubt trying to decide how long to play us. "He just went out back," says Hairy. "Borrowed my car."

I can feel the anger radiating off Vogel. "Your car. I doubt he's old enough to drive."

"Jay? Sure he is! Not very good at it mind you, but he's legal." The guy next to Hairy is staring at me and I can feel a flush creeping up my neck. It's an intense look, not a sexual one. It could just be my paranoia but it feels as if he's trying to place me, to remember where he knows me from. I drop behind Vogel so he can't see me and hope he's too drunk or high to figure it out.

"Are you his family? His relations?"

They just stare at us for a moment. "Nah. He lives up the street. Good kid."

"Do you have any idea where he was earlier this afternoon?"

One of the skinny guys pretends to think about it. "Sure, he was here. With us," he finally says.

"So, not at the variety store up the street?"

He's quick to recover. "We sent him out to buy us something at the variety store. Chips. And pop. Chips and pop."

This is all painfully familiar. When I was a child here in the East Village my uncles would send me to pick up their cigarettes at the corner store. My payment was a few coins to buy candy or popsicles. On a good day they'd let me take in their empty beer bottles and keep the return. But unless their social assistance cheques had just come in, they needed the ten cents a bottle themselves to put toward the kitty for more beer. That's how they lived: on social assistance, working cash jobs under the table, doing crimes. Every one of them, and all of their friends was a criminal or had one in the family.

"I could arrest you for obstruction." Vogel finally snaps. He's pissed off.

"I guess you enjoy paperwork," one of them taunts him. Vogel looks uneasy. We're outnumbered and I pull him away.

"You're going to let them get away with that bullshit?" Vogel hisses as I walk him out of the house. "They're obviously lying. Shielding that kid."

"I don't believe in starting a fight we can't win." Vogel sighs and starts the car. "That's just not the way it works here." I pull on his arm to lead him away. "Just give it up?!" He snaps. "Are you fucking kidding me Gauthier? We had him."

"How do you figure? If we had him, we'd have him," I laugh. "And I don't see him, do you?" Vogel has no idea about the East Village. He served his first few years on the force in Kitchener, about as far away as you can get from here. "Vogel, you've just had your East Village baptism."

"What makes you such an expert on the East Village anyway?" Vogel jerks his arm away from me then storms off. "Never knew your Community policing actually led to your being on their side." I bristle in anger, but bite my tongue. Vogel has no idea how much I know about the East Village. And he never will.

"Next you're going to tell me they aren't all bad, just misunderstood," he slams the car door shut. "Not real criminals."

"Oh, they're criminals all right. Every last one of them." I know that too well, but Vogel doesn't need to know that I spent the first eleven years of my life in the East Village, or that most of my family are criminals. And the only way I got out was by committing the worst crime possible. And I'm not going to tell him.

Vogel's mood doesn't improve when we get a call from the station. We're going to have to release the dealer in the car. There's no evidence. He's clean, his car's clean, and the kid is gone. No doubt he dropped any drugs somewhere when Vogel was in pursuit, to retrieve later.

"Shaun Pearson's father should be back from the beer store by now," I say. "And I'll bet the day's definitely not going to get any better."

Turns out the visit to Jim Pearson isn't as bad as I'd expected. He's drunk and already well into the case of beer he'd just brought back from the store by the time we arrive. He refuses to speak with us privately inside the house, so we have to deliver the death notice in front of the neighbour, who at least has the courtesy to step inside on some pretext when he realizes what we're there for.

Pearson can't care less his son is dead. He doesn't even ask us about the circumstances. He's a hateful man and it's no wonder his son Shaun's life went off the rails. Not that I believe in blaming parents for their kids' problems, but in his case I'll make an exception. Why Shaun had even wanted to visit him on Father's Day is beyond comprehension.

FIFTEEN

T**ALKING TO** J**IM** Pearson, especially coming after our visit to the East Village, has put me into a dark mood. It's the worst part of the job, dealing with people like Pearson, the lowlifes and losers, the criminals and crackheads. I can't help thinking about my escape from that life, and what that escape had cost me.

It's why I've been avoiding any follow up on Doreen's request. I don't want to go to Nick Melynk's house, or meet his parents, or have anything whatever to do with his problems. In fact I resent even knowing my cousin exists.

There's also the problem of Vogel. I've never told him anything about my past and have no idea how to explain why we'd be going to Melnyk's house, which means I'd have to go alone. And that is more than I can deal with.

Luckily Vogel is on his phone, so he's unaware of my mood. He's got a silly grin on his face, so I guess he's in love. Again. Or is it still? It's so hard to keep up.

So I sit at my desk and sip my coffee, thinking about Clive Deeping and his stolen Cadillac.

If his weird son Lionel is to be believed, the car could have been stolen anytime in the past few weeks. He doesn't even remember when he last saw it, so we'll need to ask the sister and the care worker. Maybe they'll remember when it was last in the garage.

"Why would anyone want to steal it?" I ask Vogel when he hangs up. "It's over fifty years old."

Vogel recoils in shock. "It's a classic Coup de Ville, Gauthier! It's vintage!"

"Valuable?"

"Sure, especially if it's mint, like the son said."

"So then why was it stolen, then burnt out on Neff Road? Not to mention with a dead body in the trunk."

"Not the work of your typical car thief, I agree."

"Unless… ," an idea comes to mind. "What if this typical car thief had his eye on a vintage Cadillac, and he knew the owner had recently died…"

Vogel picks up on my train of thought right away. "… and he thought the family might be busy and preoccupied with funerals and such…"

"… so he might take that opportunity to help himself to it, hoping it may not be noticed as missing for a while. Long enough to sell it on to whatever chop shop…"

"*Chop shop*! No way. Not a vintage Coup de Ville. It'd be sold intact."

"Fine, whatever he was going to do with it then. How long do you suppose it would have taken Lionel Deeping to realize the car was gone, if we hadn't alerted him?"

"Definitely long enough to move the car out of the country." Vogel ponders for a minute, but I can't help notice he keeps stealing glances at his cell phone, no doubt looking for texts. "Maybe our thief just reads the funeral notices and goes to the houses to see what he can take," he says. "Finding the car was just good luck, not planned."

"Okay, I'll buy that," I say. "But how do we explain the body in the trunk?"

"Maybe it was an accomplice?" Vogel says. "Our car thief kills his partner, dumps the body in the trunk, sets fire to the car and then drives the partner's car away?"

"Then why steal the car in the first place? Why would you set fire to a valuable car you stole expressly to sell? That makes no sense."

Vogel looks disappointed. "Yeah, you're right. Maybe it was stolen just to burn it. Maybe someone hated Deeping that much they wanted to destroy his prized possession. His son said he was a hateful man with no friends, but he might have had enemies."

"Maybe. Or maybe they stole the car, unaware there was already a body in the trunk?"

Vogel looks exasperated. "No, hear me out," I hold up my hand. "The car is stolen by our thief, who drives it around, maybe on the way to deliver it to the buyer… then finds the body."

He laughs. "What, he starts to notice a bad smell?"

"Why not? He finds the body, is terrified he'll be blamed, so he destroys the car."

"And walks back to town…"

"Sure, he walks back to town. It's only 10K. Anyone could walk that—even Deeping himself."

"Which one—the peculiar one or dead one?"

"Dead one. Old man Deeping kills someone, puts the body in the trunk then drops dead of a heart attack."

"Who would old man Deeping have killed?" I roll my eyes. "Seriously Vogel… And that doesn't get us any closer to who stole the car." I lean back in my chair, trying to ignore the ominous creaks and groans. Any day now the thing will give way and I'll fall right over. "That's the question. Who's stealing cars from dead people?"

Within an hour we get a report of vehicles that have been reported stolen from people's houses, in similar circumstances—though none destroyed like Deeping's. All of them had been recovered within a short time, just found abandoned in parking lots in town or in public parks—some before they were even reported as stolen.

"Sounds like our guy," Vogel says. "So why's he stealing the cars? Just to drive them around? It's the sort of thing a kid would do."

"Apart from Deepings *vintage* Cadillac, all of the stolen cars were older model sedans or even mini-vans. Nothing flashy. Nobody's going joyriding in a mini van. They were all just nondescript cars, unlikely to be noticed on the street." I wonder if that's the whole point.

"There are also a few reports here of cars that have been reported as *moved*, from long-term parking lots," Vogel says, pointing to the monitor. "The owners came back from vacation and found their cars parked in a different spot than where they'd been left."

I stand behind him and read over his shoulder. None of the cars had any damage to the ignition or evidence they'd been tampered with. It looks like nobody on the force had thought it plausible they'd been stolen and the reports weren't taken seriously. They were just put down to people making mistakes or forgetting where they'd left their cars.

"So… whoever this guy is, he isn't exactly *stealing* the cars." I'm thinking aloud. "He's *borrowing* them from people who aren't currently needing them? Because they're on vacation. Or dead."

Vogel considers what I'm saying, nodding as the picture comes into focus. "He wouldn't have to be in a hurry, since he'd know the owner wasn't going to be around to disturb him. If he wore gloves, he'd leave no prints."

"And it's not like he jammed a screwdriver into the ignition to start it. There's no damage to the cars. Maybe our guy's a mechanic, or at least had knowledge of cars. He took the time to hotwire it… he removed panels on steering wheel, to get at the ignition…"

"Or he had a key…" I interrupt him.

"It makes sense. People are grieving, upset. They're not necessarily going to look into the garage and see if granddad's car is still in there. It might go missing for weeks. Months, even, while the estate gets settled."

"So he could have been driving around for weeks in that car. They're not going to be missed right away."

"He could read the papers for funeral notices. But how'd he know someone's going away? Is he a travel agent?"

"Maybe he's tapped into certain groups—like Kiwanis or Rotary or one of those services that delivers hot meals to seniors. He'll learn when snowbirds go away to their places in Arizona or Florida. Their car will be in the garage—or left at airport parking."

"Let's go on a field trip," Vogel says, pushing away from his desk and turning off his computer. I've got nothing better to do, so I follow him out the door and we head toward one of the Firelanes on Lorraine Bay, just east of town. This lakeside community dates back to the glory days of the late 1880's, when wealthy families from across the border in Buffalo created one of the finest summer colonies on the lake. They built summer places in a mix of Victorian, Greek Revival, and Craftsman styles, some with private tennis courts, servants' quarters and gatehouses all on a beautiful sandy beach in a sheltered bay. Most of these places are seasonal but some have been winterized and now have year-round residents.

We park in front of a sprawling old Cape Cod place that sits on top of the dune, surrounded by old growth maple and pine trees. It belongs to Ron Whitney, owner of one of the cars *borrowed* from long-term airport parking.

I instinctively hang back and let Vogel take the lead. These are his people: old money, privileged and wealthy, with roots that go deep in the soil of the region. I may have been born in town and raised nearby, but I'm more like a weed. My people aren't welcome, sprouting up like nuisances where they aren't wanted.

"Quite the place," I mutter under my breath. "Bet he's got a big boat too."

"He's got the biggest boat in the marina." Vogel laughs. "You've seen it—the big yacht on the end?"

"Of course he does." I shake my head. "What else?"

There's no answer to our knock on the front door, so we follow the aroma of cigar smoke and find Whitney on his deck, overlooking Lake Erie. He's well fed, expensively dressed, and is nursing a glass of red wine, probably also very expensive, as is the lit cigar resting in the ashtray.

"Good afternoon, Mr. Whitney," Vogel says. "We're with Niagara Police."

Ron Whitney looks only mildly interested. Most people get flustered when the police show up, but not this guy. He's cool and controlled, like any master of the universe would be. His high-end casual clothes—especially his Gucci horsebit loafers—tell their own story, one of wealth, privilege and entitlement.

"With regard to your report of last March, regarding your stolen vehicle," Vogel continues.

"Yes, my new Escalade. Not exactly quick follow up," Whitney says with a laugh. "I made that report months ago." *A new Cadillac?* That doesn't fit with our operating theory about older model, low-tech cars.

"We've read the report of course, but wonder if you have any additional information or thoughts you could share."

"I have many thoughts, detective." Whitney smirks and inspects his cigar end, finding it has gone out. He relights it, puffing hard to get it going, in absolutely no rush to reply. Ron Whitney is smug and I decide I don't like him, not that he'd care one way or the other.

"We understand when you returned after your vacation last spring, you found the car in the airport long term parking lot…"

"Exactly. But not where I'd left it," he interrupts, sounding bored. "The car was absolutely fine, no damage whatsoever, but it wasn't parked the same way I'd left it."

"How could you be so sure?" I can't even find my car in the parking lot at the mall.

"I always write the number of the aisle on my ticket—the last thing I want to do is spend an hour looking for my car after a long flight. Where I found my car was definitely not where I'd parked it. I reported it to police of course. They thought I was nuts, but were polite and went through the motions of taking my report." He shakes his head in irritation.

"But what was completely inexplicable was that the parking fee was a mere fraction of what I normally pay."

"So, someone stole your car, drove it around for a few days…

"More like weeks…" he interrupts.

"Then brought it back and left it?"

"Exactly." He takes a satisfied puff on his cigar. "And there's more."

Vogel flips through his notes in confusion. "More?"

"Just happened a few weeks ago. I didn't even bother to report it, given your lack of interest in March." I hear Vogel sigh.

"I always keep a second car here, in the garage. A Mercedes. For guests, or maybe my own use while I'm here during the season."

"When I opened up the cottage in spring, I checked on the second car and found it had an additional several hundred kilometers on the clock and it was out of gas."

"You're very… meticulous about your cars Mr. Whitney." I have no idea what the odometer reading is on my car. I can barely remember the colour.

"I have them both serviced at the dealership regularly. Keep them in pristine condition."

"And the keys? Where are they kept?"

"On a hook, here in the kitchen," he gestures vaguely toward the house. "I have spare sets hanging there for both cars as well as in my home in Buffalo." So anyone breaking into the cottage had access to the car keys.

"And no evidence of a break-in?"

Whitney shakes his head. "It's a real mystery." He's clearly somewhat amused—or maybe he's on his second glass of wine. "Colonel Mustard in the garage with the car keys."

"And there's no way it was your wife? Or other family?" Vogel says. "I always used to return my parents' car with an empty tank," Vogel says. "When I was younger of course."

"I'm divorced. My ex-wife has no access to this property."

For the first time Whitney doesn't sound bored or indifferent. He sounds bitter and angry, which gives me a button to push.

"Where does your ex-wife live?" I ask. "Nearby?"

He meets my eye and I can see he's not going to bite. "In town," he says then he turns to Vogel and continues speaking.

"My children have their own vehicles. They seldom visit the cottage anyway." He takes another puff on his cigar and looks out over the lake. "No… someone has helped themselves to my vehicles, on more than one occasion. I wonder exactly what they got up to during that time."

Vogel thanks Whitney for his time and I follow him back out to the car, careful not to say a word.

"This guy," Vogel says when we're back in the car. "Something about him stinks and it's not his cigar." I'm relieved Vogel feels the same way I do, for a change.

Usually it's me taking a dislike to rich guys like Whitney,

the corrupt pricks who use their money to manipulate and control everyone.

"How is it that he knows exactly when his car was taken and returned, where it was parked, all of it?" I say. "It's a little too perfect, don't you think? Seriously. Nobody keeps track of that stuff: how many kilometers were on his car when he left it in the garage? How much gas he had in the tank? Give me a break."

Vogel nods. "Not gonna argue with that."

"Why would anyone be so aware of those details, unless they were setting up an alibi. Maybe he's the one who used it, or he knows who did, and he reported it as stolen, just in case it was seen?"

"An alibi for what?"

I shrug and we drive in silence back to the station. I sense Vogel is waiting for me to say something, but I keep quiet for as long as I can. Finally, I can't help myself.

"Oh, and did I mention he's a smug, self-satisfied prick?"

Vogel grins. "There you are! I was wondering when you'd say it out loud."

"I tried to keep it to myself this time," I laugh. "You're always saying I've got a hate-on for rich people."

"You do. But in this case, you're not alone."

SIXTEEN

Normally we'd have to wait for identification of the victim found in the trunk of Deeping's car. It's first come, first served in the morgue and the bodies found in the canal are at the head of the line. But the canal bodies have been sent to the Center of Forensic Studies and extra resources magically were found and directed to that investigation. It's amazing how that happens when several government Ministries are involved and the case is of huge media interest. That meant our local Coroner and FSU team were free to work on the Deeping case, which means an autopsy was conducted and the victim identified at lightning speed.

Vogel and I are waiting in the morgue for Victor Todor to arrive and share his findings. He's been appointed Coroner in Maja's place, since she's leaving on her sabbatical. I'm used to picking up the phone and calling for results or dropping by and asking Maja informally. But Todor has made it clear that's no longer acceptable, which makes me irritable.

"He's late," I grumble.

"Seven minutes," Vogel says glancing at the watch. "Relax Gauthier."

"I have no idea how I'm supposed to work with this guy. He's got no people skills. I can't get a read on him."

"Sounds like someone else I know." Vogel gives me a sly smile.

I don't bite. "I can't stand the guy," I say. "Every time I've met him he's been arrogant, condescending, rude, dismissive…"

"C'mon Gauthier. You just don't like him because he's not Maja. He's okay."

I roll my eyes. "Vogel do you have to be so amiable? It's exhausting. Can't you just get on board this one time and agree with me that Todor is a prick?"

Vogel shrugs amiably. "Okay, you're right. He's a jerk. What is he Hungarian?"

"Croatian, I think."

"I'm Serbian, originally," a voice says from behind us. "But I've lived in Canada for over twenty years."

Dammit.

As Todor brushes past us into the room he hands me a printed report. I quickly read it, mostly to avoid having to meet his eye. The body was a female and has been identified as Tracey Reid, based on fingerprints they were able to pull from one of her hands. She was a licensed practical nurse, employed by an agency that provided in-home medical and personal care. Her driver's license has her residence at Clarke Street, two blocks east of the canal.

I quickly put in a call to the station and pull up any information we can get about her and get in touch with her employer and have them send over her client list.

When I hang up, Todor glances at his watch then gives me a look. "May I continue?" he says and I give him a tight smile. *What a prick*. I don't anticipate we'll have a positive working relationship.

"It's often a challenge to match burnt human remains through DNA profile," he says. "The STRs and mtDNA sequences aren't reliably reproducible with badly burnt material. It's usually highly degraded or even completely absent—and without nuclear DNA we're only left with mitochondrial DNA for analysis…"

"Will you be able to make a match?" I interrupt him, which earns me a silent glare. He clearly enjoys the sound of his own voice.

"… which as you may know, is less informative," he continues as if I hadn't spoken. "In this case, the body was only semi-burnt, so there will be enough to match with the blood evidence you may find at a crime scene or at the victim's home."

"… And do we know the cause of death?" I interrupt. I'm not interested in the granular detail of how burnt the body was.

Todor stares at me for a moment, a look of mild astonishment on his face, as if he was watching a dog walk up the street on its hind legs.

"Cause of death was likely head trauma," Todor says. "Caused by a narrow, cylindrical object, likely metal…"

"… Like a pipe?" I interrupt again. "Someone hit her?"

Todor takes a deep breath, irritated by my interruption. "Possibly. Or she fell onto it. The angle isn't determinative."

Todor turns to Vogel and continues. "The human body is predictable in how it burns. First the soft tissue—the skin and muscle will burn, with the subcutaneous fat liquefying and providing a fuel source that keeps the fire burning until all the tissue burns away and only the bones remain. As I've said, there was evidence of severe blunt force trauma to the skull, which would indicate cause of death."

"So the victim was dead before the fire was started?"

"That is what I just said."

I take a deep breath and count to ten before I say another word. It's not that I'll say something I might later regret; I doubt I'd ever regret whatever I might say to him. But I don't need to get a reprimand, and I don't need to complicate my relationship with the Coroner's Office. After having Maja as my go-to for all this time, having her to run ideas by, and especially having her there to clarify and explain forensic matters to me, has definitely spoiled me. Her being away at Doctors Without Border is going to be a long, difficult adjustment—professionally, not just personally.

I give Todor another tight smile, turn on my heel and leave Vogel to smooth over any ruffled feathers. I don't know how I'm going to get through the next six months and all I can hope is that his rotations don't overlap with my cases.

At least our next meeting with Jun Song will be more pleasant. The minutiae of the evidence she deals with as a forensic technician is excruciating but she's able to explain it to me like I'm five years old—without the arrogance Todor has. That skill has served her well in court, since she's able to testify and explain things in a way that juries can actually understand the analysis of physical evidence from crime scenes.

Jun and her boyfriend are into all these sporty, outdoor activities like kayaking and winter camping that she keeps trying to convince me to try. She invited Maja and I to join them on an ice boating weekend last winter. Thankfully the idea of sliding at a hundred kilometers an hour across a frozen lake appealed to Maja as little as it does to me, so we managed to change it to dinner in a local restaurant, which was delicious—and much warmer.

Jun gives us a big smile when she sees us come into the crime lab and puts down the cast of a footprint she's working on.

"Perfect timing," she says as she brings us over to a table covered with materials taken from Deeping's car. "Not that it'll be a surprise to you. No question it's arson," she says with a laugh. "Odds are pretty much any car just abandoned and set ablaze at the side of a country road is going to be arson—for an insurance scam, or to get out of an expensive lease payment, or to cover up another crime."

"Like a body in the trunk?"

"Whoever did the deed clearly wasn't familiar with torching vehicles. The car's not completely burnt out."

"That's not usual?"

She shakes her head. "Rookie mistake. All cars have accelerants built into them—all over the place—and lots of additional fuel and ignition sources everywhere, so once the burning starts it doesn't usually stop."

"So what happened here?"

"The windows were up. Once the fire burned off the oxygen available in the main compartment it snuffed itself out. A bit more accelerant, more judiciously applied, and it would have all burnt until the tires melted. But…" she shrugs. "I can tell you the accelerant used was diesel. "

"And the car wasn't diesel?"

She shakes her head. "Definitely not."

"You can tell the difference? Even when it's burned?"

"Sure! We can probably even tell you the brand of fuel, given enough time. It was probably just diesel in a plastic gas can, poured inside the car, then someone lit a match…"

"So, we just need to figure out what gas stations in the area sell diesel fuel. Maybe there'll be some video footage?"

"Not just cars and trucks use diesel," Vogel says. "Some boats use it. Construction and farm vehicles too."

"And, lots of farms have their own fuel storage tanks." Jun chimes in. This isn't looking like it'll be a fruitful line of inquiry after all.

"And there was no accelerant in the trunk? On the body?"

"Nope. Just in the main compartment."

"So… it's possible whoever did this didn't even know about the body?"

"I suppose so. But then what's the motive for burning the

car? Surely that was done to try and destroy or at least disguise the body."

"True. So, we're left with a body in a trunk, fire set by person unknown, with no way to trace who did it, or why."

"Pretty much, yes."

SEVENTEEN

As we're heading over to Tracy Reid's address my phone pings with an email. It's the client list of everyone she's worked for over the past four years with the home care agency.

The patient she saw on her last day at work was Clive Deeping.

When we knock on Theresa Reid's door it's opened by a tall, young woman with long hair held back off her face with a do-rag. She checks Vogel and I out, unsmiling. We aren't welcome.

"Took you long enough," she says.

"I'm sorry," I say.

"… You should be," she interrupts, eyes flaring in anger. "I made the report last week. I can't believe it took you…"

"We seem to be a cross-purposes," Vogel interrupts. Always the peacemaker, he inserts himself between us. "I'm Detective Vogel, and this is Detective Gauthier, from Niagara Police. We're about Tracey Reid. She lived here?"

The woman's eyes narrow suspiciously. "*Lived.* Past tense. She's dead?"

"I'm sorry, yes. May we come inside?"

She opens the door wider to allow us to pass then stands with her arms folded, glaring at us. I notice she's using a cane. She catches my look and raises her chin, as if daring me to ask about it.

"I'm Pamela Visser. Tracey is my tenant."

"When is the last time you saw her?" I ask, pulling out my notebook.

"Are you fucking kidding me?" She explodes in anger. "Tracey's been missing for seven days now! I reported it to you guys!" Dammit. Vogel and I exchange a look.

"Doesn't the right hand know what the left hand is doing?" She storms over to the couch and flounces down onto it, dropping her care on the floor next to her. "Unbelievable," she mutters.

Vogel and I follow her into the living room. Neither of us says anything as she continues to swear under her breath, shaking her head at our incompetence. It's getting on my nerves; neither of us killed Tracy Reid. She needs to redirect her anger and I'm about to tell her so when I feel Vogel's hand on my arm, warning me to cool it.

"She's definitely dead?" she finally calms down enough to ask. "How?"

"What do you suppose happened to her?" Vogel asks, avoiding the question. She doesn't need the details of how Tracey Reid's body was found. Pamela Visser shrugs and looks away. She's pouting like a child.

"I called the agency she works for," she finally says. "All they could tell me was that she didn't turn up for work. One of her clients was found dead of a heart attack. It was clear she'd been there that day since the house was clean, he was dressed and the bed was changed. But that's the last trace of her."

"What can you tell us about this client—the one who was found dead?"

She rolls her eyes. "Tracey was his care worker… his children hired her to tend him, visit daily, feed and bathe him, whatever they didn't want to do themselves. Not that I blame them… he was a horrible old man. Tracey complained about him all the time. She even told the agency she wasn't going back there again because he was so abusive. He actually hit her with his cane! Can you believe it?

"Then he'd try to pay her off afterwards. I guess he felt bad about his temper tantrums.

"He gave her money? How much?"

"Whatever." She makes a face. "Tracey needed it and he had some. And, believe me she earned it, putting up with his crap…" She catches my irritated expression and shuts up. I really don't have time for her bullshit, and it's written all over my face. "I don't know exactly," she mumbles. "He gave her money for her kids."

"How many children does she have?"

"None. But he didn't know that. It was a payoff, a guilt offering."

"For what?"

"Putting up with his crap. Cleaning up his messes. Not telling his kids about it." She turns to Vogel for understanding. "She wasn't stealing! But his family found out and accused her. It was awful."

"Families, eh?" Vogel chuckles as his phone rings. He glances at the screen then steps outside to take the call, leaving me with Pamela. This could take a while, if it turns out to be Vogel's new love interest. Pamela Visser looks at me, uneasy as she realizes she's been left with the bad cop.

I take a deep, calming breath and sit down across from her. I might as well get some background about the living situation in the house.

"What do you do for a living, Ms. Visser?"

"I'm a cleaner," she says. "And I have two tenants, to help with the rent and utilities."

"Do you have records of your clients? They're not all cash jobs?"

I can't help myself. I'm cynical by nature, suspicious of temperament and my experience growing up in the East Village and later as a police officer has just confirmed all of that.

She gives me a sharp look. "I assume you mean am I being paid under the table? In a brown envelope—to avoid paying tax?" I look down at my notebook, embarrassed.

"I have a business," she continues, raising her voice. "I'm registered and I pay all the appropriate taxes. To be clear I'm required to file tax—I need whatever proof of income I canprovide, since whatever paltry disability benefits the government sees fit to give me are all tied to tax filing." She picks her cane up off the floor and leans it next to her. "So in response to your insinuation: No. Not *all cash.*"

Suddenly, to my relief, she stops herself and takes a deep breath. I'm afraid she's about to go off on a rant and I just don't want to deal with it—especially since I'm the cause of it.

"No, *fuck it,*" she explodes after a moment. "What is it with you people? Not just you cops—with all of you people who sit there, judging me because I'm a cleaner? I'm automatically a tax evader because of it? What the actual fuck is wrong with being a cleaner?"

I recoil in awe of her rage. It's impressive. It makes me like her more.

"I make good money," she continues. "Very good actually, not that it's any of your business. I work hard. I set my own hours so I'm home for my kids. Always. Everyone telling me I'm 'better than this'—like it's something terrible I do for a living. *Maybe you could get a nice job in retail somewhere. You're so personable. Have you considered a career change? Looked into job training?*"

She pulls a pack of cigarettes out of her smock and lights one. "*Fuck.* I'm not a prostitute! I clean houses and I'm good at it. I clean their mess. They make a lot of mess." She takes a pull on her cigarette, then drops it in the ashtray and stubs it out.

I've set her off and realize I better make this right, now. "My mother was a cleaner. In Wainfleet. I used to help her, after school sometimes."

I can see the rage drain out of Pamela Visser. She gives me a crooked smile.

"Sorry," she mumbles. "I didn't mean what I said."

"Yes you did. And you've got nothing to apologize for."

"I'm sorry I got ratty with you. I'm just… so tired. All these well meaning people, thinking they know what's best for me, thinking they have any insight into my life. I clean their houses. They don't know me." She gives me a sly smile. "But man, do I know them! You would not believe." She hesitates. "But then you're a cop, so I guess you've probably seen it all".

"Maybe not *all*, but yeah, I've seen a lot." *And not all from being a cop… but I don't need to share that.*

"Not criminal stuff though," she's quick to add. "My clients are all good people, at least as far as I know. They pay on time, they aren't too messy, and if there's ever an extra clean, like if they've had a party or whatever, they tip me extra. It's fine. All good." She rolls her eyes. "And the presents at Christmas. That's a nice bonus."

"Extra cash is always handy—especially at that time of year." She bursts out laughing.

"*Cash?!* I wish. Sure, some give me an envelope, but others…" She shakes her head. "I get gourmet artisanal vinegars, scented fucking candles, artistic *objets* for my house—they have no idea how I live." She waves her arm across the room, revealing her humble home. It's definitely modest and, I can't help but notice, it's really tidy for a woman with kids. I guess she's a good cleaner.

"Not exactly practical… what do you do? Regift them?"

"I mostly sell them online. Turn them into cash."

"Sometimes I get things I actually can use," she says, pointing to a luxurious cashmere throw tossed across the back of the sofa.

"It looks expensive."

"Oh, it definitely is," she laughs. "I'm pretty sure she re-gifted it to me. When she and her husband divorced she got rid of all the furniture, replaced literally everything."

"Someone's got money," I say. "How'd she afford that?"

"Divorce settlement I guess," Visser says, taking a deep drag on her cigarette. "Her ex-husband is rich. *Really* rich. Has a huge place down by the water." She thinks for a minute. "I shouldn't have said that. It's not fair. I'm sure she makes plenty of her own money. She's in politics—a local Councillor. Saw her in the paper the other day."

Margaret Lawrence. She was all over the papers before the canal murder story broke.

The front door opens and I turn, expecting to see Vogel. But it's a skinny young guy with dark hair, carrying a backpack. He ducks his head down in Pamela's direction but doesn't actually look at her, then heads down the hall to one of the bedrooms. I hear a door shut.

"One of your kids?" I sure hope not, the guy looks like he's thirty years old.

"Uh… no… I got married young, but not that young!" she laughs. "I was actually still in high school. Never finished of course. How could I? I was so consumed with playing house, then making babies. That's how I was raised."

"Church," she says in response to my raised eyebrow. "Not many of my school friends went onto post secondary." She shrugs. "I was raised in a very religious house—Christian Reform. That's what we did—got married, became wives and mothers."

"What did your husband do?"

"Farmer, at first. On his family's chicken farm. And then a long-distance trucker."

"You divorced?"

"He died."

I feel a lot of empathy for Pam Visser, a single mother, with some sort of disability judging by her cane. She's looking after her kids by working as a cleaner, renting out rooms in her home to help make ends meet.

"So… who was that young man?" I ask.

"That's just my tenant. Joshua Logan. Quiet guy, spends most of his time in his room, playing video games."

"Pays his rent on time?"

"You bet. Perfect tenant."

EIGHTEEN

THE DOOR OPENS and this time it's Vogel. The look he gives me says it's time to go, now.

"Thanks for your time Ms. Visser," I say, handing her my card and following him out the door. "We'll be back in touch if we have any more questions."

"What's up?" I ask as I climb in the car.

"We've got another disappearance," Vogel says. "From Kerr Residence."

My heart sinks. "When?"

"The resident didn't sign in last night, apparently. He went out to meet a friend, and didn't make curfew."

"I can't believe this. Why wouldn't they tell us at 11:01 last night? They are aware of what's going on!"

"You heard Joan Morton," Vogel scoffs. "She probably didn't want anyone to know. Hoped to cover it up. Or maybe she didn't want to get him in trouble."

"*Trouble*? He might be dead."

Morton is waiting for us in the lounge at the halfway house and she brings us directly into her office. She gets right to it.

"I'm sorry," she says, talking rapid fire. I guess she's nervous, and with good reason, since her facility seems to be going right off the rails. I wouldn't be surprised if it did close down, given what's happened. "We had a staff issue last night. Two staff members called in sick. They're frightened by what's going on. All of us are—staff and residents…"

"What's the name of the missing resident Ms. Morton?" Vogel interrupts. He's not interested in her explanations or excuses, nor am I.

"Nick Melnyk." My heart sinks. *Shit.* Even though I half-expected it, I hoped she'd say some other name. I catch Vogel looking at me and I wonder for a second if I've made a noise when I heard the name. Probably he knows me too well and could sense something is wrong.

"What can you tell us about him?" Vogel asks, turning back to Morton. "Anything unusual?"

"Not at all. He's always been a model…"

"Prisoner?"

"We prefer resident," she says, giving Vogel a look. "Quiet. No trouble." She's looking at the file on her desk, familiarizing herself with the contents. I doubt she even knew Melnyk.

"Nobody even realized Nick was out," she's still talking. "He didn't sign out… he just slipped away. I guess."

"There's no bed check?" Vogel asks. "To make sure everyone's accounted for after curfew? Especially recently, given what's been happening?"

She shakes her head, no doubt trying to formulate some explanation for yet another missing resident. As she said when we first met, the responsibility is all hers, and she's going to have to explain what happened—to the Ministry of Corrections, to the media and to the public.

"All I can tell you is he wasn't missed," she finally says. "There's really nothing much I can tell you about him."

No kidding. Nick Melnyk is just another case number, another budget line. I didn't like Morton the first time I laid eyes on her and I like her even less now, if that's even possible.

"He's a quiet young man," Morton says. "You'd barely know he was in the room. Nick Melnyk never caused trouble, never drew attention to himself."

"What can you tell us about him?" I ask. "His past life before he came here?" I know I can talk to his family but if there's any way to avoid meeting my cousin I'll take it.

"Sorry. If it's not in the records I won't know it." At least she's being honest. Morton flips open the file on her desk. "He's been with us for ten months now. Absolutely perfect record here, and in prison. He got his high school equivalency diploma and several college credits while in prison, and has passed several courses to make him employable upon release: forklift, scissor lift and pre-apprenticeship welding training."

"He was clearly heading for full release. There's no reason he would have broken parole…" The alternative doesn't need to be said. Morton fears Nick Melnyk will be found dead, like the other missing residents, which is exactly what Doreen was afraid was going to happen.

"Maybe he was frightened? If he suspected something was going on here, something dangerous?"

Morton puffs out her cheeks and averts her eyes. "Like what—a serial killer stalking his victims?" She laughs nervously.

"If that were the case," Vogel says. "I'd say he might be right, wouldn't you?" No wonder Doreen thought he was afraid. Nick Melnyk knew something was going on… and it scared him.

Morton drops her head into her hands, for the first time revealing some semblance of human emotion. "God. I'm sorry to be so flippant. It's just so… horrible. I can't even…"

"So, Nick Melnyk never reported anything to you? Or to another staff member? " She shakes her head. "Nick is the last resident I'd ever expect to run off. He didn't even like to leave the facility."

"What do you mean?"

"Our residents are granted a lot of freedoms," she says. "They're allowed to be out in the community, even have jobs if they can get them. Most stay out as long as they're allowed to every day—which makes sense, given that this place, despite the relative comfort, is an extension of prison.

"But Nick Melnyk was unusual. He stayed in all the time. He seemed happiest here, in the common room, talking with visitors and volunteers."

"He never went out?"

"I wouldn't say *never*. But… it was definitely less often than we usually see."

"Would you say he made friends here?"

"Oh yes, for sure. In the time he was living here, he seemed quite close to a few of our residents."

"Younger ones, like himself?"

"No, not necessarily," she says after a moment. "Nick is highly intelligent, so he could talk with anyone he chose to. He could be quite… charming. In fact, I'd say he often dominated the relationships."

"Can you give us any names of the men he became close to?"

She thinks about it. "Shaun Pearson. Tyler Comeau." A look comes over her face. "Nathan Ambrose…"

"And I bet they're all missing." Morton shrugs, staring into space. It's like she's numb. The efficient, professionally distanced woman we met just two days ago is gone.

"And there's nothing else… ?" I ask, giving her a pointed look.

"I've told you everything I know." I'm trying to decide if she looks shifty, or she's hiding something, but can't see any evidence of that.

"I assume you've informed his family?" Morton avoids my eye. So that's a no. "Please do so, immediately." It's not our job. Let Morton do hers and we'll mop up the mess.

"Please give us his family's address," Vogel says. "Should we expect the same reception as Shaun Pearson got from his parents on Father's Day?"

"No, no," she quickly says. "Nick's parents are lovely people. They've been here several times, to visit their son. They just live up in Fonthill."

I leave Vogel to take the address and leave without saying anything. I don't trust my voice to remain steady. *My cousin.*

"Want to go out there now?" Vogel asks once we're out of the building. I pretend to consider it, but the truth is I'd rather have a root canal than go out there. I could happily live out my life never meeting my cousin.

"No, it's been a long day." I shake my head, thankful for anything to delay the inevitable. "Let's let Morton give them the news first. I'm not up to dealing with a grieving family today." Vogel looks surprised, but doesn't argue.

NINETEEN

"**Let's just stop** in at Deeping's place for a quick visit," I say on the way back to the station. "I want to confirm something Pam Visser said." Vogel shrugs and pulls a U-turn on Killaley, then heads back to Coronation Drive. "About Deeping's kids objecting to him giving Tracey Reid extra cash."

There's no car on the driveway when we arrive. "Looks like Lionel Deeping isn't here," Vogel says. "Now what?"

"Let's talk to the neighbours. See what they've got to tell us about Clive Deeping. Maybe one of them noticed someone driving off in his Cadillac."

The houses on either side of Deeping's are empty. "Probably not home from work yet," Vogel says, checking his watch. Then in the house across the street I notice a curtain twitch.

"Somebody's watching," I elbow Vogel. "Exactly the kind of neighbour I was hoping to find."

We don't even get a chance to knock on the front door. By the time we've crossed the street and are heading up the front path we're intercepted by a woman riding an electric scooter. She's sped around the corner of her house to make sure she catches us before we get away. Her hair is piled up on top of her head in a messy bun and she's wearing glasses, even though there's another pair of glasses hanging from a chain around her neck.

"You're the police, right?" she barks. "I saw you yesterday, talking to Lionel." We don't get a chance to reply before she's talking again. "I tried to get out to speak with you then but by the time I made it outside you'd already gone. Today, I was ready for you!" She pats her scooter and grins. "Had it parked by the door."

"I'm sorry you had to go out of your way," Vogel says. "You could have asked Mr. Deeping for our number. I gave him my card." She looks horrified.

"Oh no! I do not want him to know I'm speaking to you. Or what I'm going to tell you. Promise me that!"

"Okay… Ms… ?"

"Laturno. Elise." She extends her hand and we introduce ourselves.

"Ms. Laturno," I begin. "We'll be discreet, I promise." Though why we have to be I don't know. It's unlikely that Lionel Deeping will be back to this street once his father's house is sold. "What is it you want to tell us?"

Elise Laturno looks around, making sure no-one is within earshot, which is absurd, given the suburban street is empty. "It's about Clive Deeping. I just never knew who to tell, and now he's dead…" We wait impatiently for her to get to the point.

"Clive Deeping was a demented old man," she blurts. "He needed to be in a home," she says. "I tried to tell them, more than once. But his kids wouldn't hear of it. His kids are both useless, crazy and greedy." I can't argue with her about Lionel. He was definitely odd.

"Why do you say that? *Crazy?*"

"You better believe it!" she says. "Coming and going at all hours. In and out of the house. Lionel's got a family and his own home. Why's he always here?"

"Visiting his father? Looking after him?"

"Please. They hated each other," she rolls her eyes. "And as for looking after him… they wouldn't lift a finger, no matter what we said."

"What you said? About what?"

"Clive Deeping was absolutely not fit to be on his own. My husband found him in the street one night, in his dressing gown, completely disoriented. We told his kids to put him into a home, but they just brushed it off. Long term care homes are expensive, and I'm sure they didn't want to spend the money."

"So they provided in-home care instead?"

"Oh no… he didn't have full time care," Laturno says. "That would be too much money. A woman just came in a few days a week to clean and help him out. And there was someone from the social services who came in to bathe him twice a week. Apart from that… .he was alone most of the time." So much for Lionel Deeping's story of how he and his sister came in every day to spend time with their father.

"And he had a violent temper! I once saw him hit that poor woman, his care worker—with his cane!"

"You saw him hit the care worker? Tracey Reid?"

"I don't know what her name is! But yes, he hauled off and hit her right on the head. Or it would have been the head but she turned just in time and it struck her on the shoulder. She was lucky."

Not sure how lucky Tracey Reid actually was, but we thank her for the information. I make sure to give her my card as we leave, in case she thinks of something else.

"Vogel," I'm thinking out loud. "What about this: The old guy has dementia, is losing it. He's hit her before. One time he does it again…"

"But this time she's not so lucky," Vogel says. "You think he killed her?"

"It's possible. He realizes what he's done, drags her body into the garage and puts her into the trunk. She wasn't a big person—just over five feet tall. I think even an old man could have managed it, if he took his time."

"Then he cleans up the mess, sits down in his chair, and has a fatal heart attack brought on by the stress?" Vogel thinks it over. "Okay… I guess that scans. But what about his car? Who took it out of the garage, drove it across town and set fire to it?"

"Someone trying to hide the evidence? The kids, trying to protect father's name?"

"I doubt it. The son didn't even realize the car was missing."

"If you believe him. They could be lying." I find it hard to imagine Lionel Deeping was acting. And he seems like such a feeble guy. But maybe the sister is a stronger personality.

"We need a warrant. Get FSU to swab the house and find evidence that Tracey Reid was killed there. Maybe we'll find the crime scene."

TWENTY

B**Y THE TIME** I'm home it's already dark and Maja has dinner ready. I'll miss that when she's gone. It means I'll be back to microwave meals or drinking my calories in the form of Sauvignon Blanc.

When I finish cleaning up the kitchen I find Maja on the deck reading the paper under the porch light.

"You'll strain your eyes," I say, aware I sound just like my mother. She smiles and points out the article on the front page.

"Look, it's you," she says. There's a shot of the crime scene at the bridge, taken when the bodies were first discovered two days ago. Since the local paper only comes out once a week, most of the news isn't exactly breaking. Still, it's a huge story that's been getting national coverage and prompting all kinds of editorials and reports about the criminal justice system. It should provide enough fodder for months for pundits to chew on.

"I'm going to light a fire," Maja says, handing me the paper. Then she piles wood into the fire pit, adds kindling and lights it while I flip through the paper.

Next to the photo is an article about the controversy surrounding the halfway house when it first opened, suggesting it should never have been allowed to open at all. The Trustees of the Kerr Estate should have listened to the citizens and ensured public safety, though honestly all I can see is that the public hasn't been harmed at all—just the parolees. Seems to me the killer is on the public's side.

There's also a photo taken at one of the Town Council meetings when they were discussing the halfway house proposal. There are dozens of people with angry faces, shouting at the Council, many of whom look familiar, which isn't surprising, given the size of our small town. I squint in the poor light to get a better look. It's Warren Kerr, his face a mask of rage as he shakes his fist at the Councillors.

"Wine?" Maja asks once the fire is going well, as if she needs to ask. She heads inside while I scan a follow up article about Margaret Lawrence and her leaked nude photos. Since the discovery of the bodies her scandal has been pushed off the front page, which makes her a lucky woman, all things considered.

"Help me with this." Maja is struggling to open the door as she's balancing two glasses of wine on top of the cardboard box I brought home from the station. It's been sitting on the floor ever since, and I've been avoiding it ever since. "You need to deal with this," Maja says. "You can't avoid it forever."

"Are you sure?" I force a laugh. "I've been doing a pretty good job of it so far."

We head over to sit by the fire pit and drink our wine before I gather enough courage to open the box. Maja pulls out a bundle of photographs and hands them to me.

The images are all in black and white, of men in suits and hats, ladies in wasp-waisted dresses with full skirts, standing in front of big cars, or in front of houses I don't recognize, some holding children's hands as they squint into the camera.

"Who are these people?" Maja asks.

"I have no idea." I stare at them, trying to decode their connection to my parents, and to me.

Then I realize they aren't connected to me, not at all. They were friends or relations of my adopted parents; they're people I've never met, never even heard of, people who are very likely dead by now.

There are photos of Christmases past, of parties with laughing faces, of tables laid with bottles of wine and plates of food, of Christmas trees, and piles of presents. My parents are in some photos, looking younger than when I knew them. There are pictures of children's birthday parties, none of them mine.

I pass them on to Maja after I've looked at them. "But you aren't in any of these," she says. "They look like they're from before you were even adopted."

"I know."

"Why did they send these to you? Are they trying to be cruel?"

"Maybe," I say, emptying my wine glass. "More likely they just kept whatever they wanted and threw the leftovers into this box."

Maja goes in to get another bottle of wine, leaving me holding the meaningless photographs. I feel cold, despite the heat of the fire and the warmth from the wine.

I don't have any photos like these, of random relatives or family parties—not from my adopted one or my birth family. If my birth family even had a camera when I lived with them, one of my uncles would have sold it for drugs. Not that there would have been any parties or Christmases like these to document.

"How long did you live with them?" Maja asks. "Since you were eleven or twelve?"

"Almost ten years. When I finished University they retired down East."

"So they looked after you, but not as long as your real mother. Your birth mother." Maja is treading carefully here… she knows she's on very difficult ground. "I guess the siblings don't think that ten years means much, that you're not really part of the family."

I feel a stab in my gut. "Maybe I wanted them to be," I choke.

"I wanted to feel like the Gauthiers really were my family. They told me so all the time. And I believed them."

"I'm sure they meant it. They sound like good people." Maja takes the photos out of my hands and wraps her arms around me. "Anyway, you've got me. I'm your family now. None of this matters any more."

But you're going away! You're leaving me! I want to scream at her. But I don't. I hope she'll come back to me. She says she will and I have to believe that.

"I'm off to bed," Maja says, giving me a kiss. "I've got an early call."

After Maja leaves I stay by the fire, staring as it burns to embers, drinking the rest of the bottle.

I dread her going away and not just because I'll be alone again. My anxiety has been under control while she's been living with me. I haven't had any panic attacks in months, I'm managing my anger and I haven't killed anyone lately—an ongoing joke I tell myself to keep it light. But I know things will get heavy again when she's gone, and I'm afraid something bad will happen.

I tell myself that tomorrow I'll call my therapist and make an appointment, but I know I'm lying. Since Maja moved in I've even cancelled a few times and I've been decreasing my meds because I feel so much better. I wonder if I'll need them more once Maja's gone; I expect I will.

God I'm tired. For so much of my life I've been acting *as if,* pretending to be someone I'm not. Hiding my past, hiding my true nature. I finally told Maja some of it—but not all. Never all of it. How could I? She loves me anyway, loves me despite what I've told her about my past.

When I was a child I worked so hard at being a perfect girl so I'd be adopted by the Gauthiers. I'd have done anything to never have to return to the havoc and chaos of the East Village, to the life I'd come from, or to the care home. I kept everything perfect: my room, my schoolwork. My foster mother would come home from work to find the house perfectly tidy. I wanted them to need me—or at least to not see me as a burden.

We want our parents to love us, to take care of us—and if they don't we think it's our fault. Never mind if they're drug addicts and criminals, we still want their love and care. When the Gauthiers fostered me, I tried to become the kind of child I thought they'd love. I created a new version of myself because I knew the real me wasn't good enough. But the work of hiding my true nature, of burying my emotions is exhausting. And I know, deep in my soul, that if anyone ever sees the truth of who I am behind my mask, they won't love me. They couldn't. Not even Maja.

No wonder I'm exhausted.

I stare at the photos, looking for clues, for some insight into who these people might be, and if they could somehow be connected to me. Of course I know they aren't; it's a fantasy. There's no one alive who even knows who they are, who can tell me how I fit in to the pictures. If I do. They are the Gauthiers' friends, not really mine. Just like my parents themselves. Yes, they loved me, but I'm not their blood. My blood is different—very different.

One by one I toss the photos into the flame, and watch as they crinkle and smoulder, finally reducing down to a tiny spark. Then in a blink they're gone.

TWENTY ONE

Friday

MELNYK'S BRICK BUNGALOW is tucked in at the end of a quiet cul de sac. It's surrounded by overgrown shrubs and mostly dead grass and looks neglected, apart from a few annual flowers tucked in next to the path. There's a pair of stone lions flanking the front path that look oddly pretentious and out of place.

"Those belong in a much bigger house, don't you think? Ostentatious. "

"My parents' have a pair like that," Vogel says. "At their new house."

"Why am I not surprised?" I mutter.

"What exactly is wrong with you Gauthier?" Vogel says, glaring at me.

"I'm sorry," I lie. "I'm just hungover."

"Right. And not only this morning." He climbs out of the car, slamming the door shut. "It's every damn day and it's really getting tired."

Dammit. I don't need to deal with Vogel's feelings, especially today. I've got my own to manage and I don't like *feelings,* even on a good day.

I barely slept last night, thanks to the bottle of Shiraz I drank, full of dread about this morning's interview with Nick Melnyk's parents. I don't want to meet my cousin Nick. I resent even knowing he exists and my brutal red wine hangover isn't making it any easier.

Head throbbing, I drag myself out of the car and join Vogel on the front porch, avoiding his eye like a sulky child. I know he's right, but that doesn't make this any easier.

"Good morning Sir. We're from…" Vogel says when the door opens.

"Have you found him?" Melnyk interrupts. "Have you found Nick?" I study his face, looking for some resemblance to my mother and I find it.

Melnyk looks exactly like my uncle, or how I remember him. It's the eyes. He has my mother's eyes. I'm frozen and unable to speak. Vogel notices me staring at Melnyk and gives me a puzzled look.

"I'm sorry. No, we haven't."

"Don't be sorry," Melnyk says. "That's good news, right? I'm afraid you will find him… and he'll be… Like those other guys I heard about on the news."

He invites us into the living room. It's nicely furnished, by someone who has spent a lot of time watching decorating shows on television.

I pick up a photo of Nick from the side table. He looks just like my mother too, and maybe even like me. The family resemblance is so strong. It's all in the eyes. Those sad, haunted eyes. I quickly put the photo back on the table, face down in case Vogel notices.

When I was young my uncle used to hang around the house and dangle me on his knee, with a cigarette in one hand and a beer in the other. I remember his rock music playing, his half-closed eyes and big grin and both of us laughing so hard. I liked him. When I was a few years older my memories are of him passed out on our living room couch when I came home from school, curtains drawn during the daytime and a pile of cigarette butts in the ashtray. He looked after me when my mother worked nights at the club, which meant I'd watch tv all night while he played cards with his buddies in the kitchen. I'd stay up until I heard her car drive up, then I'd quickly turn off the tv and run upstairs so she didn't realize I was still awake.

"What can you tell us about your son?" Vogel asks, flipping open his notebook. "Anywhere he might have gone? Any friends he might be staying with?"

Melnyk shakes his head. "I already told all of that to them, at the halfway house. There's nobody."

"And he didn't let on to you that he was thinking of running off?"

"There's no way he'd ever have done that! He's almost finished his parole. Why would he run now?"

"Maybe he was frightened?" It's certainly possible Nick Melnyk ran away to save himself. Once the news broke about the halfway house killings he might have thought it was better to take his chances elsewhere.

Melnyk's father just shakes his head and throws up his hands. He's obviously exhausted and worried. It's clear he loves his son.

"What can you tell us about Nick?" Vogel asks. "Was he a good student? Athletic?"

"No. None of that," Melnyk says, heaving a big sigh. He gets up and starts fidgeting, fluffing pillows and moving objects around. He's clearly uncomfortable and I wonder why. "My son was always a difficult child. He didn't do well in school, was in trouble a lot. We thought he had a learning problem, so we had him tested.

"Turns out he's a genius. Intellectually gifted, off the charts, but socially he was... off." My mental image of Nick is getting mixed up and I start to pay closer attention to what Melnyk's saying. If he was a genius I can't imagine why he received forklift training in prison, rather than something more academic. Something doesn't fit.

"He's on the spectrum?" Vogel asks. "Not neurotypical?"

"High functioning autism," Melnyk nods. "He's some kind of a savant when it comes to math and computation. But he has real difficulties with social interaction, with people. He was bored at school, so he'd get into trouble—that's how we first figured out something wasn't right with him."

"You got him some help?"

Melnyk seems to perk up. "We got him into a therapist. Nick was anxious, depressed… tired all the time." He's keen to explain his son, to convince us, or maybe himself.

"Kids like Nick, they spend all their energy trying to seem *normal,* like the other kids. Trying to fit in, to be accepted, to seem neurotypical. Some of them are so good at masking they don't even know who they really are anymore."

"Masking?"

"Autism often presents with this unemotional, blank affect," Melnyk says. "Masking is an adaptation strategy, a survival technique. Often kids like Nick will mimic gestures and imitate facial expressions, trying to fit in with the *normals."* Melnyk makes air quotes. "It's always been difficult for Nick to read other people. Relationships are… difficult for him. And it's not that he doesn't care about other people or have empathy—he just doesn't show it."

It's difficult to reconcile what he's saying with what Morton told us yesterday, about Nick being so charming and getting close to several other residents. Maybe there's hope for therapy after all.

"Masking delays diagnosis… it did with us anyway. We didn't even realize anything was going on with our son."

"Did the therapy help Nick… fit in?"

Melnyk laughs bitterly. "Sure. I guess. But by the time we figured all this out he'd already found a way of fitting in and seeming *normal*—smoking weed, skipping classes, hanging out with the *bad kids* at school, the other misfits. And... .one thing led to another."

"He got into trouble?" Melnyk nods and I see there are tears in his eyes.

"Nothing like supplying drugs to make the other kids like you," he says. "He may have even convinced himself they were *friends*. Those kids, they were just using my son. They put him up to it." I don't say anything. I've heard this story before, from many grieving parents who are in denial about their kids' criminal activities. It's never their kids' fault, not really, and they reject any evidence that their kids might be troubled or guilty.

What I'm hearing him say is that Melnyk didn't have any real friends, just the kids he sold drugs to. Again, that doesn't jibe with what Morton said. Was Melnyk mis-diagnosed? Who is the real Nick Melnyk? He's not at all like what he presents. Is he hiding his truth? Is he like me?

My anxiety spikes and I feel a flush of anger. That's why I didn't want anything to do with him in the first place.

Vogel looks through his notes. "So your son was arrested... for trafficking drugs?"

Melnyk isn't listening. "You know, you work hard, do all the right things, try so damn hard to get it right... ." He shakes his head, wipes a tear from his eye. "And it all goes to shit."

"Is Nick your only child?" I ask.

Melnyk nods. "We only had one. There were... issues. Medical issues. My wife couldn't go through it again."

"Where is Mrs. Melnyk?"

"She's no longer living here," he says. "We're separated."

"We'll need her contact information."

"Why?" Melnyk pushes back. "She wouldn't know anything—she and Nick aren't close."

"Why's that?" In my experience, indifferent parents lead to messed-up kids. Maybe that explains some of Nick Melnyk's problems.

"She lacks maternal instincts," he says, his lips twisted. "Maybe she blames him for the hard time she went through giving birth to him." He gives Vogel a wink and circles his finger around the side of his head.

I call him on it. "Are you saying she's got a screw loose? She's mentally ill?"

"I couldn't tell you." He shrugs. "She's in therapy." He may not be able to tell us, but he's sure hinting loud enough. It's clear Melnyk blames his wife for Nick's issues.

Melnyk picks up the photograph of his son and stares at it. "He had everything he needed, and most of what he wanted. All of our attention. Our time. Our money. We're not poor, we live in a good area, excellent school catchment area…" He shrugs. "But, you know the saying… these things miss a generation."

My heart leaps in my chest. "What do you mean?" My voice is hoarse. I'm afraid of what he'll say.

"My father wasn't a good man. He was a criminal," he says. "And I swore I'd never be anything like him. And that my kids would have every advantage I could give them. I kept that promise. But look what happened… my son…"

"A criminal?" Vogel presses.

"He was also an addict," Melnyk says, half answering. "Opiates. He was on methadone, while he was in prison, and later at a halfway house. He'd get his daily dose… But now he's gone the same way my sister did."

"What do you mean, Sir?" I ask, my voice cracking with nerves. "Your *sister*?"

He wipes his hand over his face. "She was an addict. Like my father, and his brother." I hold my breath, waiting for him to mention my mother, but he doesn't. Maybe he doesn't even know the story. Maybe it's just me.

"In and out of rehab. On the streets. The first few times I helped her out, tried to get her back on her feet. But she always fell off the wagon, again and again. She was clean at my wedding, I know that for a fact—I could see it in her eyes. They were clear. Then after my wife and I got married, bought the house, had the baby... I just lost track of her."

"What happened to her?"

He shrugs and points at the front door. "The last time I saw her, she knocked on that very door, just when my wife was feeding the baby. I answered and saw her there, on the doorstep." He shakes his head. "She was smiling at me, this pathetically hopeful expression on her face."

"What did she want?"

"I have no idea. I just... I just couldn't deal with it anymore. I don't know what she wanted but I knew I had nothing more to give her."

"What did you do?"

"I closed the door in her face and went back to my wife. Told her it was a kid handing out flyers for window washing. My wife doesn't even know about my sister. My family. My shitty, terrible family."

Believe me, I understand, I almost say. Melnyk's story is something I'm very familiar with. Put it all behind you, wipe it out, deny the past so you can change your future. Nobody's ever going to convince me it doesn't work.

"What happened to your sister?"

"She died, a couple of months later. Overdose." He stares out the window. "And I know it's my fault, you don't have to tell me it's not." Vogel starts to say something but I talk over him.

"There's always a trigger to get someone back using again. This was hers. She might have OD'd another time, for another reason, but if she was an addict she was always going to go that way, if she didn't get help."

Melnyk starts in surprise. Not what he expected to hear I guess. Then he bursts into tears. "I think about her every day," he sobs. "What I could have done to help her."

"But you were too busy helping yourself. I understand, the need to escape that life. To escape the past."

"What do you know about the fucking East Village?" he snaps. I just smile.

"I've been a cop long enough to learn." He doesn't need to know my history, and I'm not going to tell him.

Vogel turns on me once we're back in the car. "What the hell Gauthier! Why'd you have to talk to him like that? You told him his sister's death is his fault."

"That's because it is. He had a choice—save her or himself. He chose himself and his family over her." It's a choice I understand.

TWENTY TWO

I SHUT DOWN after that. Talking to Melnyk took what little I have left this morning right out of me. I need some space to calm down so I pull out my phone and start to pretend I'm checking email. Really I'm just scrolling blindly, brooding on my cousin and how his life—and his sister's, turned out.

Vogel, for all his irritating faults, has a high EQ. He notices I'm upset, but he just can't stop himself from prying.

"Are you okay?" he asks. I ignore him. "You seem upset." He drives for a few more minutes in silence then just can't remain quiet any longer.

"Is there something about this Melnyk situation that's getting under your skin? Ever since we first heard his name yesterday at Kerr Residence you've been… weird."

My head snaps up so fast I hear my neck crack. "His name!? What are you fucking talking about? Why should it get under my skin?"

"I'm not saying it *should*. I'm saying it has. I can see it and I want to know why."

"It isn't and you're mistaken."

Vogel stares at me for a moment in silence, then turns away and focuses on the road. I doubt he's convinced, based on how his brow is furrowed. He heads down Highway 140 and makes it all the way onto Welland Street, crossing the Clarence Street bridge before he says another word. Knowing Vogel as I do, I understand that must have been torture for him.

"I'm going to have to investigate you, Gauthier," he says with a smile. "Why are you always so secretive?"

"*Back the fuck off Vogel.*" The look in my eyes tells him I'm not kidding around.

"Woah!" He recoils in shock. "I'm just joking." Then he looks at me, more concerned than curious. I feel bad for a moment but it passes. He needs to stay the hell out of my private life.

We're passing the Green Bean Cafe on Clarence Street and I tell Vogel to pull over. "I need a coffee." He pulls over so fast I'm sure he can't wait to get me out of the car.

I'm waiting in line at the counter when I spot Doreen sitting at her usual table in the window.

"What are you doing here?" I ask, then catch myself. "I mean, how'd you get here?" My attempt at correcting my tone doesn't fool Doreen.

"Who pissed in your cornflakes?" she says. "What's your problem?"

"Sorry," I mumble. "People just need to mind their own damn business. I don't mean you," I quickly add when I see her hurt expression. "It's just been a crap morning."

"I find a day that starts out shitty can only get better," she says in her gravelly voice. "Usually."

"So… what brings you into town?"

"I came on the short bus," she chuckles. "The rest of them are out at the Farmer's Market."

"Not you?"

"I got everything I need at the liquor store," she says, patting the handle of her walker. "I'm good." Doreen takes a sip of her coffee, her eyes never leaving my face, waiting for me to explain.

"We just left Nick Melnyk's place," I finally say. "He's gone missing." Doreen nods, unsurprised.

"Figured that was coming," she growls.

"You never mentioned he's autistic." That gets her attention. She leans in closer so I can discreetly fill her in on everything Melnyk told us. "And the sister— my cousin, I guess? She's dead," I add. "Overdose."

Doreen nods. "That fits."

She's taking a bite of her cinnamon bun as I see a fishing hat standing above the crowd at the counter.

"Well, well," Doreen mutters. "Look who's here. Haven't seen him in a while. It's Warren Kerr," she says, following my gaze. The expression on her face makes it clear she can't stand him.

"You know him? From where?"

"Oh, just from around town," Doreen says. "He lived in the big house," she laughs. "His family is very important... Town founders and all that shit."

"What *big house*?"

Doreen bursts out laughing as she points down the street. "That one! The Kerr Residence!"

I feel like I've been blindsided. How did I not put that together earlier? "You're telling me Warren Kerr—that old guy with the fishing hat—used to own that house?"

"No, he never owned it," Doreen says. "His mother did. When she died, she left it to the town."

"Not to her own son? Are you serious?"

"Families, eh?" Doreen has a twinkle in her eye and she takes her time, sipping her coffee. I know enough to let her enjoy herself—she doesn't get out much. Let her dine out on the story.

"Word is the old lady hated her son. No idea why. But it's gotta be something big for these old families to cut the heir out of the Will... ." She finishes the last bite of her cinnamon bun and shakes her head. "Then again, who knows? It could have been something as simple as he wasn't fit to be in the family business, or carry on the tradition and all that crap."

"What was this *family business* that he wasn't fit for?" She shrugs and sips her coffee. I can never tell if she doesn't know, or if she doesn't care, or if she's making a note to find out.

"What did he end up doing?"

"Mechanic," she says. "He always was a piston head as I recall. He had an auto shop out on Killaley for a while. Sold used cars." She thinks for a minute. "As I recall at some point he got a dealership in town—GMC? Cadillac, maybe. I don't remember. Pretty sure the family helped with that. It was more prestigious than being just a lowly mechanic. Made a lot of money I hear." She watches Warren Kerr over the rim of her coffee cup. "That's usually how it works. The rich get richer."

"What was his mother like?" It is odd that she supposedly hated her son. Warren Kerr was jovial and friendly at the marina, even though he'd been a prick the first night I met him. "He seems harmless enough."

"Queen Kerr," Doreen smirks.

"Her name was *Queen*?"

Doreen gives me a look. "No! It was Katherine, I think. Queen's what we used to call her. She used to lord it over people in town, back in the day. Gotta say, she was a real bitch. Then, when she got older and more peculiar, everyone started calling her Queenie…"

"To her face?"

"Oh yeah, in the street, even at church." Doreen laughs. "But she loved it! She wore her fur coats and her jewels to the grocery store! She'd pretty much lost the plot by then."

"Dementia?"

"Who knows? Inbreeding? These old families. Maybe that's

why Warren never married—he didn't have any cousins!" She bursts out laughing so hard at her own joke I'm afraid her dentures are going to fly across the table.

I hand a coffee to Vogel as a peace offering, both for my being miserable and for taking so long. He accepts it with a grin, everything forgotten. That's Vogel for you—he never holds onto anger, unlike me. I can nurse a grudge for decades; in fact, I've been doing it my whole life.

He drives over the bridge then follows the canal down to the wharf and Sugarloaf Marina, where we leave the car and walk back the way we came, following the canal, all the way back up to Bridge 19 to where the bodies were found. I'm still angry with Vogel and I do my best to say as little as possible—in case I say something I end up regretting. Feeling angry all the time is bad enough without adding guilt into the mix.

Vogel's talking about the damn bridges along the canal again. How the Clarence Street bridge is one of the last remaining lift bridges in the country and how the bascule bridges—or maybe the jackknife drawbridges—are engineering marvels, how they roll up with the help of the counterweight. He does go on.

Vogel doesn't seem to notice, or at least he's not pushing me to engage. I'm grateful for that. One thing I've decided is that Vogel's a better person than I am and I kind of hate him for that. But mostly, I'm grateful.

"So, if you were going to drop a body into the canal," Vogel says, sipping his coffee. "You'd need a boat, as we've agreed. And odds are the boat would be heading downbound on the canal—from Lake Erie into Lake Ontario."

"It's not going to have been one of the big freighters or tankers from somewhere across the world. They're just passing through town on the canal; it's not as if they stick around long enough to get to know anyone, or have contact with the parolees from Kerr Residence." I realize that isn't necessarily true. One of the crew working on a freighter might have known a parolee, but odds are not all eight of the victims.

"It had to be a pleasure craft. A small one, just big enough to carry two people, one of them dead weight…"

"And a bucket of concrete."

"See these boats here," Vogel points to the pleasure craft tied off along the wharf and the city docks along West Street. "Any one of them would do the job."

I look up and down West Street. "Maybe there are some security or CCTV cameras on shop fronts along here that picked up something."

Vogel screws up his face. "CCTV won't help, even if we could find some cameras. A pleasure craft or a fishing boat wouldn't even be seen from street level, not if they stayed close to the side. It's what, ten feet down to the surface of the water?"

Damn. This is frustrating. Why isn't anything easy? "How can he not be seen? It's right downtown! In the middle of everything!"

Vogel shrugs. "It's a small town. Except for Canal Days, not many people are ever hanging around down here, especially after dark." He gestures up the street. "What's there to do? No bars, shops closed."

"Which makes it a walk in the park for our killer to take his boat up the canal and dump the bodies." Then something occurs to me. "What about the Seaway Commission? They've got to have cameras on the canal, and on the bridges, right? Especially if they're remotely operated. Someone's got to be keeping an eye on things, even at a distance."

"Definitely. I'll call and see what we can get."

"Apart from that," I sigh. "It looks like all we know for sure is that he didn't do it in the winter."

Vogel laughs. "It would be tough to do when the canal is frozen over."

"We need to correlate the dates of disappearance with time of year. Did any of the parolees go missing in winter?"

Vogel flips open his notebook. I knew he'd have this information. "Nope, he says after a minute. All of them were between April and December, during shipping season when the canal was open."

At least that tells me we're on the right track.

TWENTY THREE

My phone rings with an update from FSU that puts me back into a better mood.

"They found evidence of blood in Clive Deeping's kitchen," I tell Vogel once I've ended the call. "A lot of blood, that someone didn't do a very good job of cleaning up."

"And?" Vogel leans back in his seat, all attention.

"It's a match to Tracey Reid, his care worker."

"So that narrows the possibilities to the Deepings, father and son."

"It's got to be Clive Deeping," Vogel says. "He had a cane, we know he was violent and had dementia…" I nod, half-listening. Someone else has a cane… but I can't remember if it's important. "The old man lost it for some reason, hit her with his cane, put her in the trunk, then had a heart attack from the stress and effort…"

"Well, if he killed her, then someone else moved the car and body—since he was inconveniently dead at the time."

"Or someone stole the car out of the garage."

"That means we have two separate crimes, and a big coincidence. How unlucky would you have to be to steal a car that had a dead body in the trunk?"

"True. But we don't actually *know* the car was stolen… Unless you believe Lionel Deeping. It could be that someone knew what

136

happened and took care of things—removed the body, cleaned up the blood and tried to destroy the evidence by torching the car."

"Lionel Deeping, covering up for what his father did?" Vogel considers the idea. "Maybe. But I can't really see Lionel Deeping being up to any of that, do you? The guy seems incapable."

"Lots of people are more capable than they realize, when they find themselves in a tight spot," I say. "In fact, Lionel Deeping could be the killer, using his father's cane."

Vogel shakes his head, completely rejecting the idea. "What's his motive? Not sure why we're looking to make it more complicated. We've already got a witness who's told us the old man was abusive, and she witnessed him striking Reid. He sounds more likely to me."

My phone rings again. This time it's dispatch.

"We need to get over to Park Street. The computer repair shop," I tell Vogel once I'm off the phone. "Break in… and a body."

Vogel makes a face and checks his watch. "Are you kidding me?"

"Yeah, I know. We're closest."

"Figures. I've got plans tonight," he mutters as we head for the car.

The computer shop is in a strip mall, between a nail salon and an Indian takeaway I go to all the time that sells delicious *bhajis*, *samosas* and grocery items. Two patrol cars are parked in front and the FSU team is just arriving when we pull up.

"What have we got?" I ask the constable posted at the door.

"Place has been trashed. One victim behind the counter. Looks like massive head trauma. It's a mess. We think it's the owner, but he hasn't been formally identified yet."

We enter the premises after putting on protective booties and gloves. The constable is right—the place has been destroyed. Computer monitors are smashed all over the floor, display boxes of games and software are strewn around, and the glass countertop has a computer tower smashed right through it.

"Looks like someone was in a rage. Certainly an extreme amount of damage."

"Hard to say if anything's been stolen. Looks more like it's just been trashed."

"Motive might not be money. Almost seems like overkill," Vogel says glancing around the destruction. "Kill him and destroy his store?"

"Do we know his name?" I ask Vogel, who's standing over the body, carefully searching his pockets for some ID.

He extracts a wallet and flips it open, then compares the image on the driver's license with our dead guy. "Joshua Logan," he pronounces.

"Why do I know that name?" I carefully lean across the broken glass counter to get a look at our victim and recognize him immediately. "It's the tenant from Pamela Visser's place. He was a roommate of Tracey Reid's."

"Well, well," Vogel says as he starts going through the piles of papers and invoices scattered around the room. "The plot thickens."

"So, we've got a murdered home care worker, and now a guy who runs a computer repair shop. What's the connection between them—apart from their being roommates?" I have an idea forming in my mind, but it's not taking shape quickly enough. "Do you suppose he keeps a customer list somewhere? People who he's sold computers to or maybe done service for?"

"Probably," Vogel sighs. "Somewhere in this mess." There are heaps of invoices strewn around the front counter and I flag them for FSU to collect. Vogel and I then make our way through the debris to the small back storeroom.

"Most of the stock here is still intact," Vogel says. "Possibly the killer exhausted his rage before he made it back here. Or maybe he was interrupted."

"Or possibly he found what he was looking for," I say, hoping I'm wrong.

There are dozens of computers and monitors in their boxes stacked on shelves, as well as bins full of AV and HDMI cables, audio and video cards, external hard drives and keyboards, and whatever else a computer store might need.

Tucked underneath the shelves are several banker's boxes clearly marked with years and dates. They are his sales records for the past five years. I flip one open and it contains copies of all the paper invoices and well as DVDs that I assume contain spreadsheets and tax filings. Joshua Logan was clearly very organized.

"Bingo," Vogel says with a grin.

"So, this guy repairs computers." I'm thinking aloud. "If someone dropped off their computer for repair, he'd have access to all the emails, documents, photos, whatever they've got stored, right?"

"Yeees… He'd even ask for the computer passwords to he could get into them to do the repairs."

"What if someone had something to hide, something private…"

"And Joshua Logan found it?" Vogel nods, liking the idea. "Maybe he found a way to exploit that information."

"And it came back to bite him, hard."

"We're going to have to go through his customer list with a fine toothed comb. Maybe something will turn up."

We watch as the Coroner arrives and starts to examine Logan's body. Thankfully it's Lewis Yun, not Victor Todor, so I don't have to shut up and keep out of the way. Dr. Yun is one of the Region's rotating Coroners and he's usually willing to share his observations with us rather than making us wait until the post mortem.

Vogel and I give him his space and continue our investigation of the wreckage in the store.

"So Vogel," I'm thinking out loud, trying to make sense of the idea that's been rattling around the back of my mind. "Apart from them both being dead, and that they both were tenants of Pam Visser, what else connects our two victims?"

"Deeping?" Vogel takes a guess. "Tracey Reid worked for him. Clive Deeping had a brand new computer on his dining room table—possibly from this store."

"That computer could have come from anywhere," I say. "But, this store is the cheapest in town. It's always busy, and it's convenient. I've had mine repaired here. He can do most PC repairs, he installs security protection, cleans out viruses, you name it. Anyway, the sales records will prove that one way or the other." I look around the mess of papers. "Assuming we can find them."

"It should be easy to prove Deeping's computer came from this store. But the question that's nagging me is why an elderly man, purportedly with dementia, needs to buy a brand new computer. An expensive one at that."

"Maybe he wasn't even aware he'd bought it," I say. "Maybe it's not even his."

"You think Lionel Deeping's lying?"

"Absolutely I do. And I don't think the computer was his father's at all. It's Lionel Deeping's—and we need to have FSU go through it. I bet they find the online history and files are all Lionel's."

Vogel nods. "Do you remember how weird was he acting when we met him? He was so… giddy, almost hysterical. At the time I put it down to him being upset about the missing car, or maybe his father's death."

"He made a point of telling us his father spent all his time online—which makes no sense at all if Clive Deeping had dementia."

I pick up the phone and request FSU search Deeping's computer. When I hang up, Vogel is nodding in agreement.

"So Lionel Deeping is keeping secrets from his wife or partner. Maybe hiding money? Secret bank accounts? Unsavoury hobbies?" Vogel says. "If he keeps the computer—his computer—at his father's house, she won't find out whatever they might be."

"Secrets." I'm thinking aloud as an idea occurs to me. "Who else do we know who had secrets? Ones that came out recently."

"Councillor Lawrence? With the nude photos?"

Yes. It fits. "What if Deeping was being blackmailed too?" That makes sense. I shudder to think what Lionel Deeping might have been up to.

"No wonder he was behaving so strangely! If he'd been hacked and was being blackmailed, then he finds out his father's car was stolen… it must have blown his mind. No wonder he practically had a breakdown."

"It's a perfect set up: Tracey Reid could get Logan into the house at any time she was working. If there was anything incriminating on the computer, then Logan would have no problem accessing it."

"*If* he was being blackmailed," Vogel says. "And he found out who was doing it…"

"Then we need to consider the possibility that he killed Joshua Logan." I nod. "And Tracey Reid too—assuming he found out the connection between Reid and Logan."

"He probably figured that out right away. She might have referred him to the store. *I've got a friend who can give you a good price.* Or, he made sure Reid told him Logan's name before he killed her."

"We need to talk with Deeping, just as soon as we find out what's on that computer."

"Lionel Deeping's such a wimpy odd guy," Vogel says. "Tough to think of him as being capable of murder, don't you think?"

"I think we're all capable of murder, Vogel."

TWENTY FOUR

P**AM** V**ISSER ANSWERS** the door before we've even climbed the steps to her front porch.

"Back so soon?" She's smiling, clearly unaware of the news. Then she sees our serious expressions. "What's wrong?"

"We're here about your tenant, Joshua Logan."

"What? No. You mean… Tracey, right?" Confusion and denial pass over her face, until it settles on fear. She's frightened. "Did something happen to Joshua?"

"I'm sorry to tell you his store was vandalised earlier today and Mr. Logan is dead."

"Dead?" She turns on her heel, almost tripping over her cane as she stumbles inside, visibly upset. Visser sits heavily onto the couch and stares into space, a frown creasing her forehead. "I don't understand," she mumbles. "Why would he be dead?"

"We need to have a look at his room," I say. "And remove any personal belongings that might be pertinent to the investigation. Did he have a laptop or desktop computer?"

Visser stares at me, astonished. "Are you kidding me? He had a store full, not to mention his room!" She waves her arm down the hall. "I'm not feeling too well today." She gestures to her leg. "I need to sit down. Just go on down the hall, okay? Last door on the left—that's Joshua's room."

Vogel and I leave her sitting on the couch, processing the news. I see her pull out her phone. The door to his room is unlocked and when we enter we have to flick on the overhead light, even though it's still early afternoon.

It's a standard bedroom with the blackout curtains that are drawn so it's pitch black inside. There's a futon bed in the corner with an IKEA dresser squeezed in next to it. The other three walls are lined with tables, each holding a computer, monitors, hard drives, and more paraphernalia and tools than I can identify.

"Looks like he brought his work home," Vogel says. "Maybe did the repairs here, after store hours."

"Maybe more than just repairs. We need to have all this brought in. Have tech go through it." I put in a call to request FSU and tech services support to collect all of Logan's equipment while Vogel starts going through Logan's closet and drawers.

"Anything?" I ask once he's done a cursory search.

He shrugs. "Not really. His wardrobe seems to consist of black band t-shirts and work pants. And more camouflage than seems healthy."

"Nothing personal anywhere," I say, looking around the room. "No mementos, no photos. Odd."

"He was an odd guy," Visser says. She's standing outside the room, leaning against the doorframe. "Joshua wasn't… like other people."

"Can you be more specific?"

"He never had much to say. Never joined in, like if Tracey and I were having a glass of wine or whatever. And to be honest, he wasn't exactly likeable." Vogel and I come out of the room, herding her in front of us. Even though she's had ample opportunity to be in and out of Logan's room as often as she liked, given it's her house, I don't want her tampering with anything now.

Visser sits back down on the couch, clearly upset. She seems nervous. No wonder, given that both of her roommates have just been killed. The odds of that happening are astronomical and I have to wonder what exactly is going on at this house, and whether it involves Pam Visser as well.

"Did you like Joshua Logan?" I ask once we're sitting down. "Were you friends?"

"No. Not if I'm honest." She looks uncomfortable. "He was a weird guy. But I need the money and he was looking for a place to rent."

"How do you mean *weird*?"

"He was a nerd—obviously, with all his computer stuff. Sad. And a loner, a bit… *off*, if you know what I mean. Kind of a misfit?"

"What do you know about his background? Like where he lived before he came here?"

"He was in the Armed Forces," she says. "Somewhere. Doing some kind of Tech Support position. A civilian employee, not enlisted."

"Did he try to enlist?"

She nods. "He didn't get in. I don't know why."

That could be a red flag, depending on why he was rejected. Visser called him a *misfit* and a *sad loner*. Maybe the recruitment officer didn't want Joshua Logan to have training in weapons, fighting and explosives. There's more than one person who joined the military because they wanted to kill people, legally. Now I really want to know what's on his computers—and if we'll find a clue there for why he was killed.

"Did he have a car?" Vogel asks.

"No. He could walk to the store from here. I think that's why he rented the room in the first place."

There's a knock on the door as the FSU team arrives to remove Logan's equipment. I glance at Pam while Vogel takes them down the hall. She's biting her nails and I wonder if she's afraid for herself or for what we might find on Logan's computers.

"I have to go… to pick up my kids," she says, looking at her watch. "School ends in a few minutes."

"No problem," Vogel says. "The team will be here when you get back."

"Um… actually, I was hoping they wouldn't have to see any of this," she sounds embarrassed. "Would it be okay if I took them out, to the beach or something, until you're done?" Vogel shrugs and she heads down the hall, returning with two tote bags stuffed with what I assume is their swimsuits and beach towels.

"Just close the door when you're done, okay?" she calls over her shoulder as she heads to her car, an old Ford Escape SUV. She's driving away before we can say anything else.

TWENTY FIVE

BACK AT THE station, we're waiting for results from FSU and working our way through reports of stolen cars without getting any clarity on the situation. It's my turn to pick up lunch, or maybe it's dinner since it's already late afternoon, so I drop Vogel at the station and as I head over to the Trini roti shop. I'm already hungry. Driving back to the station with two Buss Up Shut rotis with sides of rice and peas, the aroma in the car is so delicious I struggle to resist the urge to eat mine on the way.

Vogel's in a very good mood when I get in. I hope it's because we've had good news from FSU and not because of his current girlfriend. He unwraps and inspects his roti while I'm wolfing mine down. I can't believe he hasn't even started his lunch.

"No hot sauce?" he asks. I toss him the paper bag with the condiments.

"Sorry. I forgot." Vogel needs everything doused in hot pepper sauce.

"Gauthier," he says through a mouthful of roti. "I've been thinking."

I can't avoid the low hanging fruit. "Nice for a change." He smirks but doesn't bite back.

"Who would steal cars like that—drive them around and then return them?" He continues as he dumps some pepper sauce onto his roti and takes a bite, then rolls his eyes with pleasure. "It's… odd."

"Someone who needs a car, doesn't have one, can't borrow one and can't afford to rent one?"

"Exactly. And why do people need vehicles?"

"To get around. To move things… ."

Vogel nods, waiting for me to catch up. When he sees I get it he breaks into a grin.

"He needs it to move things… in the trunk! He's our killer and he needs a car to move bodies to the canal? From wherever he's been keeping them. Or maybe keeping the parolees, alive, until he was ready to dispose of them."

"What's better way than to use someone else's car? Any forensic evidence from the victims can't possibly be traced back to him, if we ever caught up with him."

"Our killer doesn't have a car, and is smart enough to use other people's vehicles so he's not tied to the victims."

"We need to see if there's a match between the dates the parolees went missing from Kerr Residence and when the cars were stolen."

Within half an hour Vogel and I have created a spreadsheet. "It fits," Vogel says. "The dates match up." He points at the screen. Every one of these cars was stolen around the time period when these parolees went missing."

"Okay, we need to pull them in and test each of their trunks for forensic evidence. It's been a couple of years in some cases, but we may get lucky."

"It'll take a while to get warrants," Vogel says. I roll my eyes.

"We don't have time for that. Let's just ask nicely."

"Guess by that you mean I'll be doing the asking," he laughs. "*Nicely* isn't your thing."

For the next couple of hours Vogel and I work the phones, calling everyone on the spreadsheet who's reported their car borrowed or stolen. By the time we're done, our elation fades. We're facing another wait while FSU goes through each car—and it'll probably be days before we hear anything about what they might discover.

I get up and stretch my legs, my tight hamstrings telling me I'll regret missing my workout today. And yesterday, now that I think of it. *Damn.* No wonder I'm tense and irritable. I need my workouts to burn off my anxiety and adrenaline and help me set my world in order. If I don't keep on top of them, it feels as if everything piles up on top of me, the weight of my own life and the memories I'm carrying around all the time crushing me, grinding me to dust.

I walk outside, taking a few turns around the parking lot. Not exactly a workout, but deep breathing in the early summer evening air improves my mood and clears my head.

"Vogel, something doesn't fit," I say when I come back in. He gives me a look, sighs deeply and leans back in his chair. Vogel knows me well.

"Clive Deeping's car." Vogel nods. "Our killer needs the trunk. So he *borrows* the car, as we hypothesize. He brings it home or to wherever he keeps his victims, and is about to put one of the parolees into it when he sees Tracey Reid's corpse."

"Right."

"But then he supposedly panics, drives the car out to Neff Road and burns it? Why? Why not just return it to where he stole it from? Leave Deeping's family to find the body, eventually."

"You're right," Vogel's eyes light up. "Because by burning it he's alerted us. He's slipped up." His smile fades. "Not that it helps us, exactly. We still don't know who he is."

"No. But… maybe we can find out what he looks like." I push my chair over next to Vogel's. "We must have some CCTV footage from wherever those stolen cars were taken from, right? Like at the airport?"

Vogel gets excited. "We just got the security camera footage from the long term parking at the airport. From when Whitney's car was taken." I roll my chair around next to Vogel's and we start to screen the footage.

Within a minute Vogel is whining. "There's so much here. Weeks of this stuff. We'll need support to help screen this all." He's reaching for the phone when I intercept him.

"Hang on a minute. We only need to look at the times one of the parolees disappeared. Who's on our list as going missing while Whitney was away?"

"I get it," Vogel says as he starts to pull up the footage from the relevant dates while I go through the spreadsheet listing the dates Kerr residents were reported missing. "If we work from the dates of the parolees' disappearances, then match that with the reports of missing cars…"

"… .and possibly some CCTV footage," I say as I find a name on the spreadsheet. "Here's one. Nathan Ambrose. That's one of Melnyk's buddies, right? Isn't that what Morton told us?" Vogel nods. "According to this, he disappeared in April."

"Bingo!" Vogel says. "That's when Whitney's car went missing."

Vogel fast-forwards the video footage to a few days before Nathan Ambrose disappeared, to allow for a margin of errors with the dates and presses play. We lean forward, peering at the monitor and watching for Whitney's Cadillac Escalade to exit the parking garage.

"Whoever borrowed the car would have paid with cash to exit the lot, rather than credit or debit."

"Not that many people use cash anymore. That'll help narrow it down. I'll keep an eye on the kiosk for people who used bills to settle."

Finally we see the Cadillac leaving the lot on April 3. "That's definitely it," Vogel says, pausing the playback and zooming in on the license plate. He starts the video again, in slow motion. We see the driver's hands, wearing gloves, handing over bills to pay the bill, then the barrier is raised and he drives out of the lot.

"Can you see his face?"

"No. He's smart enough to avoid the cameras." Vogel's right. The driver is wearing a dark jacket and a baseball cap. He keeps his head down and face averted.

"From the height I'd say it's a male, maybe about six feet tall, white."

"Sounds just like Ron Whitney."

"Why would he steal his own car?" Vogel is exasperated. "That makes no sense."

"Plausible deniability," I shrug. "If he reports it as stolen, then any trace evidence from a crime that might show up one day, he's got an explanation."

"Gauthier, there's just no way Whitney is our guy," Vogel laughs in exasperation. "Why would he be killing parolees and dumping them in the canal? For fun? It's ridiculous."

"Fine, forget Whitney for the moment," I say, pointing at the monitor. "Our guy there now drives that Cadillac out of the lot and *possibly* uses it to dispose of Nathan Ambrose's body in the canal. Then he'll return it at some point over the next few days. We need to see when he returns it."

"Once we learn the days it was being driven around, before it was returned, we can look at all the CCTV footage in town, especially around the canal, and see if the vehicle turns up. Then we might get a better look at our guy. Maybe he'll have been less careful than he's been at the airport."

After another hour of eyestrain, we see the Cadillac Escalade being driven into the airport parking garage, on April 7. Once again the driver has taken pains to disguise his appearance and we can't identify him from the video camera footage.

"So, between April 3 and April 7 our killer *possibly* used Ron Whitney's Escalade to dispose of a body, *probably* that of Nathan Ambrose. Let's get onto the St. Lawrence Seaway Corporation and get access to their footage. And we'll definitely need some help looking at the rest of the footage from the streets in town for that time period. Maybe we'll get lucky."

TWENTY SIX

I leave Vogel looking at CCTV footage while I pop out to see Maja. She's going to visit her parents for a couple of days before she leaves for the Kutupalong refugee camp, and I want to spend as much time as I can with her before she goes.

When I get home I'm in such a rush I trip over the overnight bag that she's left by the door, which tells me that at least I haven't missed her. I head into the kitchen for a hug and find her portioning out prepared meals into plastic containers, ready for the freezer.

"Something you can just put into the microwave," she says. "When you're too tired to cook." My eyes well up with tears. Before she moved in I lived on Sauvignon Blanc, cheese and crackers and whatever takeout I managed to grab on my way home after work. I don't know what I'm going to do without her.

"It smells delicious," I manage to say. I don't want her to know how upset I am, how afraid of losing her. "What is it?"

"There's chicken korma, dhal, butter chicken, biryani rice. Enough to keep you alive for a while," she laughs.

"Did you get enough for your parents too?" Maja's parents are Anglicized and never cook traditional Indian food for themselves. They also don't have any decent Indian restaurants near them, so she makes a point of bringing them dinner when she visits.

"Of course, and dessert." She shows me a box of Indian sweets. "Enough to make them both diabetic. I got some for you too." She points to the counter. "To give Vogel." Maja knows Vogel can't get enough of them.

I sit on the stool next to her and watch her for a while, until she finishes packing up all the food and places the meals into the freezer for me.

"I'm going to miss you," I say. *I miss you already. Please don't go. Don't leave me.*

She smiles. "I'll be back before you notice I'm gone."

"We've had a breakthrough," Vogel says as I toss him his sweets. He opens the box and picks up a bright green square of pistachio Pista Burfi. "Mmmm. Tell Maja I love her." He licks his lips and takes a bite, then proceeds to talk with his mouth full.

"Ray Weaver, one of the victims, disappeared during Canal Days last summer, at the same time a Dodge Caravan was reported moved." Canal Days is the annual Marine Heritage Festival in town, held every Simcoe holiday weekend. It's a celebration of local nautical history and the Welland Canal, and it draws visitors from all over the province and from across the border, in cars and by boat.

"Okay," I slump into my chair and try to avoid looking at Vogel while he eats. He really enjoys his food, and a glance at his middle tells me he's going to get fat if he doesn't either step up his exercise or slow down on the sweets. Vogel's a big guy, tall and strong like a football player, but that muscle will quickly go to fat if he doesn't get it together.

"And the preliminary search of that Dodge Caravan," Vogel continues, licking his fingers. "Has turned up traces of concrete, as well as forensic sample that I'll bet Jun Song will find is a match to Ray Weaver."

"Not exactly a breakthrough," I mumble. "We knew most of this stuff a couple of hours ago."

"It's proof our theory holds," Vogel says. "We can demonstrate the killer used borrowed cars to dump the bodies, and may be able to use CCTV footage to see where the vehicles were during the periods in question. Maybe we'll even get a picture of our killer."

"It also narrows down the time when the Ray Weaver's body would have been dumped in the canal," Vogel says. "And we know it would had to have been done at night."

"We already knew that. Anyway, during Canal Days downtown is jumping until late at night," I argue. "Our killer would have to like taking chances."

"Gauthier, the guy's a serial killer who's been dumping bodies under our noses for two years. Of course he likes taking chances. This would be easy—just come right up the canal after dark. Sure there's some lighting, but there aren't many people around. Nobody's going to notice at three or four o'clock in the morning. Even the bars are closed."

"But we have extra officers on duty, doing foot patrol all night—protecting the exhibits and displays and fairground rides that line the canal on West Street."

"Sure, but remember the water level of the canal is much lower than the street. And who's going to take any notice of a boat? There are boats all over the place during Canal Days. The patrol officers are going to be watching the shops and the people on the street."

"The public marina is just below Main Street," I'm thinking aloud. "It's busy during Canal Days, sure, in the daytime. But our killer could have kept his boat tied off there with the body already on it, waiting until late at night when he could just head up the canal to dump it."

"With the victim's feet already in the bucket?"

"Sure, why not?"

"We know Shaun Pearson, and possibly others, were still alive when they went into the water. How do you get them so sit still while their feet end up encased in concrete?"

"Drugs?" I shrug. "Alcohol? Something that incapacitated them. Quickset concrete sets up in about thirty minutes."

"It's not impossible to see how that could work," Vogel nods in agreement.

"But wouldn't the boat make noise? I mean, an outboard engine… late at night… someone's going to notice, whether the street's busy with tourists or it's deserted in the middle of the night."

Vogel considers for a moment. "Not if it's an electric motor. They're practically silent."

"Who'd have one of those? Are they common?"

"Yeah, pretty common. And anyone who has a bigger boat anchored out in the harbour, who might just need a small runabout to get them into shore or the marina, could have one."

"So anyone with a dinghy." This isn't exactly narrowing the field.

Vogel nods. "They aren't exactly rare."

"Okay, let's leave the dinghy for a minute. What about a boat belonging to… let's just say… a fisherman? Or a bird enthusiast? Could they have a quiet motor?"

"Sure, why not?"

"So, what would a fisherman be out for at night? In August?"

"Walleye," Vogel says. "Lots of them come out at night, especially under a full moon. The fish come closer to the surface to feed, especially in the shallows."

I suppose we could easily find out what phase of the moon Canal Days have fallen on, but I think I've got a better idea. "Why don't we go down to the marina and find a fisherman to talk to?"

"Warren Kerr?"

"No. I don't want to tip him off."

Vogel screws up his face. "C'mon Gauthier, sometimes you've got to trust your gut. Warren Kerr's just a nice old man."

"I am trusting my gut. He's not *nice*. He's an arrogant prick. There's something off about him."

I glance out the window. Even though it's after eight the early summer sun hasn't set. "Think it's too late to visit the marina?"

TWENTY SEVEN

BY THE TIME we arrive at Sugarloaf marina the sun is setting over the trees, bathing the lake and marina in a pink glow.

"What's that saying?" I ask. "About a red sky?"

"Red sky at night, sailors' delight. Red sky at morning, sailors take warning," Vogel recites, looking toward the sunset. "Looks like it'll be another beautiful day tomorrow. There'll be a lot of boats out on the water."

It's still busy at the marina. Dozens of boats have groups on them, drinking wine and having dinner. There's a BBQ at the end of the wharf and some picnic tables have been set with red and white checked tablecloths.

"Looks like a party."

"It's like this most evenings in summer," Vogel says. "Boaters are friendly people. They like to party."

"What's the night fishing like around here?" I ask a young man who's just closed up the marine supply store and is walking towards us. "In August, specifically."

"It's great! Anytime in August you can land you daily limit on Walleye. I've seen trophy fish—up to twenty-four inches long—almost every day."

"No kidding." I should have left this to Vogel. I'm finding it impossible to show any enthusiasm for fishing. Luckily the kid is oblivious.

"It's best to fish for them at night. They're sensitive to light so you need to go after them at dusk or later in the evening. Lots of people go out at night though—fish right through until dawn. Walleye can get pretty aggressive, really go after the lures."

"They're here, inside the breakwater?"

"Depends on water temperature. If it's really warm you'll need to go out into the lake for Walleye. Around forty feet deep."

"You'd need a good sized boat though," Vogel says.

"For sure. I wouldn't want to be out in just a dinghy or even a bass boat after dark!" he laughs. "Hell, I wouldn't even go out past the lighthouse in a small boat."

Vogel's phone rings and he walks away to answer while I stay with the clerk.

I lean in conspiratorially and lower my voice. "What about around here... inside the breakwater?"

"Well, if you cast in the south east corner of the breakwater you might catch something. A lot of fish come in at night to feed. Or over off the east pier," he points. "You'll get perch, pickerel and pike out there after dark. And bass, but you can't go after them during spawning season."

"What about up the canal?"

"It's not technically allowed..." He winks. "But I'm told you can get them all the way up to past the bridges at night. They like the lights... or so I'm told."

I thank him and join Vogel.

"We've got the results of the background check on Andrew Croft, our bird guy," he says with a smirk.

"Anything interesting?"

Vogel nods, a glint in his eye. "He's got a record for Mischief and Criminal Harassment. Spent time in the Niagara Detention

Center. He was charged with Voyeurism, but they couldn't make that charge stick."

"Voyeurism? Our bird watcher is a Peeping Tom?"

"Are you up to another boat ride?"

Within fifteen minutes we're out on the water, heading for the breakwall. The last of the sunlight has illuminated the lighthouse and rocks and they're glowing gold and pink. By the time we land the sun has dipped below the horizon and within an hour it'll all be in shadow and darkness.

I can see Croft's boat is tied off in the usual spot and Vogel keeps the speed slow to reduce the engine noise—and possibly to not alert Croft that we're coming. But he's already waiting for us when we dock, and he looks angry. I suspect he'll be a lot angrier in a few minutes once he knows the reason for our visit.

"Stay in your boat!" he shouts.

This time we ignore him and climb out of Vogel's boat, disregarding his concerns. I don't care if he's upset. In fact, if he loses control that can work to our benefit.

But Croft isn't the same guy we met a few days ago. He's not twitchy and nervous, or anxious about why we're back so soon. He's defiant and belligerent, which is a huge red flag. He should be frightened, worried about why we're back again and especially about why we're ignoring his demand that we stay in the boat. He knows his criminal record makes him vulnerable in a way other people aren't, and most ex-cons are very careful around police. Generally, they try to avoid us, and when that's not possible, they make nice. So why isn't Croft concerned about why we're back?

Vogel doesn't open with his usual friendly greeting. Instead he's aggressive, and doing his best to provoke Croft.

"Taking any good photos today? Maybe of topless women?"

"What are you talking about?" Croft's aggressive and ready to get into it with Vogel. His record dates back to when he was arrested for taking photos of women sunbathing on the break-wall. I'd have thought Vogel's remark would have chastened him, embarrassed him or at the very least put him off balance. Instead, it has angered him. I can see the rage in his eyes and his body tenses as if he's going to fight.

"I'm talking about what you're doing here? Given your record, I'd have thought this was the last place you'd want to hang around."

"*Hang around?*" Croft sneers. "I'm not *hanging around* any-where. I told you, I'm here on a research project."

"Like you were three years ago?"

"It's not what you think! Those women—they had no business being here," he insists. "It's posted! There are signs everywhere."

"Why didn't you just ask them to leave? Or call the police?"

"I thought I'd catch them in the act," he mutters. "I wanted to prove they'd been there. In case they tried to deny it."

"Then what happened?" I've read the reports but want to hear his version.

"They called the cops—on me! Said I was lurking, like some pervert. I tried to explain that I was looking after the birds, but…"

"The police looked at the photos on your camera?" He nods, looking miserable. Taking photographs of young women—espe-cially those topless or in bathing suits and unaware they're being photographed, is easily interpreted by the courts as voyeurism. The assumption is they will be used for sexual purposes, or exploited in some way. But Croft had a legitimate purpose for being on the breakwall—monitoring the nests—so the court dropped the Voy-eurism charge, but still charged him with Mischief.

Croft is such a peculiar guy he probably frightened the women, and possibly the court too, if he showed this anger. He presents as mentally ill, as odd but harmless. Until you see the rage.

Unfortunately for Croft, he kept insisting he was innocent even though the women refused to believe him. He kept trying to convince them, by calling and following them and waiting for them outside their places of work, until they accused him of Stalking and he was charged with Criminal Harassment. Guys like Croft are creepy and disturbing—even if he didn't intend to do harm to the women, it would be impossible for him to convince them of it. I can barely believe him myself.

If I didn't suspect it already, it's now obvious that Croft has obsessional tendencies. And his judgement isn't great, that's clear. But apart from the concrete in his boat, and the fact that he can access the canal anytime he wants to, we've got nothing on him. No motive and nothing to connect him to the missing parolees.

"I didn't do anything wrong," Croft insists. "I was innocent and they knew it. But they just wouldn't listen…"

"And you thought you could convince them? By stalking them?"

"I never *stalked* anyone! That's not what happened," Croft says. "I was railroaded."

"Didn't you have legal representation?" Vogel asks.

"Sure I had a lawyer. A bad one." *More like a bad attitude.* But I don't say this out loud. "They insisted I get counselling! Why should I do that? It wasn't my fault! I did nothing wrong." Croft is getting more agitated. He's pacing and waving his arms and seems unhinged. It's no wonder the court found him guilty.

His behaviour—belligerent and argumentative, like he is right now, along with a refusal to comply with the recommended mitigation, is usually an immediate guilty verdict. Couple that with maybe a judge having a bad day or wanting to set an example, and boom, Croft's off to jail for six months.

It doesn't happen often with a first offender charged with a relatively minor offense, but now that I've seen Croft in action, I'm not surprised.

"How long were you in jail?"

"I was paroled after two months," he mutters. "Released into the community." Offenders serving six-month sentences are eligible for parole after they've served a third of their sentence. I guess he showed remorse, or maybe he realized his behaviour contributed to the situation. Or he just got smart and figured out how to get early release.

"When did all this happen Mr. Croft?"

He looks out across the breakwall. "It was before I started my graduate degree."

"And your parole? Where did you serve that?"

"Here," he says. "In town. I was one of the first parolees in Kerr Residence after it opened."

I'm speechless for a moment. "How was that experience?" I finally ask. It's the only thing that comes to mind.

"*How was that experience*?!" Croft explodes with rage. "That *experience*?! It was shit. It was the worst thing that ever happened to me in my entire life! It was worse than prison."

"Worse than prison? A halfway house? I find that hard to believe."

"What do you know? Croft shouts, his face a mask of bitter rage. "Those people… they're all disgusting… addicts and losers… I'm nothing like them."

I give him a moment to calm down before I change the subject. He's not going to be able to answer our questions if he's so enraged he can't focus.

"How are the birds doing?" I ask after a minute. "Keeping the cormorants at bay?"

"Doing my best." He doesn't look at me.

"What are you doing today? More nest building?"

Croft shrugs and says nothing, but I tell he's calmer.

"We wonder if you can answer a few more questions for

us. About anything you might have seen at night, out there on the breakwall."

He looks shifty. "I'm not out there at night…"

I know he's lying. "Mr. Croft, we know you're out here all the time, looking after the birds. I'd bet we could even find confirmation of that in your research notes, if we got a warrant for them.

He gives me an angry look, but realizes he has no choice. "I sleep out here sometimes," he says. "Protecting the nests."

"So, you see people out on the water, fishing, at night?"

He makes a face. "They're out there all the time. Twenty-four seven," he says. "Coming too close to the rocks, scaring the babies."

"Anyone in particular come to mind? Boats or people you might remember, that maybe you've seen a few times?"

He shakes his head. "They all look the same to me."

I glance into the bottom of his boat. The bags of concrete are still there.

"Do you drive, Mr. Croft?"

"I don't own a car." He looks wary and I wonder why he didn't just give me a yes or no.

"But you have a license?" He nods, eyes narrow. "How did you get your boat down to the marina, without a vehicle?"

"I borrowed a car."

Vogel and I thank him and climb back into the boat. I feel Croft watching us until we're well out of sight.

"He's our prime suspect. He's got it all: motive, methods, opportunity… and he's really weird." Vogel says, glancing over his shoulder as if he thinks Croft could hear him. "Sleeping on a rock to protect the birds?!" He shakes his head. "That guy is definitely off. He's not wired like the rest of us."

"His anger definitely isn't rational. But it doesn't make him the killer. Just obsessive."

"Well our killer is obsessive, and we think he uses borrowed cars to dump the bodies. Croft borrows cars—he just told us. And he's got a grudge, and a lot of anger toward Kerr Residence."

"I wonder if that grudge extends to him killing parolees?" I say. "It definitely makes him a person of interest. He's got a boat, concrete, a possible motive. Where does he live now?"

"He rents a farmhouse, out by Willoughby Marsh."

"Isolated. Private, exactly what the killer needs."

TWENTY EIGHT

Saturday

I'M AT THE station before seven, fully expecting to find it empty since it's the weekend, but to my surprise I find Vogel at his desk, talking on his cell phone. So it's not work related. If he were in last night's clothes I'd assume he'd had a great date, but the fact that he's freshly showered and changed tells me it ended early. I wonder briefly what's up with his new woman then realize I'm not really that interested. They come, they go, and none of them stick around for long.

I didn't sleep well. The bed seemed too big and I know I'll have a hard time getting through the day, despite the extra large Americano I've got in my hand. And the task at hand today is to go through Joshua Logan's customer records, something so tedious and painstaking I doubt I have the capacity for.

Our operating theory—and one we haven't proven yet—is that Logan was blackmailing his customers, any one of whom might have killed him and trashed the store, looking for whatever Logan has on them. The enormity of that task is overwhelming. And even if we have the manpower and the motivation to do it, what person on his customer list is going to admit to being black-mailed—especially if it implicates them in Joshua Logan's murder?

Just when I'm about to tear my hair out, Vogel hangs up and gives me a huge grin. I guess everything's fine after all.

"Good morning. All set for a day of excitement?" I manage a grunt and take a sip of coffee.

Before I get a chance to answer, Vogel gets another call, this one on his desk phone. He answers, putting it on speaker. It's Jun Song, from the Technological Crime Unit.

"We've started taking Joshua Logan's computers apart," she says. "I think you're going to want to come in," she says. "You need to see what we've found for yourselves."

"We've already been in touch with the Cyber Crime Unit," Song tells us when we arrive in her lab. "And it looks like the Canadian Anti Fraud Centre will have an interest."

"The CAFC?" Vogel whistles in surprise. "What was Joshua Logan up to?"

"Well, two separate points of interest that we've come across," Song begins. "First," she turns her computer monitor around so we can more easily see it. "Your guy was an *incel* creep. There are some alarming emails and searches on his personal computer." She indicates some emails on the screen and we lean in to read the screen for ourselves while she continues. "This is next level. Extreme right wing, Proud Boy, anti-female, anti-immigration, white supremacist, promoting violence, end of the world crap—which tells us a lot about who this guy is and what he's comfortable with."

"I guess Pam Visser wasn't kidding," I say, reading through some of it. "He's definitely unlikeable."

"We also found a number of these keyloggers in his stuff—both at home and in the store." She holds up a handful of small plastic devices about the size of a USB drive.

"What's a keylogger? Some kind of spyware?"

"It's a piece of hardware, like a circuit, that gets inserted into the computer. It logs all keyboard activity, running in the background all the time, copying passwords, web history, emails, photos, financial information, passwords and PINs, bank accounts, credit cards… you name it. And, since it's embedded into the internal hardware it's not dependent on the operating system—and it can't be detected by any virus protection or software."

"And the user wouldn't know it was there?"

She shakes her head. "They'd have absolutely no idea. Anti-virus can detect software versions of spyware but not hardware. They're easy to detect if you know what they look like, but who'd think to look for it?"

"You'd have to have physical access to insert it into the computer, right? " Vogel says. "Which is easy for Logan to do since he ran a computer repair store."

"Yes, but it's a little more complicated than that," Song says. "The device logs the data to an internal memory, so it needs to be physically retrieved afterwards. He'd need to have access to the house or the computer to get it out."

"Or," Vogel says. "He'd have to wait for it to come back into the store for repair or service. Which might take a while."

"He'd definitely be playing a long game, if he was willing to wait months or a year to get his keylogger out, or even to see what's on it."

"Seems inefficient. Waiting that long."

"Unless he had easy access to the properties," I say. "Like through a care worker? Or a cleaning lady?" Vogel and I exchange a look.

"Do you think he was using the data himself? What would he do with it? Blackmail?"

Song shakes her head. "It's typical cybertheft. I think it's more likely he sold the data to someone else—to a third party who knew how to exploit it. Joshua Logan would have been part of a larger scheme. His job was done once the computer left his repair shop, or once he'd retrieved the keylogger and delivered the data."

"But maybe there was blackmail involved," I argue. "With Logan taking advantage of some incriminating information he found. It would have been a bonus— a chance to make some extra money."

"Possibly," Song continues. "We've retrieved Joshua Logan's banking information. He has a history of many large cash deposits into his personal accounts."

"Payment, I guess," Vogel says. "For delivery of the data, from the mystery *third party.*"

Song shrugs. "Possibly."

"What about this *third party*?" Vogel says. "How do we figure out who they are? Can you follow the money?"

"We've been over Logan's bank accounts—I doubt if the deposits are traceable. The amounts were all in cash and each less than ten thousand dollars, " Song says. "Also—some more bad news I'm afraid—there were no fingerprints left at the scene of Logan's murder. It's a dead end."

"So we have no way of finding out who this third party is," Vogel says. "Or whether Logan had definitely been blackmailing anyone?"

"If we can figure out who's being blackmailed," I'm thinking out loud. "That might be a step in the right direction. But I have no idea how that would work. Should we put out a media release? Invite everyone being blackmailed by parties unknown to come forward?"

"Gauthier, are you okay?" Vogel laughs. "We already know someone—Margaret Lawrence, remember?"

We find Councillor Margaret Lawrence—or former Councillor Lawrence—in her office in Town Hall where she's packing up her personal items and moving out. I barely recognize her since she's wearing jeans and a t-shirt and hasn't done her hair. Basically she looks like any woman on a weekend, rather than a high-profile Regional Councillor and successful businessperson.

"Look, I've lost my job," she says once we've introduced ourselves and taken seats. "I've lost any hope I ever had for a career in politics—and believe me, that was my dream since I was a kid. It's humiliating."

I've seen the photos that were leaked and from my experience they're pretty tame stuff. They're not what I would call porn; they're more like boudoir photos if anything.

"This won't be much comfort to you," I say. "Given what's happened. But this will blow over." I'd say it already has, given the discovery of the bodies in the canal. "There's always a new scandal to distract people. This too shall pass."

"Maybe for now. But whenever the media wants to they can pull them up again. They've been shared all over social media and the internet never dies. I'm done." She buries her face in her hands. "It's even worse for my kids—they have to deal with it at school. Can you imagine? Nude photos of their *mother*?"

"Is your husband managing okay?"

"I expect my *ex-husband* finds it all hilarious." She laughs bitterly and jumps to her feet. "Look I need to keep moving," she says as she starts piling some boxes by the door. "Do you mind?" I shake my head, completely understanding the need to act, to do something physical to stave off dark thoughts and anxiety. "The joke is," she continues. "I had those photos taken for him—as a birthday gift. When we were married of course." She slams down a box on the pile, with more force than necessary.

"Something else I regret." She turns to us. "If I didn't know better I'd suspect he's behind this. He's the only one who had copies of the photographs, apart from me and of course."

"Not the photographer?"

"No, he gave me the negatives. The police checked him out anyway. He runs a successful photographic service that I doubt he'd want compromised by this kind of scandal."

"You seem very sure it wasn't him," I say. "Do you have any idea who leaked them? Or who was trying to blackmail you?" She shakes her head.

"No… No. I don't know who did it." It feels like she hesitates for a moment and I wonder what she's not saying. But I don't push.

"I got texts, from a private number. Untraceable, apparently." I've read the reports. The investigation hit a dead end when they found the communications had been sent from a pay as you go cell phone. And, since she'd refused to pay the blackmailer there'd been no opportunity to catch them in the act of retrieving payment—either in cash or by wire transfer.

"Where do you get your personal computer serviced?" I already know the answer to this; we found her name in Joshua Logan's files before we left the station.

Her eyes flash. She's an intelligent woman and figures out where my question is leading. "Are you suggesting… that's who leaked the photos? That computer repair guy? He's the blackmailer?" Vogel and I try to look non-committal, but she's too smart.

"He's the only place I ever took my computer to," she says, slumping into her chair. It's almost as if she's relieved it wasn't someone else she'd been suspecting. "Are you going to arrest him?"

"I'm afraid he's dead."

"Good, I guess. Too late for me though."

"Do you have any idea who might have benefitted from blackmailing you?"

"Whoever wanted the money, presumably," she laughs. "He demanded ten thousand dollars. And my ex-husband definitely enjoyed my embarrassment. The pig even sent me flowers when the photos came out."

"Harsh. Who's your ex?"

"I thought the police knew everything," she laughs. "Ron Whitney. The biggest prick in town."

I can't argue with that statement.

We'd found a few other prominent names in the store's repair records, when we were looking for Margaret Lawrence's. It's not likely that everyone who had their computer serviced at Logan's store was being blackmailed, or that everyone had something to hide, but you never know.

I take a minute to frame my next question properly.

"I wonder if you are aware of anyone else, perhaps on the Council, that might have been under similar pressure?"

"Pressure? Blackmail, you mean?" She shakes her head, then stops and stares at me. She thinks for a minute, considering whether she should say anything.

"I have no idea what it means—and I don't want this to come from me, you promise? Some of these people were in opposition to me—with respect to public policies. It would look like sour grapes."

"At our last meeting, one of the other Councillors—Arjun Devi—suddenly changed his position on an issue we've been debating for months. Just out of the blue, without comment or explanation, he voted in favour of a development proposal we've been protesting for over a year."

"Do you think he might have been under pressure? Maybe a threat of exposure?"

"I have no idea. Honestly. It was just so unexpected."

I make a note of the name. "Arjun and I were colleagues. Friends, even. He noticed my new laptop at one of our sessions a few months ago. I told him where I bought it. I recommended he go there, since the prices were so good and—I thought—the service excellent.

"He wanted some anti-virus protection installed. Was worried about some data loss. Wanted to make sure it never happened again. My god…"

"What kind of loss?"

"I have no idea. He told me afterward he'd brought his laptop in there to have it cleaned it up, and he added some RAM or a new video card or something. He bought a new tablet as a gift for his wife, too. My god… he thanked me for the recommendation. I feel awful."

TWENTY NINE

"**So, do we** think Arjun Devi was being blackmailed? Is that why he changed his vote in Council so suddenly?"

Vogel shrugs. "One way to find out. Ask him."

I put in a call to his office but I'm told he's out, so I make an appointment.

"I guess we can look for his name in Logan's files while we wait. " I groan inwardly at the idea of going through more files, looking for connections and overlaps.

"What about Tracey Reid," Vogel asks. "Was she involved with Logan's scheme? Seems a bit of a coincidence that she's dead too. "

"It could just be Reid referred her clients to Logan, innocently. After all, they were roommates. His store was conveniently located here in town and his prices were reasonable. Maybe the connection between them really is just coincidence. This is so frustrating," I grumble, raking my fingers through my hair. "Anyway, I thought we had Deeping as the likely suspect in her murder."

"We can't have it both ways," Vogel says. "Either Tracey Reid was killed by Clive Deeping—and her connection to Logan is just circumstantial and she's innocent of the cybertheft and blackmail operation, or she and Logan were both killed by the third party, who's running the whole game."

"There is another option," I say after a minute. "Both could be true. She could have been involved in the operation, if only by referring customers to Logan, and she still got killed by nasty old man Deeping. Just back luck."

"And, to add to the mix, none of these options explain how she ended up in the trunk of a burnt out car."

We brood in silence for a few minutes, trying to figure out a way through this mess. Finally Vogel breaks.

"We've got to pick a lane Gauthier. In the end it doesn't matter much if Reid was involved or not, at least not this minute. We know Logan was, we have evidence tying him to the data theft."

"And we need to visit Lionel Deeping again, and rattle his cage. Let's ask him about blackmail, see how he reacts."

"But first we need to find out if Arjun Devi's name shows up in Logan's files. And let's look into who benefits by that proposal going forward? Maybe that will take us somewhere."

Vogel's computer pings announcing an email, which he reads then chuckles in amusement.

"Come and take a look at this," he says. "It should interest you."

It's from the Technological Crime Unit. They've cross-referenced the list of Reid's clients her agency provided with Joshua Logan's customer records and found what they think is a disproportionately high number of matches.

"Keep scrolling," Vogel says with a smile. He can be so infuriating sometimes. I keep scrolling the pages to last year and the year before that, when a name practically leaps off the screen: Mrs. Howard Kerr. Queenie.

"Warren Kerr's mother?" Vogel says.

I remember what Doreen told me over coffee. "And no doubt she could afford full time in-home personal care. I understand she got a bit peculiar when she was old."

"Looks like Tracey Reid looked after her for a long time, until she died."

"I don't suppose there's anything there, beyond another damn coincidence. This is a small town and there aren't many agencies that provide in home care."

"True," Vogel agrees. "And anyway, she's been dead for what, three years? It's not like we can interview her and see if she'd been blackmailed."

I start to pace in frustration.

"So, regardless of who killed Tracy Reid, we still believe that she helped Logan gain access to the computers and the client's homes. This email supports that…"

"What about Pam Visser?" Vogel interrupts.

"What do you mean?"

"C'mon Gauthier. She lived with both of the victims. She must have known about what was going on. She may have even participated in it. She's got her own list of clients, just like Reid—people she cleans houses for—maybe she set some up with Logan as well."

Instinctively I reject Vogel's idea. "Why would a single mother take that risk? Working with a lowlife like Logan…"

"Money, of course," he interrupts me. "I know Pam Visser told us she didn't like Joshua Logan and that they weren't friends, but what if she's lying? What if they were working together?"

I remember Visser had looked very upset when we told her Logan was dead. But maybe that was really fear—terror that she'd be next.

"It's possible," Vogel continues. "They were in the extortion business together. She's a cleaner, who's able to legitimately go through her clients' houses when they aren't there, looking for incriminating things."

"So where does that leave Pam Visser? With her two tenants

dead and possible involvement in this crime? She's in danger, Vogel."

Vogel rolls his eyes. "For all we know she's the killer," he mutters under his breath. I choose to ignore him.

A few minutes later Vogel laughs out loud. "Gauthier," he says shifting over so I can see his computer. "Come take a look at this."

It's a breaking news piece, a live press conference with former Councillor Margaret Lawrence. The chyron across the bottom of the screen read: Blackmail Shame Scandal. Vogel unmutes the volume.

"I'd prefer to hide my head in shame over this… but I'm not going to, Lawrence says. "I'm a fighter and I'm going to figure a way forward. Probably not in politics," she pauses for the laugh, just like someone used to working a crowd. She's a natural politician. I'd be surprised if she didn't run again after an appropriate time.

"She didn't waste any time," I say. "Must have the local media on speed dial."

"I feel it's important at this time to let the public know that I'm not the only Councillor who's been pressured in this way," she continues and I lean in to hear what she's about to say.

There's a loud burst of questions from the media scrum and she holds up her hands to try and quell them. "As I've said, I was blackmailed. An individual attempted to extort money from me and I refused to comply. That cost me… a lot." She looks chastened, but yet strong and defiant. I expect she's practiced that in front of a mirror. Again, another surge of questions and the click of camera shutters.

"But another Councillor didn't stand up to them. He suddenly changed his vote on a controversial issue—one we've been fighting for years and the reason for that is because he was being threatened, just as I was.

"I don't believe it," I say. "What a shitty thing to do."

"Believe it," Vogel shakes his head. "She just dropped Arjun Devi in it. Hope he can swim."

I can feel anger flaring in my chest. "She's hanging him out to dry. Why would she do that?"

"Probably saw an opportunity to salvage her reputation, by ruining his."

"The bitch just outed him on television and there's no proof it really happened."

"Relax Gauthier. She didn't name Devi."

"She may as well have. It isn't hard to figure out who she's talking about!"

Margaret Lawrence is still on television. "I want people to be aware of what happened to me, and understand that cyber stalking and cybertheft is a real thing, and it's happening everywhere. Either through phishing or software or online scams. Or, at disreputable computer repair stores that have access to all of your hard drives once you drop off your computer to them. Which is what happened to me—and it could happen to any of you."

"Stupid woman. What does she think she's doing?" I turn away in disgust. "If Joshua Logan wasn't dead already there'd be a lynch mob in front of his store! She doesn't even know for a fact that he's the one responsible for the data loss."

"She's angry," Vogel defends her. "Don't you…"

"It's irresponsible!" I shout over him. "And vindictive!"

"Gauthier, just stop," Vogel holds up his hand. "I know you're angry…"

"*Angry?* I'm not angry."

"Gauthier, you're always angry. Afraid—you're angry. Worried— you're angry. Hungry—you're angry. Your emotional range runs between mild irritation to fury." I'm too stunned to speak. "Maja is leaving in a few days now, and I know that's hard. But you've got to let up. Give all of us a break—especially yourself."

I'm too stunned to respond. *Who the fuck does he think he is?* Vogel starts to look uncomfortable after a moment but then he sticks out his chin defiantly, daring me to argue. I turn and leave the office, without saying a word.

I'm driving out of the station lot when Vogel runs up to the car, pulls the door open and jumps in.

"Where are we going?" I'm relieved he doesn't bring it up and instead chooses to pretend it never happened.

"To Visser's house. To find her client list."

Vogel nods. "Okay. I thought you didn't think Visser had anything to do with it."

"To compare it to the others. We've got Tracey Reid's patient list. And we've got Logan's customer list. If we see where the overlaps are…"

"But what's the point of that? Logan's dead. The blackmail scan is finished."

"Maybe one of those blackmail victims killed Logan."

When we pull up in front of Pam Visser's house her car isn't in the driveway, but we knock on the door anyway. There's no answer and I'm peering in the front window when the neighbour shouts over.

"She's gone," he says.

"Any idea when she'll be back?"

"Never I'd say," he laughs and ambles over. "She cleared out in the middle of the night. Loaded up her car and left." Shit. She's running scared. She knows something and is afraid for her life.

"Do you know Ms. Visser?" Vogel asks. "Any idea where she'd go?"

"No idea where she went. Out west? Down east? Up north?" He laughs. "Why? Is she in trouble?"

"No," I say. "We've just got a few questions."

The neighbour gives me a skeptical look. "You're the police, right? I read about her tenant—that computer guy."

"Did you know him?"

"Hell no! That guy was a weirdo. Goth, or whatever you call them. I had no interest."

I smile my thanks and Vogel and I head back to the car. I turn back at the last minute.

"Do you know what school her kids went to?" Maybe we can learn something from their teachers about where she was moving.

"Kids? She never had any kids." The neighbour shakes his head and ambles back onto his lawn.

Vogel whistles. "No wonder her house was so tidy," he says. "Now, why do you suppose she'd lie about that? And what else did she lie about?"

"So what do you suppose was in those big tote bags she took *to the beach* the other day?" Vogel continues. "Money? Hard drives? Keyloggers?" I shrug, but don't argue. "It's obvious she was involved in the scam," Vogel says. "That's why she took off."

"Maybe she's just afraid."

"Yeah, of getting caught."

"No. Afraid for her life."

Vogel rolls his eyes. "C'mon Gauthier! Get real."

"If my tenants were killed I'd be afraid too," I say, realizing how weak it sounds. "It doesn't prove she knew anything about what Logan was up to. Maybe she's afraid the killer or this mysterious *third party* would think she was involved." I hit the steering wheel in frustration. "*Dammit.* How are we going to find her client list now?"

"We can put out a APB…"

"She's not a suspect, Vogel! She's just a person of interest at this point." Vogel is clearly frustrated with me, but he doesn't argue.

"Okay then, an ATL," he sighs and reaches for the radio to call for the Attempt to Locate.

THIRTY

WE DRIVE BACK to the station in silence. I'm not willing to acknowledge what Vogel said to me before we went to Visser's, and it's made me so angry I refuse to even think about it.

We're at a dead end, again. Twelve dead bodies pulled out of the canal, and no idea who their killer is, where or when they were killed, or why. Two more unrelated murders, possibly connected by a blackmail and data theft operation. One person of interest has disappeared.

And, as the icing on the cake, the minute I arrive back at the station, DS Agu appears at my side, looking for an update. I'm not looking forward to telling him all about Visser's disappearance. Luckily my phone rings, saving me for a moment. It's Jun Song, from FSU.

"We've had a look at the data on one of the keyloggers," she says.

"And?"

"You'd better come down here. See it for yourselves."

When Agu, Vogel and I enter the tech lab, there's a strange atmosphere in the room. Song escorts us to her computer while the other techs make themselves scarce or pretend to be busy with something.

"It's not pretty," she warns us. She's right.

On her screen is a series of images of men, sprawled on a bed and posed in fur coats and hats. They are clearly dead. One is a close up of a young man wearing lipstick and eye makeup, with his long hair swept back and held in a glittery clip. Vogel recognizes him immediately.

"That's Shaun Pearson." Agu exhales loudly and I can hear him swear under his breath. "Where did these come from?"

"One of the drives we found in Joshua Logan's room," Song says.

"I guess we've just found the motive for Logan's murder," I say. "And the connection between his death and the Kerr Killer. Logan found these trophy photos and tried to blackmail the killer."

Something doesn't feel right about that explanation. "But it's a different kind of murder," I argue. "The destruction at the store, the rage, the way Logan was savagely beaten. It's almost as if it were committed by someone else."

"Someone else?" Vogel argues. "How likely is that?"

Agu holds up his hand before I can answer. "I see your point. The killings in the canal are discreet, planned, precise. The murder of Joshua Logan, and the destruction at his store, aren't similar."

"With all due respect, Sir, why would they be?" Vogel argues. "When he was planning the canal murders, he was completely in control, every aspect of the crimes were anticipated—clinically. But this… this discovery or threat by Logan would have triggered him, sent him over the edge. He wouldn't have been able to react in his typical manner. He'd lose it, go nuts, kill Logan in a rage."

Agu nods, conceding Vogel's point. "It certainly feels better than the option of having another killer out there."

"Exactly!" Vogel says. "What are the odds of that? Two murderers?"

A horrible idea creeps into my mind. "Maybe he's got an accomplice? Or an apprentice."

The room falls silent. We've been operating on the assumption that the Kerr Killer was working alone. The idea that he may not be is too horrible to contemplate.

"And the accomplice murdered Logan…" Agu groans in frustration.

"It has to be a different killer," I insist forgetting to be diplomatic. "The man who planned and executed the murders of these parolees was in control of every aspect of those killings. But when the trophy shots were found, he completely loses control? I can see him killing Logan, sure, but not this way. He would have stalked him, made Logan disappear, like he did the parolees."

"Why not? Time wasn't on his side. He couldn't take his time to plan… he just reacted."

"And he definitely couldn't risk calling the blackmailer's bluff—like Margaret Lawrence did. This is a lot worse than nude photos—it's proof he's a serial killer. Whoever he is."

"So," Agu is thinking aloud. "Our killer was going about doing his business of murdering parolees, dressing them up, taking these photos and dumping their bodies when suddenly he gets a call from someone demanding money or his secret will be exposed."

"He probably didn't even know how the photos were discovered in the first place, but he's clever enough to deduce how the photos leaked out… through Logan…"

"Logan must have called him," Vogel says. "That's how Margaret Lawrence was contacted."

"How? When? Can we trace that?"

"We already know Margaret Lawrence was called from a pay as you go cell. It's unlikely we'll find anything conclusive."

"Still, check Logan's phone records," Agu says. "His personal phone and the business. He would have acted quickly, once he found the photos, wanting to cash in. Go back to a week before he was killed, no need to go back farther. It won't be a long list, and somewhere on it will be our killer's name."

THIRTY ONE

I'M HEADING OUT of the station when Vogel stops me. "Where are you going?"

"I can't just sit around waiting for Logan's phone records," I say, keeping my voice down. I wasn't about to argue with DS Agu just now, and I don't need him to learn I disagree with him. "I'm not even confident they'll turn up the killer's name so easily."

Vogel rolls his eyes.

"Logan wasn't stupid," I argue. "He would have known how incendiary those trophy shots were and that whoever took them wouldn't hesitate to kill him. Logan would have been smart enough to not leave a trace."

"So what's your plan?" Vogel shakes his head, but still follows me out to the car, reluctantly.

"We need to keep looking at suspects we've already flagged, like Croft for a start. It can't just be random chance that he lived at Kerr Residence, or that he spends all his time on the water and has a boat."

Since we're just around the corner from Kerr Residence our first stop is to speak with Joan Morton. The lounge is full of people, sitting on chairs in a circle—it must be a group counselling session. They all stop speaking and watch us, not bothering to disguise their interest. If I'm not imagining it, I'd say the place looks busy, with many more residents present. Nothing like a scandal or mass murder to bring in the crowds.

The way Morton quickly hustles us into her office tells me she's nervous about why we're back again so soon. Good. I don't like the woman and maybe a shot of fear will shake her up and make her do her job instead of hiding behind a desk.

"Is this about Nick Melnyk?" She says once the office door is closed. "Have you found him?" *Alive* is left unsaid.

"We're here about a different resident, from a couple of years ago." Morton heaves a deep sigh of relief.

"Do you remember Andrew Croft?" Vogel says. "He served out his parole here…"

"Yes." Morton's lips are pinched. "I remember him."

"Really? It was over two years ago." I'm surprised. I had the definite impression she didn't remember any of her residents, but I don't say so.

"Mr. Croft left a strong impression."

"In what way?" She doesn't reply but starts looking through some files on her computer, probably looking for Andrew Croft's.

"What can you tell us about him and about his time here?"

"He was one of the first parolees we had here—in our first intake." She doesn't look up from her computer screen. "He's one I failed with. It didn't feel like a great start."

"Failed how? Did he end up back in prison?"

"No, no. He remained here the required time then re-entered the community upon his release, and we never heard from him again."

"So why is he a *failure?*"

Morton brushes it off. "No, I misspoke. He's not the failure—*I'm* the one who failed. Maybe I'm being silly." Vogel and I watch her, waiting for her to elaborate but she just shakes her head as if she's trying to decide how honest to be. Then she blurts out what sounds like the first genuine statement she's made to us.

"Andrew Croft was uncooperative, unremorseful and obstreperous. He really challenged all of us here. I'd bet every one of the counsellors here remembers him—and not fondly.

"He's highly intelligent," she continues after a moment. "I suspect now he was clever enough to *play the game* while in prison, in order to gain early release. But, once he was here he no longer felt obliged to play along."

"What does that mean, exactly? How was he *obstreperous*?"

"He argued all the time, with all of us, about policies and procedures, and health and safety, and quality of meals and excess noise, you name it. He was extremely difficult." Her lips twist in disgust. "He claimed we were in it for the money."

"In what exactly?"

"This place. Kerr Residence. He *did his own research* online and was always presenting me with documents and annual reports that *proved* he was right."

"You're privately run?" This is a huge surprise to me. "For *profit*?"

"No!" Morton insists. "We're a non-profit agency. I explained that to him, several times, but he just… refused to accept it. Andrew Croft is a big conspiracy theorist. He's paranoid."

"How do you suppose he got that impression?"

"Community Residential Facilities like ours are run by non-governmental private facilities. We sign service contracts with the Ministry of Correctional Services that pay us a certain amount per day, per resident. That revenue covers housing expenses and supervision, life skills counselling, substance abuse treatment and even employment counselling. You've seen what we offer here." She looks to both of us for approval. I can't speak for Vogel, but she's not getting mine.

"And he didn't think the tax payers were getting their money's worth?"

Morton sighs. "He sneered at everything we provided. Said that sitting around in peer groups telling lies, or hanging out playing cards and smoking with criminals was a waste of his time."

"Criminals," Vogel chuckles. "Unlike himself."

"Naturally. He never participated in any group or private sessions. He just sat them all out and complained the entire time he was here."

"So why would Croft do that?"

"I have no idea, honestly. I don't know what he was hoping to prove." She shakes her head. "He claimed that since we operated for profit, our interest was not in helping residents reintegrate into society upon release from parole. He claimed that Kerr Residence was gang-infested, full of drugs and alcohol, and that the residents weren't properly monitored and everything was poorly supervised overall. Oh—and that the staff members were either incompetent, indifferent or criminal. Or all three." He even wrote letters of compliant to the Ministry." No wonder she dislikes him.

"That can't have been good for the launch of this facility. Do you think he made these complaints hoping to shorten his time here?"

"It wouldn't have made one bit of difference in the length of his sentence," Morton says. "Even though—speaking personally and off the record—I'd have loved to get him out of here as soon as possible."

"Could it have made it longer? By his being a pain in the ass?"

"No, not unless he did something really serious. Being a nuisance makes no difference to his parole." She leans back in her chair, shaking her head. "That's what Andrew Croft is. A nuisance. And obsessive. And he holds grudges. I was very happy to see the back of him when he was released."

"What kind of grudges?"

"Oh, the usual thing," Morton brushes off the question. "Against people who got him in trouble. Not his fault, blah blah."

"So, you aren't aware he spends most of his time just a few block away—out on the breakwall? Working with the birds?"

Morton's professional mask cracks. "I thought he left the province?" Her voice is high, revealing her alarm. "That he went out to the coast, to finish his degree?"

"He did. Then he came back."

Morton's eyes dart back and forth. She's frightened, but of what? Andrew Croft seems like a creep, but she's just told us he was more of a nuisance than a danger. Unless she's lying.

"Ms. Morton?" She doesn't respond. "Is there a problem?"

Vogel leans forward and lowers his voice, which could be seen as an invitation to confide in him or a threat, depending on your state of mind. Vogel is good at figuring out how to get through to people, how to break down their barriers. My style is less subtle; I'll either smash through or go around, whatever's faster. Morton's bureaucratic armor definitely needs to be broken down, and I'm happy to let him take the first shot.

"Croft claimed Kerr Residence was not a safe environment," she finally says. An alarm bell rings, faintly, in my mind. "He said our residents were in danger…"

"From what?" Vogel asks. "Anything specific?"

Morton just shrugs and I lose patience. "Nick Melnyk said it wasn't safe here either," I say. "His father told us he was afraid." I can see Morton close down, her lips pinched in anger.

Morton stares down at her hands for a moment, reluctant to respond.

"Ms. Morton?" I prompt. "Do you have anything to say about that? Why would both Nick Melnyk and Andrew Croft feel Kerr Residence isn't safe?"

Morton rolls her eyes and glances at her watch. I lose all patience.

"Are you finding this tedious? Do you have somewhere to be?" My voice is dripping with sarcasm. "I don't think we need to underline the fact that we've found a dozen bodies in the canal…"

"I've already told you about Andrew Croft," she interrupts. "He's a little shit. I wouldn't give any credence to anything he said."

"And Melnyk? Is he *a little shit* too?" She doesn't meet my eye. "You told us yourself he was a model prisoner."

"Resident," she snaps. "And there's no reason to credit whatever Nick Melnyk's father may have told you. The boy was troubled."

Vogel makes a show of consulting his notebook. "He's a quiet young man," he reads back Morton's own words. "*You'd barely know he was in the room. Nick Melnyk never caused trouble, never drew attention to himself.*" Morton looks away.

"You also said '*Nick is highly intelligent. He could talk with anyone he chose to. He could be quite… charming.*' Doesn't sound like *a little shit* to me. What about to you DC Gauthier?"

I smile at Vogel, shaking my head. "Nope, not to me either."

I'm also having a problem with that statement of yours Ms. Morton," Vogel continues. "According to his father, Nick was high functioning autistic. He had social difficulties, problems with relationships. That doesn't sound like a *'charmer who could talk with anyone,* does it? It makes me wonder if you have any idea at all about your *residents.* "

Morton glares at Vogel. She's lost control of her anger and her professional mask finally falls away.

"Nick Melnyk was not *autistic,*" she snaps. Her voice is shrill and she's very flushed. "High functioning or otherwise, regardless of what his father may choose to believe. He's manipulative and, in my opinion, he has antisocial personality disorder."

Vogel recoils in surprise as she continues to rant. "He only has *problems with relationships* if he doesn't see any way to exploit them. He's a sociopath…"

Listening to her shrieking about Nick Melnyk sets my teeth on edge. If I disliked Morton on our first two interviews I despise her now. What kind of a person who works in social services would go on like this, about one of the people in her care? I'm feeling very defensive, very protective of Melnyk, not that I've ever even met him, nor that I want to.

"Ms. Morton," I interrupt her before she says anything more inappropriate. "By your own admission you barely even knew Nick Melnyk. He's only been here for a short time since being in juvenile detention. A sociopath? He was charged with trafficking…"

"*Murder*," Morton interrupts, her face a mask of confusion. "Nick Melnyk was charged with culpable homicide."

"What did you just say?" I feel the room start to spin as I feel the tunnelling that means I'm about to have a panic attack. I'm short of breath and my heart is pounding, so I fake a coughing fit and tip my head to Vogel steps in while I step out of the office. I slip an Ativan under my tongue and lean against the door until my dizziness subsides.

"Murder," Morton repeats as the door closes behind me. "Nick Melnyk killed a child."

Vogel doesn't ask how I'm feeling when we're walking back to the car, and I'm grateful. He took over the rest of the interview while I'd pretended to listen, but what I was thinking about was how Nick Melnyk, my cousin's son, is a killer. And how, once the shock wore off, it doesn't really surprise me. After all, Nick Melnyk is my blood relative.

"So Melnyk's father lied to us," Vogel says once we're in the car. He got all the information from Morton when I was hiding out in the hall, trying to manage my panic attack. "He wasn't sent to prison for trafficking."

"Or he really believes what his son said," I say. "Parental denial?" That's probably the same story he told everyone. No wonder that's what Doreen heard. "So what exactly did Morton tell you? "

"He gave a little kid some cannabis gummies—fed him the whole packet apparently, and the toddler died."

"From overdosing on cannabis? That doesn't seem likely." There have never been any cases of death by cannabis overdose.

Vogel shakes his head. "The kid vomited, choked and asphyxiated. Melnyk didn't show any remorse in court. Laughed and said it was *just a joke*, which didn't win him any sympathy from the judge."

"No, I guess not." I feel anxiety licking my gut. No remorse. *Just a joke.* Sounds like a sociopath to me.

"Even though he didn't technically sell the drugs to anyone, they charged him with trafficking since they were given to a minor..." Vogel shrugs. "He was also charged with manslaughter—culpable homicide. Presumably he didn't mean to kill the kid, but since he died as a result of a criminal act..."

"Wasn't Melnyk a minor himself when this happened?"

"He was in high school." Vogel nods. "The Crown pushed for him to be tried as an adult, given the seriousness of the crime. But, the dead kid was from a family in the East Village, broken home, single mother..."

I finish Vogel's sentence for him. "And Melnyk was from a *good home*, with loving parents, who could a afford to pay a good lawyer, so he got off easy."

"He didn't get off all that lightly I guess. According to Morton's records Melnyk was sentenced to ten years—rare for a juvenile offender—eligible for parole in five. He was supposed to have been moved to federal penitentiary when he turned 20 later this year, but his family and lawyer lobbied for him to instead be moved to Kerr Residence to serve out the remainder of his sentence."

I don't know what to think, much less say. I don't even want to look at the situation, since it just reminds me of my own mental health issues and my own past. The last thing I ever want is for Vogel to find out any of it. But I know in my gut that the cost of looking away will be too high.

"Maybe Melnyk's father is right. He learned how to present as normal, to try and fit in, whatever it took. God forbid Melnyk might not even know who he really is."

"Or he's finally figured it out… .and that can't be good."

THIRTY TWO

"**Vogel, we need** to talk to Andrew Croft again."

He looks astonished. "Shouldn't we follow up with Melnyk's father?"

Vogel's right but I just can't face more right now. "We're closer to Croft," I reason. "Marina's just over there." Vogel nods and heads for the water.

"Croft sure sounds like he could be our guy anyway. Obsessive, has an unhealthy interest in the Kerr Residence. Maybe even a motive of revenge that goes back to his time there."

"And he has a boat, and concrete, and he's admitted to being out on the water at night."

Even though my reason for avoiding Melnyk is personal, it's always reassuring in some degree that my instincts are right. Andrew Croft felt wrong from the minute I met him out on the breakwall. Learning about the Mischief and Voyeurism and Stalking wasn't entirely a surprise, nor was hearing Joan Morton tell us how he'd behaved while at Kerr Residence.

"I don't suppose we need to ask where he is," Vogel says as he starts the car.

"Nope. He may rent a farmhouse out by Willoughby Marsh, but he lives at the breakwall."

When we arrive at the marina, Vogel passes me the keys to his boat. "Want to drive? You might as well get some practice."

I'm tempted, but shake my head. Even though I got the hang of driving out on the open water, I don't think I'm capable of backing up the boat and navigating my way out of the marina. Vogel smiles and gets behind the wheel, then we're underway and heading toward the marina exit.

"No wake," I joke, happy he's going slowly, but in truth I'm happy to stay in safety of shallow marina for that much longer. I'm not looking forward to reaching deep open water.

"No worry," Vogel replies.

We have to stop for a minute as the huge yacht on the end is pulling into its berth. Whoever's piloting slips into the berth expertly and has turned into the narrow slip with one try. When he comes around, he sees us waiting for him and gives us a jaunty wave. It's Ron Whitney at the helm, just back from a day on the open water.

Once Whitney has cleared the way, Vogel pushes forward on the throttle and we head toward the breakwall. I can see Andrew Croft's boat tied off in its usual spot, and Vogel steers toward it, scaring off the flock of cormorants perching all over the lighthouse and Croft's boat. Within a few minutes we're pulling up alongside and Vogel jumps out with surprising agility for such a big guy and ties off his boat, then helps me climb out onto the rocks.

This time, there's no Croft waving his arms and shouting at us to go away or stay in the boat.

"Where's Croft?"

We look down the breakwall and there's no sign of him. "His boat's here…"

At the pile of rocks where Croft said he was building nests is a flock of screaming seagulls, fighting over something and wheeling up into the sky.

"Looks like he wasn't kidding about the nests needing protection," Vogel says, sounding concerned. "Those gulls are tearing things apart. Are there fledglings still in the nests?"

"Not for long I'd say." I squint and try to get a better look at what's going on with the gulls and if there's any hope for whatever's still in those nests. When I see red fabric I instantly understand what I'm looking at. I set off at a run toward the gulls, waving my arms and shouting.

When I get to the nesting area I see Croft, lying sprawled face down. His t-shirt and jeans have been slashed and his back and buttocks sliced open, the deep gashes gaping open revealing red flesh, sinew and bone. The rocks are covered in blood—likely what's attracted the gulls. There's no way he's still alive.

"Jesus!" Vogel gasps when he catches up. "Who'd do this to him?"

"Lucky he's face down," I say. "The gulls would've gone after his eyes." I've seen that in a corpse a few years ago and the image still features in my nightmares.

I inch forward, careful to not disturb the crime scene while Vogel calls it in. There's a blotch of dried blood and matted hair on the back of Croft's head, which probably means whoever did this knocked him unconscious before he was killed.

"Looks like a lot of rage here," I say to Vogel, once he's off the phone. "There are dozens of slashes on the body."

"Who'd Croft piss off that badly?"

"Maybe he saw something that he shouldn't have? And maybe he tried to exploit it?"

"Gauthier, you've got blackmail on the brain," he says. "What could a crazy bird guy have to do with the blackmail operation?"

"Yeah, you're right. Still. Maybe it's not connected to Logan's scheme, but he might have seen something when he was out here babysitting the birds one night."

"Okay… ."Vogel thinks about it for a moment. "And he didn't think it was significant…"

"Until we brought it up—the last time we spoke with him."

"So, what then? He tried to get money out of someone?"

"Or maybe he just had a word with them about it. From what Morton said, he was a stickler for rules, regulations, protocol."

"And they didn't like what he had to tell them?"

"Or more like they wanted to make sure he never told anyone else."

Vogel and I sit on the breakwall, under the beating sun and exposed to the wind and the water, waiting for FSU to arrive. I wish I'd brought my sunscreen. I swear I can feel myself freckling and burning.

"Now what?" Vogel says. "Our prime suspect is dead."

"Look on the bright side."

"There's a bright side?"

"It narrows down the list…"

"Yeah, from one to none."

Within the hour the coroner arrives and unfortunately Victor Todor is on call today. Vogel hears me swear when I see Todor climb out of the police boat, with Jun Song just behind him.

"Hi Constable Song," I say, intercepting her on the way to the crime scene. I ignore Todor but from the expression on his face he doesn't notice; I'm invisible to him anyway. Song smiles and walks partway with me, but I know enough to hang back once we get within twenty feet. I watch from a distance as the FSU team starts setting out markers and taking photographs and Todor examines Croft's body.

Now that I'm over the surprise of finding him I can see the blood on his body and all over the rocks is already mostly dried.

That could be because he's lying in full sun, or because he's been dead for some time, or both. The gashes are long and wide, as if they've been spread open, or as if his skin has contracted. It occurs to me that maybe the gulls have something to do with that as well. If they've been feeding on his corpse it stands to reason they'd have pulled open the wounds to get at the flesh.

I don't see anything else on the pile of rocks—no weapons or tools that could have been used to strike him down. But it would have been a simple thing to toss whatever it was into the lake. I'm sure it'll be impossible to find.

Todor finishes up with the body and leaves FSU to complete their job. "Cause of death looks like exsanguination," he says. "Multiple slashes, quite deep, on both the front and back of the torso. Made by a narrow, sharp blade, approximately six inches in length. Something like a fishing knife."

"And the head injury?" I ask, which earns me a glare from Todor.

"Not fatal," he says. "Likely incapacitated him, before he was stabbed."

"How long ago? Vogel and I just talked to him earlier today."

"Not more than three hours, based on liver temperature, rigor and lividity. He would have died sometime early this afternoon."

So, just after Vogel and I left him.

THIRTY THREE

Vogel and I pull away from the lighthouse even before they've removed Croft's body. My last sight of the breakwall as we head across the water is that of dozens of technicians in white protective coveralls climbing all over it. If Croft were still alive he'd be having a fit.

Back at the station I sit at my computer and stare at the screen, at a loss. Now that Croft is dead it feels like we've hit a wall. I don't know where to go next.

"Heard back from tech," Vogel says, reading a document he's picked up from his desk. "They've got the phone records from Logan's store. Just need to call everyone and follow up."

"That should go well," I grumble. "They'll all say he called to say their computer is ready for pick up, what was wrong with it, what the repair will cost, that kind of thing."

Vogel laughs. "Nothing like keeping your expectations low. Maybe we'll get lucky."

"Seriously? I don't imagine anyone would admit to having Logan say 'by the way I found some photos on your hard drive you might want to pay me to keep quiet about'."

Vogel shrugs and passes me the list. I scan it, still managing my expectations. It doesn't seem within the realm of even remote possibility that anyone would admit Logan had found anything on their computer.

A name pops off the page: Deeping. Well that fits. "Deeping had a brand new computer, probably bought at Logan's store. And of course Tracey Reid worked for him… and her body was found in his car."

"Except Clive Deeping was dead and buried by the time Logan was killed," Vogel says.

"Not him! The son—Lionel Deeping. He's the one who bought the computer, not the old man. I'm sure he kept it at his father's place for privacy."

"From whom? His wife?"

"From whoever. Think about it Vogel, it all fits." I'm getting excited again. "His father lived alone, in a big house. There was lots of room to take his victims."

"And nobody noticed? C'mon! The old man lived there and he had a care worker looking after him. Somebody would have noticed if Lionel Deeping was bringing men into his father's house or using it to dispose of their bodies." What about the nosy neighbour…"

"Laturno. Elise Laturno."

"She'd never have missed that. Not in a million years."

Vogel has a point. Still, we need to consider it. "Do you have those trophy photos?" He passes me the file and I start to flip through it, focussing on the background in each image, relieved to be able to look past the victims.

There isn't much to go on. It looks like a plain white wall behind them. Maybe it's a basement? Is that a mattress? A bed? Maybe we can find a chair like the one he's posed on.

"We need to check out Deeping's house," I say. "See if we can find any rooms that match these."

Before I can pick up the phone DS Agu walks in and demands an update.

"What have you found out about the most recent missing parolee?" Agu glances at the board. "Nick Melnyk."

"We've spoken with his father, and with the staff at Kerr Residence, Sir. Typical situation—parent minimizing the crime, but it appears he was doing well, heading for full release, no reason to run, unless he was afraid."

"Just need to follow up with his mother. Maybe she can shed some light."

"What are you doing here then? Get on your way."

The Food Bank is in the community centre in the heart of the East Village—just around the corner from where Vogel and I chased Jay a few days ago. We're able to find a parking space around the back of the metal warehouse and make our way past two large trucks backed up to the loading dock and up the concrete stairs. Two young guys are heaving trays of bread off the back of the truck and piling them onto folding tables. I recognize one of them and nudge Vogel.

"Anyone you know?"

He laughs. "Jeff Miller. He must be doing his community service. Food bank would qualify for his hours."

Miller looks up, catches sight of Vogel and visibly startles, his face pale. "Relax," Vogel laughs. "It's all good. We're looking for Wendy Melnyk."

Miller doesn't react. He just stares at Vogel, mouth open, as if he hasn't heard. Guilty conscience if I've ever seen one but at the moment I'm not interested in what he's hiding.

"She's just in the office." His co-worker elbows him. "I'll take you through." He puts down a crate of bagged hamburger buns and leads us away from Miller and into the warehouse. I glance over my shoulder and see Miller slump in disbelief. He's just had the scare of his life. I guess it's his lucky day.

As we go through the clear plastic strip curtains and enter the warehouse I can feel the temperature drop. The space is well organized, with tall metal shelves all stacked with canned goods, dried pasta and cereals, diapers and toiletries.

The office door is closed and the worker peeks through the window, pulling back quickly. "She's on the phone," he says. "Sorry."

"No problem, we'll wait." He stands with us, rocking back and forth on his feet, unsure if he should just leave us. The irony of him suspecting two police detectives might steal something isn't lost on me.

"Busy time?" Vogel asks, just as I'm about to send him on his way. As usual, he's always happy to engage in chat.

"Not really," he says. "Kind of a lull now, between Easter food drive and Thanksgiving. That's when the food drives remind people to donate—holiday guilt."

"So you get a break?" Vogel chuckles. "Get to kick back a bit? That must be nice."

He gives Vogel a look. "People need to eat every day, not just at holiday time. We have a lot of families who depend on us…"

"Of course!" Vogel interrupts, blushing. "I didn't mean to…"

"Food insecurity is a huge issue," he talks over Vogel. It's clear Vogel's careless comment has touched a nerve. "People have to decide between paying their rent and eating that week… kids going to school hungry."

Suddenly I feel sick. I'm dizzy and have to lean against the wall. I swallow, remembering how often I did exactly that. I'd go to school without breakfast most days, and often without dinner the night before, in the same clothes I'd worn for the past two days. My face flushes with shame when I flash on a memory of the teacher pulling me aside at the end of a school day, prying in a well-meaning way while the other kids giggled in the corner. My vision is narrowing… I'm heading into a panic attack. Deep breathing. Keep breathing I tell myself as I reach for my medication.

"We supply several schools with Breakfast Club and lunch programs—but of course, that's only during term," the worker is still lecturing Vogel. "Now that school's out and kids aren't getting that help."

Vogel looks uncomfortable—he realizes he's put his foot into his mouth. He peers into the window, looking to see if Melnyk's mother is off the phone yet.

"Where do you get the food from?" I force myself to ask, to engage in the conversation and keep myself focussed.

"Food drives. Grocery stores, farmers and bakeries donate unsold surplus food—like you see that truck out back."

"What's the most popular thing?" Vogel asks. "What don't you ever get enough of?"

"Never enough baby food or pet food. Or feminine hygiene products," he answers instantly. "It would be great to get things that regular families have: cake and cookie mixes, coffee and tea, protein bars." He shakes his head and I can tell he's about to launch into a rant. "We sure get a lot of peanut butter and dried spaghetti and jars of sauce. I guess it seems practical, but people can't live on that… they need protein and produce and…"

Suddenly the office door opens and we're spared whatever he was about to say.

"Wendy Melnyk?" I say to the woman standing in the doorway. She's wearing fingerless gloves and a fleece vest over a jacket. I guess she's about to head back into the freezer. "Can we have a word?"

She looks wary but unsurprised. I suspect she's used to getting bad news.

"Police?" She tips her head and indicates we should follow her into the small office. It's about the size of a closet, but there are two chairs and I can just manage to shut the door once we're all inside.

"Is it about Nick?" She doesn't seem fazed. More like she's been waiting for us for a long time. "What's happened?"

"He's gone missing from Kerr Residence," I say.

"Since when?"

"Thursday, three days ago," Vogel says. "We were wondering whether you'd heard from him."

"You should speak with his father."

"We have. Has your son been in touch?"

"Unlikely." She gives me a look. "We aren't… close."

"When's the last time you saw Nick?"

She shrugs and shakes her head. "Couldn't tell you exactly. A year ago?"

"Your husband told us…"

"We're separated," she interrupts, holding up her hand. "I can imagine what he told you." I'm taken aback at her hostility.

Vogel takes out his notebook. "Your husband told us Nick is autistic…"

Wendy Melnyk bursts out laughing. Vogel and I exchange a glance. She laughs until tears pour down her cheeks and I start to wonder if she's having a breakdown. Suddenly she just stops, as if someone's flipped a switch.

"Nick's not *autistic*," she finally says. "That's just what my husband thinks. He's spent a lot of time and energy making himself believe it."

"He's not?" Vogel prompts after a moment.

She takes a deep breath. "Nick has a personality disorder. My son's a sociopath."

I feel myself recoil in shock. Even though we'd heard the same thing from Joan Morton earlier today it's difficult to hear Melnyk's mother talk that way about him. I feel a flare of rage and it's all I can do to stop myself from saying something to her. I look up and catch her staring at me. She smirks.

"I know what you're thinking," she says. "What kind of a mother could say that about her own son?" I avoid meeting her gaze. "Look," she continues after a moment. "Nick's neurodivergent, sure, but not in the way his father wants to believe. My son has ASPD—Anti-Social Personality Disorder."

She sees the blank expressions on our faces and continues. "Nick has no conscience. He'll lie and manipulate and cheat and he just doesn't care because he isn't capable of thinking like you or me." Her face is flushed and she's becoming agitated. "He has no sense of remorse, or guilt, or obligation…"

"So, not autism?" Vogel interrupts, flipping through his notebook. "Your husband said he'd been diagnosed…"

She shakes her head, looking away in exasperation. "We took Nick to several doctors, when he was young. The take-away wasn't consistent, ever. We heard autism, ADHD, etc etc. The only diagnosis my husband was able to accept or entertain was autism. Much better than the alternatives."

I want to reject what she's saying, to put it all down to her being a bad parent or neurotic or making excuses for herself somehow, but… I can't. It's resonating within me, deeply, and I have to turn away, keeping my back to them as best I can for privacy in this tiny office. I pretend to make a call as take some calming breaths. I think of my birth family, the ones whose blood I share with Nick and his father. What is that familial stain? Is Nick Melnyk bad, like I am?

"Have you ever met a neurodivergent person—one who's on the autism spectrum?" Wendy Melnyk is asking when I rejoin the conversation.

Vogel shrugs. "I don't think so. Maybe?"

"You'd know, probably. I mean, you're both trained observers, right?" I can't tell if she's mocking us. "There are all sorts of indicators of autism: odd or inappropriate eye contact or facial expressions or voice volume. Being socially awkward.

"Nick's not like that. He has charm, when he wants to use it. Someone with ASPD is very socially aware—how else can you manipulate people so effectively?

If you're naive enough, he'll brainwash you into believing everything he says—and believe me, Nick completely brainwashed his father, gaslighting him every day."

"But not you?"

She laughs. "Oh I wasn't immune. For a long time I believed Nick. I really wanted to, you know?" She shrugs. "But then... I don't know. I just started to see through his bullshit. That's when I started therapy."

"Family therapy?"

"No. Personal. I needed help... to survive." I look into her eyes and see she's sincere. Like her husband with his sister, like me with my stepfather, she had a choice and she decided to save herself. I get it, but still can't quite believe her. Maybe she has an axe to grind with her ex-husband. Or maybe Nick Melnyk is as troubled as his mother believes, but that doesn't mean he's not in trouble, or that he ran away from Kerr Residence because he was afraid. Maybe she doesn't even know her son anymore—he was in prison after all, and how long has it been since she even lived in the family home? Or maybe I'm just in denial.

"We went through it all, for years. Trouble with school, with the other neighbourhood kids. I made excuses, blamed the teachers, the other parents, whoever I could to avoid facing the truth. But then..." her voice trails off.

"Then?" Vogel prompts her.

"When he was ten I caught him in the backyard putting firecrackers into the mouth of a frog he'd caught. He played it off when I yelled at him, like it was no big deal. And he was young at the time, so I tried to let it go. But then our cat disappeared. I never knew what happened to it, but… I just felt in my gut that it was Nick."

"He got older, starting doing drugs, skipping school. He was always oppositional, defying me—not his father so much. I think because he knew I didn't believe him anymore."

"When did you and your husband separate?"

"A few years before Nick was arrested. He would have been around thirteen or fourteen."

"Did you see much of him after you moved out of the family home?"

She gives me a look. "I came to court for his trial, playing happy families like his lawyer wanted. But apart from that, I didn't see him." So there it is. No visits. No birthdays. No Christmas. Maybe she doesn't know her son at all. I don't know what to say about that… so I say nothing and let Vogel carry on.

"Your husband said Nick was afraid of something at the halfway house, something that might explain why he broke parole, to run away to safety. You don't have any insight into that?"

"I read the papers," she says. Her voice has dropped to a whisper. "There's a serial killer at Kerr Residence, isn't there?" She shakes her head, her lips twisted. "I don't think Nick would run away, no."

"You don't believe he's in danger?"

"Detectives, you haven't been listening to me. My son *is* the danger."

THIRTY FOUR

"Wendy Melnyk isn't likely to win Mother of the Year," I say once we're back in the car.

"And her story doesn't really line up with her husband's. Which I guess you'd expect, all things considered."

"But it does with Morton's—she did tell us he had lots of buddies at Kerr Residence, which fits with that whole *capacity for charm*."

"Maybe one of those buddies put him onto a safe place to stay once he ran away?"

"If any of those buddies are still alive."

Vogel drives across the Clarence Street bridge to Town Hall so we can meet Arjun Devi at his office.

"I'm not even sure why we're meeting with him now," Vogel says. "We know Logan was the blackmailer and how he's dead. It's not going to get us any closer to finding his killer."

"It might. Maybe Logan wasn't acting alone? Maybe Devi can tell us how he was contacted—that could lead us to the killer. Maybe." I don't have much hope either, but one of us needs to stay positive.

"We also need to follow up on Margaret Lawrence's claim that he had been pressured to change his vote on the development proposal," I say. "Just because she told us so—and hinted in her press conference no less… doesn't make it true."

"You're still are pissed off at her?" Vogel laughs and I ignore him.

"You know, the more I think about it, the less I trust her. You saw those photos… they were so tame, so inconsequential… kind of pretty, actually." I turn to face Vogel. "Maybe she even leaked them on purpose to create a media sensation—one where she could look noble and be a hero, coming out against cyber bullying or whatever."

"That is ridiculous. What woman would allow nude images of herself out in public? Not to mention jeopardizing her job, her position in government?"

I'm not convinced. "She wasn't fired, she quit. They wouldn't dare fire her for that. I wouldn't be surprised if she's planning on a provincial or even federal run?"

"Gauthier, when did you become so cynical and angry?"

"I wasn't born this way."

Arjun Devi was elected to Municipal Council based on his expertise as a local tax accountant and his promises to cut wasteful spending and better manage the fiscal resources of the community. I have no idea if he's been effective in his role but from the spartan look of his office it's clear he doesn't spend money on appearances. The furniture in his lobby, what little there is of it, is from a discount office supplies store, and there aren't any blinds on the windows, or cushions on the chairs, or rugs on the floor. It's about as basic as can be without actually being empty. I wonder if that's to reassure his clients—and the public who elected him—that he's not frivolous and wasteful.

He welcomes us into his private office—no better furnished

that the outer space, clearly curious about the reason for our visit. I guess he hasn't seen Margaret Lawrence news conference yet.

"Has anyone attempted to blackmail you, Mr. Devi?" I cut right to it.

His eyes widen in shock and he opens his mouth a few times, but no sound comes out. "Or perhaps they've tried to influence how you've voted on certain Council decisions?"

Devi grabs for the glass of water on his desk and drains it.

"Mr. Devi? Can you please respond?"

"Who told you?" His voice is quavering. "How do you know?"

"That's not important," Vogel says gently. "But you aren't the only one."

A sharp gleam appears in Devi's eye. "It's Margaret Lawrence, isn't it? It has to be." He starts nodding and talking to himself. "Those photographs. Of course!"

"Mr. Devi. Answer the question." I'm not as kind as Vogel. "Now."

"Do I need a lawyer?"

"You aren't under arrest," Vogel says. "We're only making inquiries." *For now* remains unsaid. "Your cooperation will be appreciated. And noted."

Devi takes a deep breath. "A few months ago I got a call from a man. I don't know who it was. He said he had some…" Devi searches for the right word. "… *information* I wouldn't want to be made public." He interrupts himself and raises his hands. "Please don't ask me the nature of it—I won't tell you. I can't."

"Did he demand money?"

"No, not money," Devi shakes his head. "He wanted me to change my vote in Council. The vote about the zoning change downtown, to allow a redevelopment proposal to go forward."

"Proposal to do what?"

"A consortium wants a change of use for the Imperial Bank building downtown."

"Isn't that a heritage property?

"Yes. They've applied for the Council's permission to make certain alterations and to make it part of a luxury condominium development. We've been fighting them for over a year now."

"And now they've won?"

"Not yet. Thankfully I wasn't the only vote against them," Devi says. "There are still two others, but now it's not as strong a majority. And…"

"And you think the blackmailer might now be going after them?" I finish his thought. "Assuming they're able to find anything incriminating, of course. One can't apply pressure without a lever."

Devi drops his head into his hands. "Yes," he mumbles. "It's so… shameful. I have no one to blame but myself."

"And you have no idea where they might have accessed this *information* they used against you?"

"No idea."

"What can you tell me about this consortium? Are they local companies?"

"It's made up of two regional developers, one from Toronto and another numbered company that I believe is a shell corporation representing a US-based individual. I'm afraid I haven't been able to find out who that is."

"Do you have any suspicions?" I press. "Surely you know who's interested in developing the area."

"I couldn't say," he demurs.

"Perhaps we'll have better luck," Vogel says. "Can you please provide us with what you do have?" Devi looks panicked. "Rest assured, we won't mention your name Mr. Devi."

Devi looks through his files and puts some documents into a

file folder. "They tried to purchase the Kerr Residence a few years ago, before it went to the community," Devi says has he hands the folder to Vogel. "But they weren't successful—the Trustees were protective of the terms of the Estate. Rightly so, of course."

He seems reluctant to let go of the documents, as if by doing so his secrets will be revealed and he'll never be able to take them back. And he's right. I see Vogel tug the file out of Devi's hand.

"Do you know who is behind this extortion?" he asks. "Will you arrest them?"

"We'll do our best," I assure him but he doesn't look hopeful.

"When things first… went bad," he shakes his head. "For Margaret, with those photographs, I thought…" His voice trails off and he stares into the middle distance.

"What did you think Mr. Devi?"

"I thought it was something to do with her divorce. A personal vendetta."

"Her divorce?"

"It was… acrimonious."

"You assumed her husband had leaked the photos?"

"It seemed plausible," Devi shrugs. "He's a vindictive bastard."

"You know him personally?"

"No, not personally at all. Just from business, from local politics. We've been in opposition on a number of issues."

"What's his name?"

"Ron Whitney." I look over at Vogel, who's not doing a very good job of pretending to be surprised. "But I don't really believe he'd have leaked those photographs of his wife, no matter how bad things were. They have children together! What kind of man would do such a thing?"

"Let's go on a fishing expedition," I suggest once we're back in the car. "But not in your boat."

"Sure. Where to?"

"It's time we circle back to talk to Ron Whitney."

Vogel looks skeptical. "Why? We don't have anything on him."

"C'mon Vogel!" I start to count on my fingers. "Here's what we have: One. Logan and Reid lived with Visser. Two: Visser worked for Lawrence—she told me. Three: Lawrence's ex-husband is Whitney. Whitney benefits from blackmailing his ex-wife…"

"How?" Vogel interrupts.

"By humiliating her. Punishing her in the divorce. Maybe he didn't like the nature of the settlement? Who knows?" Vogel rolls his eyes. "And Four: it's possible Whitney also benefits from the blackmail of Arjun Devi."

"We have absolutely no proof of that," Vogel says.

"True, for the moment, but I won't be surprised if we find that he's involved with that consortium. But we do know that consortium benefitted from Arjun Devi's change of vote—and Devi was blackmailed into doing so. The other person we know who was blackmailed is Margaret Lawrence, who is connected to Whitney. That's got to be worth a visit."

Vogel considers for a moment then starts the car and heads in the direction of Lorraine.

"What are we fishing for?"

"Not sure, exactly. I'd like to know more about his relationship with his ex-wife for a start. There's also the strange way he seemed to be so certain about the details of when his cars were *borrowed*." I make air quotes as I say the word. "C'mon, knowing the mileage on his cars and the exact amount of gas in the tank? As well as the amount he paid for parking? That's just… weird."

"Maybe he's just extremely meticulous and detail oriented," Vogel says.

"Like most serial killers."

Vogel shakes his head. "I can see him maybe being connected

to the blackmail, that's not a big stretch. But killing parolees? C'mon."

"We know borrowed cars were used to dump the bodies. We know his was borrowed."

"Doesn't mean it was him. We don't have any forensic proof back that his vehicles were involved."

"Yet." *Why is Vogel having such a hard time seeing Whitney as capable of murder?* "But, I wonder if he benefits somehow from the Kerr Residence being shut down? If Whitney's part of the consortium that lost out on the property, it's got to be worth exploring."

"Gauthier, I think you're just trying to wrap everything up in a nice package—the blackmail and the Kerr Killings. They might not even be related, except co-incidentally. Anyway, you've met Ron Whitney. Does he strike you as a guy who'd murder parolees? I can't see him dumping them off his yacht, do you?"

"Doesn't necessarily mean he got his hands bloody. He could have had someone do the dirty work."

This time when we arrive, Whitney answers the front door and invites us in. He's in a jovial mood and practically insists we have a tour of his home.

"This was part of a church in Pennsylvania," he says, stroking a large carved wooden beam that's been used as an internal support in the great room. "I had it brought in, along with some other similar architectural pieces. I feel they add a certain… gravitas… to the interior. Don't you think?" *What the actual fuck is he talking about, gravitas?*

"Has your family lived here long, Mr. Whitney?" Vogel asks.

"Not in Lorraine, no. But we go way back on the other side of town. My people had a place in the Humberstone Resort, since the 1930's.

My brother has our parents' old place, over on Tennessee Avenue." He's boasting but trying to seem so offhand and casual about it that I almost don't notice. Tennessee Avenue is one of the most expensive bits of real estate in town, the houses dating back to the late-1800's, when wealthy tourists from the American South would come up to escape the summer heat. They'd bring their servants and entire household entourages to spend the summer enjoying the resort's private beach, tennis courts, bowling alley and casino.

"But I like the size of the building lots over here on this side of the canal," Whitney continues. "More space. More privacy. So I built this place on the site of an old cottage that burned down years ago."

"It's new?" Vogel's always the diplomat. He's engaging with Whitney about the design and building of the house while I'm trailing behind like a bored kid at a museum. "I'd never have known. I just assumed it dates back to the early resort cottages of the area."

"I've tried to make it look older, but with all the modern amenities," Whitney smiles in that smug way he has. "Used antique pieces and architectural salvage from all over, to give the impression of age."

As he shows off the butler's pantry and kitchen I wander over to look at a collection of family photographs he's displayed along a sideboard. They clearly date back to the glory days of the Whitney family, based on the vintage automobiles and fashions. There's one of a woman wearing a long fur coat, standing next to a couple who look vaguely familiar.

"That's my mother, with the Roosevelts," Whitney says from behind me. Then he points to another photo of her, wearing an evening gown with elaborate jewels, and a different fur coat draped over her shoulder. "This is her, at the April in Paris Ball. And this one here…" He and Vogel move down the sideboard, looking at the collection of family photographs.

I can't be bothered to even pretend interest in Whitney's photos of his rich family being fabulous, so I go over to the large window facing the lake. From here, high up on the dune I can see right down to the sandy beach. It's empty, which is surprising for such a beautiful sunny day then I remember the beach along here is private, for the personal use of the cottage owners.

When I was a teenager my friends and I would sneak onto these private beaches when we knew the owners were away. It wasn't hard to figure out who was in residence but if we ever got caught we'd just pack up and head over to Nickel Beach with the rest of the unwashed.

We'd drive out there in our parents' cars, pop the trunk and set up speakers so we could play music and we'd lie in the sun, slathered in Bain de Soleil suntan oil. This was back in the day when a tan was a good thing to have, the darker the better. Not that I could ever achieve more than the faintest hint of bronze, and only then after I'd burned and peeled a few times. I don't want to even think about the sun damage I'd done to my fair freckled skin, much less the increased risk of melanoma I have to look forward to.

"Are you married Mr. Whitney?" I blurt, interrupting his lecture about his family history. "Oh, no. I forgot. You said you were separated."

I'm not subtle, I admit that and I'm also a bad actor but it doesn't really matter. I got what I wanted when I see the look on Whitney's face. His eyes narrow and his nostrils flare in anger.

"Your ex-wife is Margaret Lawrence, is that correct?" Whitney nods. "The woman who's been in the news lately, resigning over some nude photos that went out over the internet?"

Whitney shrugs with exaggerated indifference. "Serves her right," he mutters.

"You wouldn't know anything about that, would you? Sir?" I

need to be careful. I want to poke him but not piss him off so much that he tosses us out and stops cooperating. I know Whitney's nice guy act is only superficial. It's clear that if you scraped Whitney his veneer would come right off, exposing the beast underneath.

Whitney doesn't bite. "Our divorce has been… difficult," he says. "On me and on our children. And those… photos… have not helped matters."

"Is there a custody issue?"

"Hardly. Our children are teenagers now. Custody is shared. Anyway, why are you asking?"

"It must be difficult to look after a place like this," I say, not really answering his question. "Living alone. Especially if you travel so much… for your work."

Whitney nods. "I have help, naturally."

"Local people? They come in and clean for you?"

"Yes. And look after the garden. Make sure the place is safe during the off-season as well. I've been lucky so far," he says. "No break ins."

"You know," I say. "I'm looking for someone to clean at my place. Maybe you can give me a name? Assuming you're happy with yours of course."

"Pam Visser," he says and I have to look away so he doesn't catch my grin. "I'm very happy with her. Or I was…"

"Was? She's no longer satisfactory?"

"She just quit. Left town," he says with a frown. "I've got to find a new cleaner myself."

There's an awkward pause and Whitney looks from Vogel to me, expectantly.

"So…" he prompts us. "What is the reason for your visit today, Detectives? I can't imagine you've finally made some progress on the theft of my car."

I don't know what to say. Beyond deciding to come on this

fishing expedition to Whitney's I haven't prepared a plausible excuse for our visit. Luckily Vogel still has his wits about him.

"We'd like your permission to have our forensic team look over your vehicle," he says. Whitney laughs in his face.

"Is that a joke? Now, months after it was reported?" I wonder if he's resisting because he's got something to hide.

Vogel shows more diplomacy than I could ever muster, but then he always does. "No, Sir. We're following a new line of inquiry." Whitney raises his eyebrows.

"Whatever. The keys are hanging by the door. Pick them up on your way out."

"Not sure why you started needling him about his wife," Vogel says once we're back in the car. "What did you think you were accomplishing?" His criticism makes me bristle.

"Hey," I try to laugh it off. "We got a two-fer. Now we know he's behind her blackmail…"

"We do?"

I try to ignore his tone, but he's irritating me. "*Please*, you saw his face. Who else benefitted from his ex-wife being humiliated?" Vogel shrugs. "And we've also got a clear connection to Joshua Logan, through Pam Visser." I glance at Vogel for confirmation he's heard what I said, but he's doing his best to ignore me.

"It also confirms one important thing," I continue as Vogel reverses out of the driveway and turns onto the Firelane. "Ron Whitney's an arrogant prick." Vogel doesn't bite. It's obvious I've pissed him off.

We drive for a while in silence. "You can't seriously think Ron Whitney is behind this," Vogel finally says. "He's a successful, wealthy businessman. What does he need to get involved with some lowlife like Logan for?"

Vogel's got a point. They didn't exactly move in the same social circles, but I instantly push back. "What, because he's rich he can't be a criminal? In my experience the more money the wealthy have they always want more." Vogel glares at me. It's our old argument, the one we'll never settle, flaring up again. I take a deep breath and try to stay calm.

"Maybe Whitney is the third party—the one who buys and sells the computer data Logan stole. Pam Visser could have been the go-between, they'd be at arm's length. That way Whitney wouldn't be directly *involved with some lowlife like Logan*." I glance at Vogel, who's keeping his eyes on the road. "Logan inserted the keyloggers into computers, in houses accessed by Pam Visser and Tracey Reid."

"So… you're suggesting Whitney might not even have known about the blackmail operation," Vogel finally says. "He's just buying and selling data and the rest was Logan's side game."

Clearly Vogel finds it more believable that Whitney would be the third party behind it all, but not that he'd get his hands dirty with blackmail.

"Except for the fact that his ex-wife was a target!"

We drive the rest of the way in silence. Once Vogel has parked in the station lot he turns to me.

"Our current thinking is that whoever killed Joshua Logan was a victim of blackmail, right?" I nod. I don't think I'm going to like where he's going with this. "Probably Logan tried to blackmail the wrong guy this time."

"Okay…"

"So why, if he was behind the data theft or blackmail, would Ron Whitney kill Logan? He needs him. It can't be that easy to find someone with Logan's skills and with ready access to people's computers. Killing Logan puts an end to the scheme."

"Maybe it was already played out?"

"I suppose that's possible. How many people could they extort in a small area like this?"

"Everyone has secrets. Some even worth killing to keep."

As soon as we're back at our desks Vogel's computer pings as an email arrives.

"From the financial team." I notice he's not smiling. "They've found out who's in the consortium."

"And?"

"It's made up of Niagara area developers, along with one from Toronto, like Arjun Devi told us."

"And that mysterious US shell corporation, the one that interests us the most?"

"Is led by Ron Whitney," he says. "But it doesn't prove anything." My head almost explodes. Is he kidding me?

"Of course it does," I laugh incredulously, staring at Vogel. "That's two blackmail scams he directly benefits from—against his wife and Arjun Devi."

"We have no evidence for either."

"What's wrong with you Vogel?! Whitney is linked to both cases!"

"Maybe, but we still need to have proof!" He leans back, rubbing his eyes in frustration and fatigue. It looks like he hasn't been sleeping much either lately. But that doesn't explain his stubborn refusal to look seriously at Whitney as a suspect. My heart is racing and I feel my face flush. I'm losing my temper with Vogel, but I take a deep breath and try to reason with him.

"Vogel, somehow Whitney arranged for the blackmail against Devi so his development could go forward." He may be stubborn, but I can be obstinate too, especially when I know I'm right. I can feel it in my bones.

"*Arranged for blackmail?* It's not like calling an Uber!" Vogel laughs at me. "There's no clear connection between Whitney and Logan. It's all circumstantial."

Sometimes Vogel has no imagination. He's not willing or able to think beyond what's right in front of him and he's always plodding along, conscribed by rules. It's frustrating trying to figure out answers while having to drag him along with me.

"C'mon Vogel, it's obvious and you know it." I know I sound sulky but I'm past caring. "I'm sure he's involved in the other murders too."

"That's just… nuts. Where did you get that idea?"

"Ron Whitney and his consortium benefit by having the Kerr Residence shut down," I try to say calmly, methodically. "Their original goal is to take over the property and develop it, right?" Vogel nods, warily. "And now that's increasingly likely that will happen, right?"

Vogel stares at me in disbelief. "Are you actually suggesting that Ron Whitney not only blackmailed his wife and Arjun Devi, but he's behind the murders in the first place? To get Kerr Residence shut down?"

"I'd say it's inevitable that it'll be closed now. Especially as things become public—like the lax way it was being run, or god forbid any of those trophy photos leak to the media. *Qui bono*, Vogel?"

Vogel leans back in his chair, shaking his head. "No way. I can't see Ron Whitney as our guy."

"Why not? I'm sure he's capable. And if not him, then maybe he hired someone to do it, if he's too rich to get his hands dirty?"

"C'mon Gauthier. Killing all those parolees? Posing their bodies and taking those trophy photos?"

"Why not? He wouldn't be the first rich guy to kill people, or to get off on it."

Vogel is just shaking his head, rejecting everything I say. It's infuriating.

"I can see him hiring someone to stir up public pressure, maybe pay for some protesters or ads. But… beyond that…"

Finally I snap. "Have you no imagination Vogel? Can't you see? Or are you only capable of seeing Whitney as the wealthy scion of a family who had dinner with the Roosevelts?"

"Cut the class warfare crap Gauthier," Vogel snaps back. "It's not Whitney. We need to take a closer look at Pam Visser."

"*Visser*? Why? Because she's a cleaner and not someone rich and powerful?

Vogel glares at me, then he erupts, slamming his hand down on his desk in anger. "Because—as you said yourself, she's the link between Whitney and Logan," he says, his voice getting louder. "And between Tracey Reid and Logan, and even between Margaret Lawrence and Logan. And because she's disappeared. And because she lied to us."

"There could be a good reason for that…"

Vogel tosses some papers at me. "The lease on her house in not even in her name. And that car of hers, the old Ford Escape? It's registered to someone else. Pam Visser's in the wind. It's like she didn't exist."

"She's a possible victim. She could very well be dead."

"Or she could be our killer." Vogel takes a deep breath and tries to calm down. "I don't think you are seeing this clearly," he says, first looking over his shoulder to see if anyone's listening. "You're not objective."

"What are you talking about?"

"I heard you tell Visser your mother was a cleaner," he says. "I never knew that."

"So?"

"So, maybe you're empathizing with Visser too much," he says. "Cleaner, single mom against the world… ."

"What the fuck are you on about Vogel? I wasn't raised in a single parent family…"

"I didn't know that," he mumbles, looking embarrassed. "But that's exactly what I'm talking about. I tell you all about my life, about my past," Vogel says. "About my school days, and my Dad and I going fishing, the boats on the canal, duck hunting, whatever. But you still keep me at arm's distance—even though you tell Visser, this person you've only just met. What? She's your friend? Your comrade in the class war?" I stare at Vogel, trying to process what he's saying, to understand where this is coming from.

"I'm your friend, Gauthier. We've worked together for years. But from you, I get nothing back. You're a closed book. You never let me in."

I don't even bother to reply or acknowledge I've heard him. It's all I can do to keep from crying so I keep my head bent behind my computer monitor so he can't see my face. After a few minutes I've calmed down. I gather my stuff and get ready to leave. Vogel looks up at me, expectantly.

"Well, *friend*," I give him a fake smile. "I've got to go."

"Seeing Maja?" Vogel's got his conciliatory voice on, trying to make nice with me, to smooth things over.

"Yes," I lie. "She's making a nice dinner."

I'm going home to an empty house. Maja's still visiting her parents and I'll be alone, again.

THIRTY FIVE

FUCKING VOGEL, THINKS he's so smart. It's after midnight and I'm still angry. My call with Maja was strained because there was a houseful of people at her parents, and if I was in a terrible mood before I called it was even worse when I hung up. I'm home alone, which I suppose I have to get used to, again. But I'm restless and can't stand the idea of a night home on my own. Too much dread and doom.

I'm not able to sleep and I think about opening a bottle of wine, but I know it'll go down too fast, which will just feed my anxiety and I'll end up feeling like crap in the morning. I can't find any distractions at home; there's nothing to watch on television, no books that hold my attention. I need to do some exercise, something physical to take my mind off things and to burn off some adrenaline and cortisol. So I put on my running gear and head off into the night.

It's partly this case that's triggering my anxiety. Visiting Kerr Residence, learning about my cousin and his son's existence hasn't been easy to deal with. But that's not the worst of it: Ever since the date of Maja's inevitable departure has been creeping nearer and nearer I've been feeling more out of control, more tense and yes, more angry, like Vogel said. I feel the pressure inside me building and I have to release it somehow—like a valve. So I exercise myself to exhaustion and I've had to use my emergency medication more times in the past week than I have in months. I know I should call my therapist and increase the frequency of my visits but I keep putting it off.

I haven't felt this way since before Maja moved in with me. This restlessness, this itch I can't scratch, this sense of dread, and the knowledge that what I'm really afraid of is myself.

I remember a time years ago, before I joined the police. I was young and working in a bar part time to earn money for school. It was hell for me, a timid and inhibited girl who'd spent most of my life hiding from my past—from what happened to my mother and from what I'd done.

One night a persistent guy kept hanging around, asking for my number, refusing to take no for an answer. When I was taking out the trash at the end of the night I found him waiting by the dumpster behind the club. He grabbed me and made it clear he wasn't taking no for an answer and was going to take what he wanted.

So I broke an empty bottle over his head and when he was down I hit him with another and another, then I put the boots to him. I kicked him and kicked him and as he lay there bleeding I went into another place. In that moment I became someone else. I became the one with the power, the one in charge. And he couldn't get away and I continued kicking, just like I'd seen Ray do to my mother. The rage I'd held in all those years, the anger that had become a part of me erupted and he paid the price, like my stepfather did.

The next day I came into work, terrified that it had been reported, that the police would show up any minute. I was afraid, and ashamed of what I'd done. But I was even more ashamed when I realized how much I'd enjoyed doing it.

When I was taking out the trash at the end of the night I made sure to bring a busboy with me, just in case. I saw the puddle of blood there, where I'd left him the night before. I was afraid he'd be back, this time with a weapon, or with friends. But he never showed up again. Now I doubt I'd even recognize him.

I'm always angry? Vogel has no fucking idea how angry I am. Or how much damage I can do.

I run down to Lakeshore road, past the yacht club and Sugarloaf Point, and I'm all the way out to Reebs Bay and Oakwood cemetery before I finally start to feel tired. But I keep going; I need to run until I'm way past tired, past thinking and past feeling. Then I can sleep.

So I double back, and head up Quarry Road, onto Killaley and back into town. When I arrive at the skate park, exhausted, sweating and gasping for breath, I realize this is where I was heading all along. I walk along the side of the canal, up to Bridge 19. I check my fitness watch: 12.7 Kilometers, but it feels like 20.

I walk up to a park bench and stretch out my hamstrings and quads, but my eye keeps being drawn to the bridge. Painted battleship grey it fades into the darkness but the outline of its curved steel structure and massive bulk of the counterweight is visible in the streetlights. The rollers flank either side of the roadway, open and dotted with huge metal studs. They look lethal… but are protected on the other side of the pedestrian walkway, behind a frost fence. Still… if you were walking on the bridge itself when it was being raised, you'd risk being crushed under the merciless grinding rollers.

I look down at the dark water… it's so quiet here, apart from the rustling of leaves on the maple trees in the park. There's nobody around at this time of night and it's not hard to know how the killer was able to dump the bodies without being seen. Twelve men, dumped like trash into the canal. And now we've got another man missing from Kerr Residence halfway house—Nick Melnyk.

I haven't wanted to think about my cousin's son. I suppose it's denial; I never wanted to know he existed and now he may not. I have to wonder—-is he dead too? If so, where's his body? Did the killer decide to dump it someplace else? Then my blood runs cold. What if he's already got a second dumping spot he's been using? What if there are more than the twelve bodies we've found?

My heart starts to race and I feel nauseated. I have to lean on the bridge trying to catch my breath and calm down. *It can't be possible.* I try to convince myself. There are only eight men missing from the halfway house. No more. The other four men are still unidentified, but we know they aren't from Kerr Residence. So, if we're working on the assumption that he's targeting parolees, there can't be any more. Except for Nick Melnyk.

I console myself with the hope that maybe he hasn't been abducted, that maybe he just ran away because he's afraid. But the clock is ticking. We need to find him, and the killer—before he's dead, if he isn't already. It may be that he's just not been disposed of yet.

Would the killer risk dropping another body in this same place? Using the same method? It seems unlikely after all this publicity, with so much police presence. But we know nothing about this man.

We don't know his motives, or what need he may feel for risk. Maybe the thrill of daring to do it again, in exactly the same way, is exactly what he's looking for?

He could do it. In fact, it would be easy. FSU and police have left the scene. The media and even the curious public have stopped nosing around. The bridge and canal are operational again and it's not like we've added security cameras or have surveillance on the location. Everything is just back to normal. It's as if nothing ever happened here. For all we know, the killer will keep dropping bodies here, in this same spot, until he's caught.

I step onto the pedestrian walkway and cross over to the other side of the canal, giving the rollers a wide berth and even though there's no danger to me I speed up to get across the bridge as quickly as possible. Then a siren sounds, the lights start to flash and the roadway barrier comes down. As I watch, the enormous concrete counterweight lowers and the bridge starts to swing upward, tilting until it's vertical.

A huge red freighter passes under the bridge, lights on in its wheelhouse. Usually shipping is done by eleven or so and the canal is closed to traffic, but on occasion there's a delay or malfunction downstream at one of the other locks or bridges and the canal operates until much later. Nothing stops on the canal until all ships are clear.

While I wait for the freighter to pass under the bridge and clear Lock 8, I notice the bridge tender house standing next to the canal. It's a heritage building, I remember Vogel saying. I really should try listening to him once in a while. What else did he say? Since all the canal bridges are now operated remotely, there's no need for anyone to be in the control tower and the tender house is unused. Its windows are boarded up with sheets of plywood and it's fenced off from the bridge and roadway. A prominent sign is posted on the fence:

No Trespassing under the Canada Marine Act.

This Area Under 24 Hour Video Surveillance.

Restricted Area.

Authorized Persons Only.

An impulse comes over me. I quickly look around, first checking the location of the CCTV cameras and lights, then I climb the fence, dropping down on the other side. I keep to the shadows and walk over to the bridge tender house.

There's a heavy chain and padlock on the door that hasn't been tampered with. I go around the building, checking all the windows on ground level. On the last one, the one facing the water, the sheet of plywood is loose. I'm able to pull on the bottom corner and open it enough that someone could easily slip inside, and given that the window faces the water and is invisible from the road or bridge, they'd never be noticed. I don't even hesitate.

Once I've squeezed past the plywood it's pitch black inside. I pull out my phone and use the flashlight app to look around. There's nothing here but a few old chairs, some boxes stacked in a corner and a dusty table. Then I see there are footprints in the dust and the hairs on the back of my neck stand up. Someone's been in here recently.

I crouch down to inspect the floor and see there are several sets of footprints, with different treads. Who knows if it's from the same person or different people, coming and going over the years since the tender house has been closed? I creep along, keeping my back to the wall and following the footprints that lead toward an open door.

I slip into the room. There's no one there and the only sound I can hear is my own breathing. I shine my light around the room and it lands on a heap of junk piled in the corner, under a tarp.

I lift the tarp, afraid of what I'll find underneath and breath a sigh of relief when all I find are bags of concrete mix, empty plastic pails and coils of rope. My heart pounds with excitement. Is this it—the place he prepared to dump the bodies? It's next to the canal, it's unused, and it's unlikely anyone would notice him here or what he was doing. He somehow got the victims in here, alive or dead, then got them back out, onto the bridge or into a boat, then dumped them?

No, that can't be right. It's too much work.

Not to mention that he'd have a hell of a time getting them in through the boarded up window—and out again. He might have lured them in, but how?

I start to back up out of the room, trying to minimize any trace evidence I'll leave behind. No point making FSU's job more difficult that it has to be.

Once I'm back outside, I take another look at the heavy welded steel chain and padlock securing the door. It occurs to me that this isn't necessarily the same one that was put in place when the control tower was shut down years ago. If someone used a pair of bolt cutters to remove the original chain and lock, then replaced it with a similar one he had the key to, he'd be free to come and go at will, using this door. No need to climb in and out through the window.

I'm standing in the shadows, thinking about how the killer might have been able to do it… when I see the plywood on the window push open. I squeeze back into the darkness. As I watch, a man slides out silently, then drops down onto the ground. He looks slim and young, and I can't see his face clearly in the darkness. So he'd been inside the entire time while I was looking around and he now knows we've discovered this place. He'll never be back. If I don't stop him now we might lose him for good.

I leap out of the shadows and grab hold of him, twisting his arm around his back, then identify myself and order him to stop. As I realize I don't have my police radio to call it in, nor my cuffs to restrain him, he struggles free and runs around the building. By the time I catch up with him he's scaling the fence and even though I'm tired I've got the advantage of the adrenaline flooding through me. I'm in lightweight running gear and he's wearing heavy work boots, so it's harder for him to climb the fence. I pull on his leg, trying to bring him down but he kicks free and flings himself over onto the metal grid of the bridge walkway. I'm right behind him as the siren sounds and the lights start to flash as the bridge is coming back down. The heavy counterweight is rising, the rollers grinding, as he turns to face me. He's got nowhere to go. He can't cross the canal until the bridge is all the way down and if he wants to run the other way he'll have to go through me—and that's not going to happen. I can tell he's young, barely an adult, with dark brown hair, but I can't see his face. He's clearly terrified of me.

"I'm a police officer," I shout, my hand out. "I'm not going to hurt you."

Why would he believe me? I just jumped him and twisted his arm behind his back.

He's in a panic. He looks behind him at the water, and above at the metal bridge slowly descending—too slowly, then he decides to go for it. He leaps onto the fence dividing the walkway from the metal roadway trying to get across before the roller crushes him. Before he makes the leap he looks directly at me and I get my first good look at his face.

I recognize him instantly. It's his eyes— his sad, haunted eyes. They're just like my mother's, just like those I saw in the photograph at his father's house. It's Nick Melnyk. He's already gone—over the fence and under the roller without a look back at me.

I hesitate for a second, terrified of the heavy studded roller but then I'm over the fence, chasing him again as he's running up the bridge span. It's now lowered to around forty-five degrees, so he's running uphill, hoping that by the time he gets to the end the bridge will be down. But he's at the top well before the bridge is level with the road. He pauses, calculating whether he can make the jump to the opposite side and whether he'll able to land without breaking his ankle.

I'm able to take advantage of that moment of hesitation to catch up with him and for a brief moment we're next to one another, thirty feet over the canal, twenty feet, fifteen feet, and just when I think he's not going to do it, that he's too frightened to make the leap, he goes for it, springing into gap, arms windmilling and legs kicking against the air. I'm after him in an instant. But I haven't given it enough thrust or I haven't got enough strength left in my legs and I'm falling, into the dark water of the canal.

By the time I've surfaced I know he's long gone, not that I can see anything but the gleaming dark water and the metal road above me. The bridge is now down and as I tread water a few cars drive over, the metal grid humming and rattling, as if nothing has happened.

THIRTY SIX

Sunday

"**Why am I** hearing about this now, hours later? For god's sake Gauthier! Do we really need another demonstration of you going it alone? Taking unnecessary risks? Why didn't you call me?"

"Stop making it a big deal," I say. "It was handled." I give him the side eye. "Not worth getting you out of bed."

Vogel glares at me. "I was home. Alone." I don't push. Is it already over? If so, it's quicker than Vogel's typical romantic timeline. This time it's only been a week or so.

After I ended up in the canal and the suspect had run off I had to swim several hundred yards before I was able to find a spot where I could climb out of the water by grabbing handholds on the concrete wall. I refused to allow myself to think about the dark water below me, or about what we'd found there just a few days ago, but once I was on dry ground I was overcome with revulsion so strong my legs gave out from under me. The disgusting thought of rotting corpses floating around me almost brought on a panic attack, and I didn't have any rescue medication with me. I did my rescue breathing and practiced every damn CBT exercise my therapist had taught me over the years until I was able to think clearly.

Luckily I was able to find my phone—I'd dropped it on the

walkway in the fight so it hadn't ended up in the canal with me. I called it in and within minutes a paramedic team from the fire station showed up—it's less than a kilometer away and they got there before the patrol cars. I wasn't injured, just wet and cold, but they gave me a warming blanket and distracted me until the police arrived. After I gave my statement, I got a ride home, where I took two showers, threw everything I was wearing into a garbage bag and tossed it outside.

The idea of being in that water, close to where the bodies were floating for months, haunted me for hours. I understand the water is always flowing, that it's been changed over many times over and there's literally no trace of the corpses, even on a molecular level, but I'm still disgusted. Filth and mess is one of my triggers, so my anxiety disorder went into overload and I was awake most of the night.

So here I am at the station, wired and exhausted operating on about three hour's sleep and all I can think is that this is how my life will be for the next six months while Maja's away. Not necessarily ending up in the canal every night, but being unable to sleep, definitely. And the consequences of that are never good.

Vogel has already called FSU to go to the bridge tender house to investigate. The building also needs to be properly secured.

"Vogel," I say after a minute. "I saw the guy, clearly." I take a deep breath. "I think it was Nick Melnyk." *My cousin's kid.*

"Are you kidding me?" Vogel leans forward and lowers his voice. "Are you sure?"

"I'm sure. I remember him from the photos at his father's house."

Vogel studies my face for a moment before he speaks "Melnyk. Is he our guy?"

"How can he be? He's only been at Kerr Residence for ten months. These murders have been going on for over two years."

I feel my face flush as my heart starts to pound. *It can't be*

Melnyk. It can't. If he's involved somehow, if he's investigated and they find the connection to me… It can't be him. I reach into my handbag and slip an Ativan under my tongue, praying I don't have a panic attack right here in the station.

"Headache," I mumble.

Vogel leans back in his chair, studying me. "What's going on Lucy? Are you protecting this kid? Because I've gotta say, if he's involved somehow… ."

"No," I interrupt, starting to backpedal. "He's not involved. I'm not even sure it was him. I may be wrong. It was just a feeling I had. Heat of the moment stuff, you know?" I'm talking fast, trying to convince Vogel I'm mistaken. The last thing I need him to do is go to Agu and tell him what I've said. "There's no way Melnyk could be our killer."

"Gauthier, we know there's something wrong with him. His own mother thinks he's a sociopath!"

"Maybe she's a bad mother."

"What's really going on here Lucy?" I flinch at Vogel's using my first name. "Why don't you want to look at him? What are you keeping from me?"

"Nothing. There's nothing."

Vogel gives me a look but doesn't say anything more. But I know he doesn't believe me. He turns to his computer and pretends to work, but I can feel his eyes on me.

I do the same, keeping my head bent behind my monitor and avoiding eye contact. No matter what Vogel says, or how logical it sounds, I can't believe Nick Melnyk's involved. I don't care what his mother said; I'm not even sure I believe her. He looks like my uncles. He has my mother's eyes. He's a blood relative. How am I supposed to accept that he's involved somehow in the killings at Kerr Residence?

Hours pass slowly at the station, especially on a Sunday afternoon, when fewer staff are on duty. Even though many of us are pulling overtime as we work to solve the canal murders, there's a deserted feeling. We're all in waiting mode, waiting for forensic results to come in on the stolen cars, waiting for word on Pam Visser's disappearance, waiting for something to happen. I hate it.

Since we've got no ideas on how to move forward on any of our lines of inquiry, we're moving into job creation mode: Looking for things to do, that preferably don't involve paperwork.

I can feel my anxiety growing the longer we have to wait around for results and there's nothing I can do about it. It's not as if I can go to the gym to have a workout so I end up pacing around the station, which gets on everyone else's nerves. I can feel the tension between me and Vogel mounting too, which doesn't help matters.

Finally DS Agu waves us in for an update. I've never been happier to see him and I practically run right over Vogel to get into the briefing room.

"First, we've had no information or sightings of Nick Melnyk." Agu points at the newest photo addition to the white board. "He could be in hiding somewhere nearby, or, we can't ignore the possibility he may be another victim." I see Vogel is glaring at me from across the room and I know exactly what he's thinking: Why haven't I told Agu yet about who the guy was on the bridge last night?

"Unfortunately," Agu continues. "There's nothing revelatory about what DS Gauthier found last night in the bridge tender house," Agu says once he's in front of the white board. "The construction materials, the concrete, the buckets and the rope are all generic and could have been purchased anywhere. They may or may not belong to the killer. They could even have been left by some construction crew at some point. And, in any case there's no forensic evidence on them that's useful. "

"When was a crew last in there?" Vogel asks.

Agu shrugs. "We're still waiting to hear back. We're making inquiries with the St. Lawrence Seaway Corp and with their construction/maintenance crew, but so far nothing.

"The bags of concrete aren't new, but they haven't hardened yet, which they will do if left for too long in the bags in a humid environment. So, that tells us it was purchased within last few months."

"But that's definitely long after the tender house was sealed up," I interrupt.

"Yes, but it's possible the bridge tender house is being used for legitimate storage. We can't conclude it's the killer." Agu senses my frustration and he looks at me to emphasize his point as he speaks. "I really don't see there's any likelihood the killer used the bridge tender house as his base of operations. It doesn't appear to be used recently."

"What about the guy DC Gauthier caught in there last night?" Vogel says and I tense. Why is he bringing this up? I thought I could trust him.

Agu looks exasperated. "There could have been any number of explanations. A homeless guy, looking for a place to sleep? An addict look for a place to shoot up? A vandal? I understand the timing is suggestive, but we just can't assume…"

"Sir… ?" Vogel raises his hand to interrupt and I know what he's about to say. "DC Gauthier thinks it might have been Nick Melnyk." I glare at Vogel and he looks away. *Bastard.*

"DC Gauthier?" Agu says. "Is this correct? And you haven't said anything?"

"I… I wasn't sure, Sir." I'm mumbling, frustrated and angry. "In the moment, it was dark. But…"

"But?"

"Yes, Sir. I think he looked familiar. He looked like the photos we saw of Melnyk at the family home."

Agu looks disappointed. "That's it? You *think* he looked like a photo?" He rolls his eyes. "That's not much to go on." Then he moves down the board and points at Pam Visser's photo and I exhale in relief.

"We still don't know where Pam Visser is—and nothing conclusive forensically was found on Logan's body or in his store."

"She could be anywhere, laying low," Vogel says. "Hell, she could even be at one of her client's homes if she knows they're away."

"And have we been able to find her client list?" Vogel and I shake our heads.

"We spoke to one of her clients yesterday," I say. "He told us she'd quit."

Agu nods. "It's important we track her down. She's connected to both Tracey Reid and Joshua Logan, and then she suddenly leaves town. She may be at risk, or she's hiding her involvement."

"She was a cleaner for Margaret Lawrence," Vogel says. "Which connects her to the blackmail. I'd say it's clear she's involved."

"Possibly," I mutter, but Agu still hears me.

"You don't agree DC Gauthier?" Agu's deep voice reverberates through the room. "Is there something you want to share with the rest of the class?"

"We only have Ron Whitney's word that she'd called and quit," I say, shooting a dirty look at Vogel. "Her involvement might just be circumstantial, because Logan was her tenant."

"Ron Whitney?" Agu interrupts. "What's he got to do with it?"

"Nothing," Vogel snaps.

I quickly fill Agu in on my suspicions about Whitney, from his involvement with the consortium and the development proposal at Kerr Residence to the blackmail of his wife and Arjun Devi. To my disappointment, Agu doesn't look convinced.

"What if he killed Visser?" I press. "And Tracey Reid and Joshua Logan?"

"Really?" Agu says. "You see him as a possible suspect?"

"Yes, Sir. I do." Agu looks to Vogel, who shakes his head.

"C'mon Gauthier!" Vogel loses it. He jumps to his feet and raises his voice in frustration. "Visser is obviously behind it. She packed up and disappeared right after Joshua Logan was killed."

"I think if both of my tenants were killed I might do the same thing. She may in hiding. Or dead." Vogel rolls his eyes.

"She probably isn't even disabled." Vogel slumps back into his chair and lowers his voice. "I bet that cane is a prop and she's just making some fake disability claim."

"That's quite the accusation," Agu smirks as a constable slips in and passes me some papers. "Any evidence of that?" Vogel shrugs, glancing at the documents.

"Anything?" Agu asks again. Vogel looks away.

"We executed those warrants for all the missing cars we've identified," I say. "The ones that correspond to the dates the parolees disappeared."

Agu nods. "Still working the theory that the killer steals vehicles in order to dispose of the bodies."

"Of the cars that we could still trace," I say.

"Not all of them?" Agu interrupts.

"One has been scrapped, two sold and the new owners aren't local. We could still test them, if needed, but it looks like we've got enough proof our theory is correct: The killer is using stolen cars to transport victims."

"There's blood evidence and concrete dust in all of the cars we had tested," I say. "That ties them definitively to the body disposal. And FSU has found the same set of fingerprints on all of the cars.

The only reason I can think of that the same prints would be in each car is if they are the killer's. Unfortunately, they aren't in our system."

"So one killer, using borrowed cars, but unknown to us," Agu sums up, looking impressed. "That's a good start." I duck my head to hide my proud smile. I can't help it—it's a knee-jerk response whenever he's pleased with what I've accomplished, probably what other people feel like when their father praises them. I don't have a father and Agu's not my Dad, but I can project as well as anyone.

"But, where does he actually mix the concrete?" Agu continues. "It's a messy job. You'd need a garage or a shed."

"A basement?" Vogel suggests.

"Maybe… but it would be a pain to drag a body up and down again. Let alone a bucket of concrete—unnecessarily difficult and heavy. I think a garage or shed makes more sense." He's right.

"So what's our motive? Why is this guy killing these men?"

"He's got a hate on for the Kerr residents," Vogel says. "And the mental health clients."

THIRTY SEVEN

Monday

THE DAY I'VE been dreading for months is here and I don't have any idea how I'm supposed to manage it. Maja is leaving.

I'm trying not to cry, so I've been following her around the house as she does her last minute packing with a smile pasted on my face—one that I hope looks supportive and loving. Then I catch sight of myself in the hall mirror and realize I look like a ventriloquist's dummy, so I drop the act as assume my standard resting face: watchful and suspicious.

"Don't look like that," Maja says as she checks whether she's got her passport for the fifth time.

"Like what?"

"Sad. Please, don't be sad Lucy." She gives me a hug. "I love you. I'll be back and I'll be safe and I'll call you like we arranged." We have no idea what kind of internet service the refugee camp will have so any promises she's made to call or email might end up broken.

"I'm not sad," I lie. *I'm heartbroken. I'm terrified she won't make it back.* "I'm happy for you, that you're doing what you dreamed of."

"Liar," she laughs as she taxi pulls into the driveway. She didn't want me to drive her to the airport and part of me is relieved. It would just prolong the pain of goodbye.

I lift her backpack and carry it out for her while she brings her carry-on. She turns before she climbs into the back of the car and pulls me into a deep hug as I cling on for dear life.

"Look after yourself," she whispers in my ear. "Don't do anything reckless. Stay safe and I'll be home to you soon."

Then the car backs out of the driveway and she's gone.

It takes me an hour to pull myself together enough that I'm presentable, then I head into the station. Of course Vogel's already there and there's a coffee sitting on my desk.

"You'll need to microwave it," he says. "It's gone cold." I'm grateful he doesn't mention why I'm late; he knows what today is. Much better to just carry on as if nothing is any different.

"We've got a report back on Pam Visser," he says. "Some background."

"Anything interesting? Different from what she told us?"

"Well, she's a widow, that's true. But her husband wasn't a trucker or a farmer. He was a thief who died in prison last year."

"What killed him? Another prisoner?"

"Hepatitis." I can tell Vogel is trying not to say I told you so. "She does have two kids though—that wasn't a lie. They just don't live with her."

"So, she's still technically a single parent. Where are the kids?"

"With the grandparents, in Fort Erie."

"So, she's scamming child benefit too?" I laugh out loud, a desperate hysterical sound that makes Vogel's eyes widen in alarm. It's not funny. Nothing is funny, especially today.

What a piece of work Visser is. No wonder she was so defensive about her tax filings, making a point about how she isn't paid in cash on her cleaning jobs. She was very careful to keep up her public face, when all the while she was a criminal. I know I need to apologize to Vogel, to admit he was right and I was wrong. But I just can't find my voice.

"Want to guess what her husband went in for?" I throw up my hands. "Debit card fraud," Vogel grins, then starts to read from the file. "He and two other criminal geniuses were caught at the casino. There were reports of suspicious activity at several automated tellers machines inside the casino. Over a two-hour period they visited all the ATMs, withdrew tens of thousands of dollars in cash from compromised bank accounts, using fake debit cards. They were arrested with dozens of fake cards on them, as well as the owners' names, client numbers and PIN numbers."

"Pretty stupid to do it at the casino," I say. "There's all kinds of security, hundreds of cameras, security guards on site, and casino staff trained in surveillance."

"Like I said, criminal geniuses."

"So… this definitely changes things," I manage to say. "Looks like Pam Visser knew how to use stolen bank data and possibly once shared it with her husband. She's not a victim here. She could be on the run because she's afraid—two people are dead."

"Do you think she could she be the third party—the one behind it all?"

"It's possible," I say, but it doesn't feel likely. Not that I can trust my feelings. Clearly my intuition about Visser was completely wrong. "Or, maybe she's working for them."

I feel like kicking myself for my gullibility. I'd liked Pam Visser and she'd certainly fooled me. I projected my past onto her: daughter of a cleaning woman, working class poor. I've been played and it's pissing me off. And now what we've learned about her husband's criminal life there are even more points of intersection.

When I went away to University I got a job at a bar to help pay my expenses. Even though I was on an academic scholarship, it didn't cover all my costs—and my parents didn't have any money.

Two of the other girls at the bar were working a scam with some guys they knew. They both carried a small skimmer in their pocket that they'd use to scan credit cards. Between them they probably did around fifty cards a night, and they got paid for every card they'd scanned. I thought their deal looked pretty sweet, but they never asked me to come in on it.

I now realize I must have had a good angel sitting on my shoulder, protecting me from my own greed and stupidity. I'd probably have ended up in jail with them when they were arrested a few months later. But by then I'd been fired before I could join them, when the management found out I was underage. I guess it just proves you can take the girl out of the East Village, but you can't take the East Village out of the girl.

THIRTY EIGHT

I NEED TO get out for some fresh air. Putting a smile on my face and focussing on my work is really tough. All I can think about is Maja. *Where is she now? In check-in? Has she boarded the flight? Is she in the air yet?* I can't stop checking the time until I know the plane is in the air and I'm sure her phone is turned off. I'm not just worrying about her, I'm waiting, hoping that I'll get a text telling me she's changed her mind. Or at least that she loves me. I get neither.

I make an excuse and head out to my car then drive aimlessly up the highway as fast as I dare. When I get as far as Welland I turn around and head south until I see a sign for the GMC Cadillac dealership. That gives me an idea so I pull off the highway and head along Killaley. I want to ask about Ron Whitney's cars—and this seems like the closet dealer to town.

I remember that one of these dealerships once belonged Warren Kerr, possibly even this one. I park out by the service bays, and avoiding reception and the sales desk, I head straight into the service area hoping to meet someone who's worked there for a while.

I wait by the service desk for a few minutes for someone to notice me, and when no-one does, I lean across the counter and have a quick look around. There are customer service orders and parts orders in cubbies and assorted keys on hooks, all clearly labelled and easily accessible. Anyone could take a set and make a copy if they felt like it. When the service manager finally shows up I show her my ID and head back into the garage while she takes a phone call.

A mechanic in blue overalls is shaking his head as he peers at a diagnostic readout. His nametag reads Bill. Behind him is a shiny new Audi with its hood open.

"Expensive?" I say, looking over his shoulder.

He laughs. "You better believe it. With this many trouble codes he's not getting out of here for less than five thousand. But for some people, that's pocket change."

"Pretty sure that's what I paid for my car. I can't imagine a repair bill that high," I say as I show him my ID. "I wonder if you can give me a few minutes?

"Happy to take a break," he smiles. "I'm guessing it's not about a car repair."

"Sorry. Have you worked here long?"

"Sure," Bill says. "I've worked here for over ten years."

"Do you service Ron Whitney's cars here?" The change in Bill's manner is palpable. He recoils and his eyes narrow.

"Why? What's he saying about me?"

"Nothing that I'm aware of. Have you heard he's been saying things?"

"No." He's quick to deny it. I give him a skeptical look and wait. "Fine," he grumbles after a moment. "Whitney made some complaints about the service. And about us using his cars when he's away. Idiot."

"He accused you of borrowing his cars?"

Bill rolls his eyes. "The guy's a fool. I service better cars than his every week. If I wanted to joyride I'd go out in that." He points across the service bay to a Ferrari up on a hoist. "A five year old Escalade? Please."

"He told us it was new." I'm sure that's what Whitney said. Why would he lie about it? Bill just laughs and throws up his hands.

"What about Warren Kerr? Did you know him?"

Bill laughs. "Old Warren? What's he done?"

"I'm just following up on an inquiry."

"Sure I know him. He's always coming around, ever since he sold the shop. Can't stay away, I guess."

It's clear from Bill's body language that he doesn't like Warren Kerr, even though he's trying not to say anything. Honestly, I'm relieved to have my opinion seconded—Vogel obviously likes Kerr so I've started to believe it's me. I little validation never hurts.

"So Warren Kerr's a pain in the neck?"

Bill shrugs and I can tell he's choosing his words carefully. "Well, he's got an opinion of how things should be run." He still can't help rolling his eyes.

I decide to go all in and see if Bill opens up. "I get it. He acts like he's mayor of the marina, running things, into everyone's business." But Bill doesn't bite, he just smiles and shakes his head. He's not going to share anything more.

"He visit you often?"

"Not me, specifically. I think he's just checking up on the place. Or he's bored. He spent a long time here, owned it for years. It's kind of sad, to be honest. The way he hangs around, talking to whoever will give him the time, drinking the complimentary coffee."

Bill lowers his voice, in case anyone's listening. "I think part of the sale was his help in *transitioning* the business. I doubt the new owner needs or wants his help but he feels sorry for him so he doesn't say anything." Sounds like Warren Kerr is a pest, exactly the same way he's been hanging around the station, asking questions and getting in the way. He's a retired guy just trying to fill his day.

"How long did he own this dealership?"

"Twenty years, maybe? He was a mechanic before that, forever. Worked here for a long time before he bought the dealership—his whole life, really."

"I guess retirement is difficult to adjust to."

"You must be kidding," Bill says. "I can't wait to have that problem."

THIRTY NINE

"So? Kerr was a mechanic for years," Vogel says as we walk out to the car. "He's bored, with nothing to do except fish and talk about cars."

"If anyone knows how to hot wire a car it'd be him. But he wouldn't even have to," I persist. "If he spends all this time hanging around the dealership, it would be easy for him to steal the keys and have a spare set made, for when he thought he might want to *borrow* a car. And he knows all the customers, since he's sold them their cars or worked on them for years. He'd know where they live, where they go on vacation, and possibly even when."

"Ok Gauthier," Vogel sighs. I can tell I'm wearing him down. "There's a logic to what you're saying, but I really can't see Warren Kerr being our guy… seriously?"

"Cadillacs all have nice deep trunks… perfect for bodies…"

"Maybe there is something fishy about him," Vogel can't help but laugh. "The way he's always hanging around the marina and the station, trying to find out what's going on. But seriously, Kerr's an old man… "

"A strong old man…"

"Who lives in a condo apartment. Where would he mix the concrete? Or hide the bodies? It just doesn't fit."

I can't argue with that.

"There is something *fishy* about him… ." Vogel winks. "He told us he didn't have a car…"

"But he does have a boat…" I interrupt. "He wouldn't need a car if he's borrowing them."

"Anyway Kerr said he never takes the parolees out on his boat to fish. They always fish from the dock."

"He *said* that, yes. But lots of people lie, Vogel."

"If he took them out onto his boat, and dealt with them there, there'd be a lot of forensic evidence on his boat—blood, DNA and concrete."

"Our killer's too smart to not think of that. If he borrowed cars then maybe he borrowed boats too." I have to admit Vogel's got a point.

"We haven't checked into Kerr's property records. We just took his word for it when he said he'd downsized and moved into a condo."

"You think he's lying?"

"One way to find out."

The property search quickly turns up a condominium apartment on Sugarloaf, registered to Warren Kerr, as well as an address on Canal Bank road. It's a detached house near the canal and the bridge.

"Believe me now?"

"It could be an income property," Vogel says. "Maybe he rents it out?"

"True. Let's go check it out."

We drive up to Main street and across the feeder canal, then down Canal Bank Road past Kerr's house. It looks deserted. The curtains are drawn and the grass in front is dry and needs to be cut. There's a long gravel driveway leading up to a wooden garage at the back of the property, which is heavily planted with overgrown shrubs and trees.

"It's private. Not overlooked."

"He could easily mix the concrete there and hide the victims. Nobody would see a thing."

"And then use one of the borrowed cars to get the bodies down to his boat when he's ready to dump them. Tidy, no mess on his boat if he uses a tarp. And nothing to connect him to the car he borrowed."

"Think we've got enough to get a warrant?"

"No. It's all speculation. All we've got is a nosy old man who volunteers for the halfway house, who once owned a car dealership and who happens to have a boat. And a house in town."

"He has the means, and the opportunity, but what's the motive?"

"He's a Kerr. The Kerr Residence halfway house was once his family home. He protested against it, now maybe he's trying to get it closed down, in his own special way."

"He's killing parolees because he wants the facility to close?"

"Maybe he's obsessed with family, with his history? Maybe he thinks these parolees are somehow a stain on his heritage, on his family pride."

"Just like Whitney you mean?" Vogel sighs. "Lay off that Gauthier. Whitney is not our guy. He has no motive."

"Neither does Kerr. All we've got on him is he's got a boat, and a house, and some strange family history or relationship with his mother…"

"What are you talking about? What relationship with his mother?"

"Whatever the reason was for him not to have inherited the Kerr Residence. It's his family home. I guess I forgot to mention it…" I remember with shame my temper tantrum the day Doreen shared that information with me.

Vogel considers for a moment, unoffended. "Interesting. So why didn't his mother leave him the house when she died?"

"She was a nasty old bird?" I shrug. "She didn't like him?"

"If that's true it says a lot. It takes a lot for a mother to cut him out of his inheritance, or to dislike him that much. Especially with these old families."

Vogel's right. I think of Nick Melnyk and his mother. What did it take for her to tell us her son is a sociopath? Was it true, or was it malice?

"I heard she was demented in her last few years," I say. "Maybe she embarrassed her son, caused some scenes and it caused a rift. Everyone used to call her Queenie because she wore her fur coat to the grocery store. And her jewels... ."

I stop mid-sentence as an idea is scratching around in my head, but Vogel keeps talking. He doesn't seem to notice I'm not longer listening.

"Vogel," I interrupt him. "Remember the trophy photos? The creepy way the victims were posed—in fur coats and jewels?"

"I wish I could forget."

"Whitney had photos of his mother all over the place, in fur coats, tiaras and jewels."

Vogel's eyes widen. "Well, okay, but... that's a reach isn't it?"

"Isn't it kind of odd how Ron Whitney was going on about his family history and his mother and all the illustrious people she hung out with in the US?"

"You think Whitney is our guy because he has some obsession with the past?"

"Maybe just with his mother." I start thinking out loud. "And Ron Whitney also has a big secluded house and garage that he could use. And he's younger and fitter than Warren Kerr. He'd have an easier time of the physical aspects of these crimes."

"And he's got a boat." Vogel adds, considering.

"He was strangely specific about the details of his cars supposedly being borrowed? It was as if he was setting up an alibi, in case he needed one."

Vogel nods and I think I'm convincing him. "Ron Whitney also wanted the halfway house to close, so his consortium could develop the land. He's got the same motive as Warren Kerr."

I can see Vogel's resistance drop. "And Whitney has a connection to Visser," he says. "And his ex-wife was the first blackmail victim…"

"… which clearly connects him to Joshua Logan and Tracey Reid—and the blackmail scam. Kerr doesn't have any connection…"

"As far as we know. We haven't got through the computer store's sales and service records yet." True. The search might still turn up something.

Vogel does a U-turn and heads out toward Lorraine Bay. "I think we need to have another chat with Ron Whitney."

FORTY

WHEN WE ARRIVE at Whitney's place on the Firelane in Lorraine, Vogel suggests I stay in the car and goes in to speak to him on his own. He hasn't forgotten how I'd done my best to get under Whitney's skin on our last visit. I have to admit that might not be helpful, and since I'm not really interested in another one of Whitney's trips down memory lane, it suits me fine.

The Firelane is quiet, apart from birdsong from the tall oaks and maples that shade the car from the hot sun. The properties around here have mostly been left to nature and they're thick with ferns and bracken. Most of the homes have been handed down through generations of family and that has helped preserve the natural ecology. But it appears that only goes so far. Up the lane I can see a few lots that have been levelled and laid to lawn, which just makes them look and feel out of place.

Whitney's house sits high up on the dune, overlooking the water. It's sheltered by mature trees that screen it from the road, protecting his privacy. Unless I make an effort to peer through the foliage I can barely see the house from where we've parked. A path snakes up the hill to a stone patio by the door. Vehicles are left here at the bottom, next to Whitney's garage and coach house, which I guess must be a pain on grocery day. Then I realize he probably has them delivered.

After a few minutes I get restless, so I climb out of the car and peek into the garage window. I'm expecting to see his Cadillac and whatever other expensive car Whitney might drive, but to my surprise there's also a Ford Escape sitting next to it. A Ford Escape just like the one Pam Visser drove off in when Vogel and I last saw her.

My heart starts racing and I take a photo before heading back to the car. I'm tempted to text it to Vogel, to alert him to the fact that Visser might be there. But then I think better of it and start up the hill on foot, trying to remain out of view. What is Visser's vehicle doing here?

Halfway up the hill I meet Vogel, who's on the way back down.

"Is everything okay? What's going on?"

Vogel shakes his head and keeps walking so I have no choice but to follow him back down the hill.

"Something's going on," he says once we're inside with the doors closed. "Whitney was tense, acting very strangely. Not his usual blowhard self."

I show him the picture on my phone. "Visser's car is in his garage. No why do you suppose that is?"

"Maybe he's hiding her?"

"Or holding her prisoner." Vogel gives me the side eye, but I am legitimately worried about Visser, even though I know she lied to us.

"Either way, if she's in there with him now, we need to find out why." Vogel's brow is furrowed. "He couldn't get me out of there fast enough."

"Looks like he's hiding something," I say, pulling out my phone. "Move the car down the lane, out of sight. I'll call for back up." But Vogel isn't listening.

He's already scoping out the dune, looking for access points. It's not like him to be so quick off the mark and I wonder if he's trying to prove something.

"Slow down Vogel," I say, keeping my voice down. "What's the rush?"

He just rolls his eyes. "Says the queen of going it alone, rushing into situations blind."

We split up and head back toward Whitney's house. Vogel heads down to the beach and is going to come up the back of the dune, while I skirt along the road and start to climb up the wooded hill facing the Firelane. It's so quiet here, apart from birdsong and the gentle sound of the waves breaking on the shore I'm careful where I place my feet, making sure I don't step on any dry branches or make any noise that might alert them inside.

I make it to the wall of the house and start to creep toward a window, staying down in a crouch. I'm at the far end of the building, at the opposite end to where we'd met Whitney, so I'm guessing it's one of the bedrooms which I assume is empty, so I carefully stand and peer inside, looking for Visser or some clue to where she might be. The room is empty, so is the next one and the next. I strain to listen at the windows, but they're all closed and I can't hear anything. Finally I've made it back to the front door and I turn the corner, heading to the back of the house and the large windows overlooking the deck and the lake.

Across the deck, I see Vogel is already in position, hunched over at the top of the steps that lead down to the lake. He's tucked himself just to the side of the sliding glass doors, and it looks like he has a view inside, unlike me. He signals to me and I stay put, crouching out of sight behind the stone wall that surrounds the deck. I wait, listening hard for any sound from the house.

I can hear two people shouting inside. One of them is Whitney and he's loud enough that I can hear snatches of what's being said. *To hell with you! I'm not done—and neither are you until I say you are.* If he's arguing with Visser, it sure doesn't sound like she's being held against her will.

Suddenly they stop shouting and their voices are too quiet for me to hear. So I creep closer to the house, even though I out of the corner of my eye I see Vogel shaking his head, warning me off. I want to get a better look inside.

I can just see the back of Whitney's chair, next to a side table. He's holding a lit cigar and a glass of red wine is sitting on the table. Looks like he's pretty relaxed.

I hear Whitney's mocking voice. "What are you going to do about it?"

"I didn't kill them."

"Are you sure? I assumed you did."

I'm frustrated, unsure what to do. I wish Vogel and I could figure out a plan, but he's too far away. Then I feel my phone vibrate with a text. It's Vogel—at least one of us is thinking.

What's going on?

I realize Vogel can't hear or see anything in the room.

He's accusing her of killing Logan and Reid."

I'm texting Vogel as quickly as I can, trying to figure out our next steps when I hear twigs breaking in the undergrowth. I know without looking it's Vogel—he's impatient with texting and wants to see what's happening for himself. And he's not exactly being quiet.

I glance up and see both Visser and Whitney have stopped arguing and are turned toward the window. They've heard it too. I hold my breath and flatten against the wall, hoping they don't come over for a closer look.

"Me?! Funny rich guy," Visser says, turning away from the window.

I watch as Whitney puffs on his cigar and takes a sip of wine. "What do you want?" He's not afraid of her.

"I want money, to get away."

"Why should I give you money?"

I feel Vogel creep up next to me. He's so much taller than I am he's able to peer over my head and see for himself what's happening between Whitney and Visser.

"Oh I think you'll give me what I want," Visser says as she pulls out a gun.

Whitney looks distinctly unimpressed. He puffs on his cigar and stares Visser down.

"I'm not giving you a dime," Whitney says.

"What should we do?" Vogel whispers. "If we go in, she'll shoot him. Or even worse—shoot us." I kind of like the idea of Whitney being shot, but certainly don't want Visser to shoot me.

"Let's knock on the door," I whisper back.

"What?!"

"Yes. You—or me—go to the front door and knock… that'll draw him out."

"Why wouldn't they just ignore it?" Vogel's got a point, but I push on.

"… And when Whitney answers the door… the other one of us goes in the back and takes Visser by surprise."

"Seriously? If Whitney does come to the door when there's a lunatic with a gun in his living room, he'll just keep on walking… get in his car and drive away… to safety." Again, fair point.

"Not Whitney. He's not afraid of Visser, or of us." I can tell Vogel hates the idea, but he's not coming up with anything better.

"Who knocks?" He finally says. "Let's do rock paper scissors…" Lucky Vogel can't see my eyes roll.

"No, he likes you Vogel, you knock." Vogel shakes his head and slinks off through the ferns and undergrowth. In a few minutes I hear the doorbell ring. Both Whitney and Visser start in surprise, then ignore the bell, as predicted.

Vogel rings again. Then he knocks.

"Mr. Whitney?" I hear Vogel calling through the door. "I know you're home. Please come to the door. I have some more questions for you."

Then Whitney's cell phone rings—Vogel is calling. Whitney reaches over and mutes his phone.

"I'll share the information you have on Devi." Visser is sounding desperate, and desperate people do stupid things—not that Whitney seems to notice.

Whitney laughs. "That's nothing to do with me, and there's no evidence to tie me to any of it. Joshua Logan stole Devi's data and, and sadly, he can't say different because he's dead. You, however, are deeply implicated."

"You'll have to prove that," she'd doing her best to sound tough, but it's clear he's right. "I had nothing to do with any of it."

"He lived at your house! He did your bidding."

"Like I said. Prove it."

I watch as Visser and Whitney glare at each other. Visser holds the gun, still pointed at Whitney who continues to look unimpressed. I'm surprised Visser doesn't shoot him just to get that smug look off his face.

Vogel doesn't stop knocking until finally Whitney pushes himself out of his chair, and looking Visser dead in the eye he walks to the front door, as if daring her to shoot him. She doesn't.

I can hear the rumble of two male voices, but can't distinguish what's being said. Visser is pushed up against the wall, trying to remain out of sight.

While Visser is distracted I'm able to slip across the deck and in through the sliding doors without her noticing. I can hear Vogel and Whitney, their voices loud enough to mask the sound of me creeping across the room to get behind Visser.

I hear Whitney laugh out loud then the back of the door slams against the wall as Vogel pushes his way inside.

"You can't just barge in here!" Whitney shouts. Vogel ignores him and in those moments I see him stride into the living room as Visser steps out from the wall and raises her gun. I dive in, hoping to knock her over as I see Whitney push Vogel in front of him to use as a shield. Visser goes down, just a second too late as Vogel takes the bullet and falls to the ground.

FORTY ONE

"**VISSER'S IN JAIL,**" I say quietly so the patient in the next bed can't hear. "The Crown is still figuring out what exactly to charge her with."

"And Whitney?"

"You can guess," I shrug. "He's been bailed—by his very expensive lawyer. But I hope there will be some charges for the blackmail. I depends on what Devi and Lawrence say, and whether they are willing to testify." *And whether we can actually tie him in somehow* is what I don't say aloud.

"I guess this puts the consortium on ice, in any event."

We sit in silence for a while, so long I think Vogel might have fallen asleep.

I've spent most of the last day in hospital, sitting in the waiting room outside the surgical ward. Vogel was in surgery for a long time, so long I was afraid he wasn't going to make it. The bullet went through him in a perforating wound, which I'm told is much better than a penetrating one, where they'd have to go looking for it.

He'd taken the bullet in his glute, but it had knicked his hip and taken a turn, tumbling on its way through his torso. He'd had a CT scan to help find the bone fragments, then they'd repaired the secondary damage to his bowel and liver. They had to remove his spleen and took his appendix out while they were in the neighbourhood. He was lucky—if the angle of bullet was slightly different it could have hit his spine, or an artery, but… it didn't. He's going to be okay, and all things considered, this isn't that bad. He'll be back at work in a few months.

And I'm grateful for that. My eyes fill with tears and I have to take a deep breath. I wipe my eyes discreetly, so Vogel doesn't notice. Finally I can't stand the silence any longer.

"I didn't learn how to ride a bike until I was thirteen," I blurt.

Vogel stares at me, brow furrowed. "Did you hit your head Gauthier? Are you feeling all right?"

"We were poor. Really poor," I'm rushing to get the words out before I lose my nerve. "Couldn't afford a bike when I was a kid." Vogel is silent, watching me. "But when I was thirteen I moved in with a foster family. That's where I learned." I take a deep breath. Fuck this is awkward. I'm not sure how this is supposed to work.

"Why are you telling me this?"

"You said I never share anything about myself. About my past."

"Okay…" His brow is furrowed but he doesn't press for more. He doesn't ask me what happened to my family and I'm grateful. It's like he knows how difficult this is for me.

Then he bursts out laughing. "I had to get shot in the ass for this? For you to tell me about riding a fucking bike?" He winces in pain, but can't stop laughing.

I don't know what I'm supposed to say. *I tried?* I get up to leave but Vogel grabs my hand to stop me.

"Thanks Gauthier. It's a start."

"Could you please do me a favour?" he asks, pointing to the closet at the end of his bed. "Just pass me that plastic bag. The one with my personal effects." I do and he fishes out his keys and hands them to me.

"Please water my plants and move my car back home for me?

It's sitting at the station. And toss my milk and stuff out of the fridge. It looks like I'll be here for a while. Oh, and I need my phone charger too. I think that might be in my desk at the station though…"

I bet he needs his charger, though I'm not sure what the cell service is like in here. It might be a challenge for him. Knowing Vogel he'll want to keep texting the new woman, maybe invite her to see his war wounds. It's not every day a detective gets shot—even if it's in the ass. Though, given his track record I wonder if she'll even stick around, now that he'll be out of commission for a while.

The nurse technician comes in, pushing a cart stocked with vials and equipment, so I know it's my time to leave.

"Just need to take some blood," she says.

"I think I might have some left," Vogel attempts to flirt with her. I've got to hand it to him, he never stops trying.

"See you soon," I say on my way out. "Tomorrow I'll bring food. Text me what you want."

"Hey, Lucy," he calls after me. I stop. "Please promise me you'll chill out. Stop taking chances, stop going it alone… you know. The whole Gauthier thing."

"Well, since I now haven't got a partner, I don't see how I can avoid going it alone," I laugh as the door closes behind me.

I pick up Vogel's car, park it in the underground garage at his building, then water his plants and empty his fridge, as instructed. I look around for some other chore to keep busy, but Vogel's apartment is so tidy there's literally nothing else that needs doing. He's even made his bed, which I've got to say, I find endearing. I do the same, every day. That simple task calms my nerves and makes me feel like there's at least some small thing I can control.

I wander over to the window and look out at the view. He's

on the tenth floor, overlooking the lake, and I watch the boats out on the water and the jet skis race back and forth, one pulling a wakeboard.

I'm not sure where the investigation is going now. Thanks to Pam Visser's confession as she's angling for a plea deal, we've got the blackmail part figured out. It's pretty much what we'd already concluded: Joshua Logan found incriminating or embarrassing files on customers' hard drives, he inserted keyloggers, and extorted money from them. Both Visser and Reid got him access to the houses, and referred customers to him, including Ron Whitney. Whether Whitney was actually the *third party* behind the blackmail or not is an open question. Visser has certainly accused him, but without hard evidence it's her word against his. Whitney's not talking—thanks to his expensive lawyer, and I'm not confident we can get him on any charges.

It looks like whoever killed Logan and trashed the store is a potential blackmail victim, but Visser says she has no information. She admits to referring Margaret Lawrence to Joshua Logan for service, and to introducing Logan to Whitney in the first place—but she has no knowledge of whatever went on between them. It's plausible. She is *just a cleaner* after all. And since Whitney had the most to gain, my money's on him.

We've also come up empty about the deaths of Joshua Logan and Tracey Reid.

And, we aren't any closer to finding the Kerr Killer. Given the trophy photos discovered on the keylogger, it seems likely Logan tried to blackmail whoever murdered our parolees, and got killed for it. But there's nothing on the photos themselves that gives us a clue to who he is, or where the photos were taken.

I watch as the sun starts to dip toward the horizon, a ball of orange and pink, the horizon glowing red. But to the south, far across the lake, the horizon is dark and ominous. I know I need to get moving or risk getting caught in the rain.

It's only a couple of kilometres to my place from here and it's a nice walk along Sugarloaf Street. The wind is picking up, but the air is still warm and sweet with the aroma of early summer flowers. It's my favorite time of year and normally Maja and I would be planting our vegetable garden. But it didn't happen this year, since she was going away. I thought about doing it alone, and imagined how happy she'd be to have home grown food when she's home in six months. But what if I got too busy and forget to care for it? How bad would it be for her to come home and find a garden of dead plants?

On impulse I turn down the drive and head into Sugarloaf Marina, where I sit at one of the benches overlooking the water. Here in the sheltered harbour the water is still and a colony of gulls is roosting on the surface, heads tucked under their wings, oblivious to the coming storm. I realize why I've been lingering; Maja and I used to watch the sunset from here. Suddenly I'm overcome with a wave of sorrow, missing her so intensely I can hardly breathe. I don't want to go home to an empty house, to a house I know Maja isn't going to be returning to for months.

Out beyond the breakwall I call see waves are picking up, and the line of the southern horizon is black with storm clouds. Thunderstorms are predicted for this evening as a system is moving up from the south. I watch as dozens of boats are already heading back into harbour.

Lake Erie is shallow and it can go from calm water to ten-foot waves in a matter of minutes, so it's never a good idea to take a chance if a storm is coming in. I see the waves are already around three feet high and the rising wind is whipping up whitecaps across the lake.

I'm surprised to hear a boat engine start up and when I glance over, I see it's Warren Kerr's boat. It looks like he's heading out for a night of fishing. Why would he be heading out when everyone else is coming into shore? A storm is coming. I wonder if that's a good time to fish and make a note to ask Vogel next time I visit him in hospital.

The boat reverses out of the slip and I can see it's definitely Kerr at the wheel, wearing his old fishing hat. I think I see a silhouette in the back window; it looks like he's got someone else on the boat with him, which strikes me as odd.

I run across the parking lot to get a closer look as Kerr pilots his boat right past me on his way out of the marina, heading for the lake.

As it goes past I see for the first time the name painted on the back of his boat. *Queenie.* Queenie Kerr, his mad mother, wearing her fur and jewels as she walked down Main Street. My pulse quickens. Warren Kerr named his boat after his mother. His family home, his rightful inheritance, didn't go to him. It became Kerr Residence—a halfway house for parolees. Kerr fought against it, and now it might even be closed, thanks to the Kerr Killer murders.

As the boat leaves the marina and heads for the breakwater I see he's got another person with him, a young man who turns his head to watch me. He raises his hand and waves, and I see a familiar crooked smile. It's Jay.

FORTY TWO

I'M TOO SHOCKED to wave back. What's Jay doing on Kerr's boat? Kerr said he never took parolees out on the water. So why is he now? And where are they going?

I feel the weight of Vogel's keys in my pocket and without thinking I run toward his boat to follow them. For a moment I freeze. *What the hell am I thinking? I can't drive a boat!* But then I put the key in the ignition to start it and when the engine turns over I just do exactly what I've seen Vogel do. I put it into reverse and start to back it up but it doesn't go anywhere. Then I realize the boat is still tied off to the slip, so I cast off the rope and pull the throttle back. The boat responds immediately and I'm able to back it out of the slip and throw the throttle into forward.

Kerr isn't in any hurry; he's slowly moving through the marina, heading for the breakwall, and from there out into the lake. I know I've got to stop him but I don't even know what I'll say once I catch him. I have no reason to detain him, but I know without any doubt that Jay's in danger.

I push the throttle forward and keep my eye on the speedometer as the needle creeps up. Five knots, ten knots, approaching fifteen knots and I can feel the boat is slapping against the waves, but I don't dare slow down until I'm close to Kerr's boat. It looks as though he's stopped just past the breakwall. Maybe he really has just decided to do some fishing. Or maybe something more sinister is going on.

Kerr's still at the wheel, talking with another person—probably Jay. Then he turns and sees me. He must have heard my boat approaching. This is the moment. If there's nothing going on, he'll just wave and smile. But instead I see he shouts something and starts his engine. He's making a run for it. He pushes on his throttle and starts heading out past the breakwall, out into the lake. Whatever he's up to he doesn't want me to know about it.

I'm already going faster than he is so I'm able to steer Vogel's boat in front of Kerr, hoping to cut him off or at least slow him down. As I come around in front of him I hear a grinding crunch as Vogel's boat runs aground on the rocks around the breakwall. I don't have time to think about what Vogel's going to say. Anyway he never taught me how to stop.

I scramble out onto the rocks and run toward Kerr's boat. He's had to stop and reverse in order to back away from my wreck, so I've just got time to catch up with him and as I leap from the breakwall onto the rear deck of his boat I can see the absolute terror in his eyes.

"Stop!" I shout at him over the roar of the engine, but he ignores me and turns his wheel hard, trying to steer around Vogel's boat. "I said, Stop!" I shout in his ear and grab the wheel so he can't turn it. He hangs on and tries to shoulder me off until I reach for the key and turn off the ignition. The engine dies. The only sound is the rising wind and waves lapping against the boat. We're adrift. The water is getting rough and the wind is blowing my hair into my eyes. The storm is coming in fast and it's quickly growing dark.

Kerr just stares at me in silence and I realize there's nobody else on deck but the two of us.

"Where is Jay?" I ask. Kerr doesn't say anything, but I can see him tense up, his hands tight on the wheel. I turn away to look around again, confirming the bench seats and table behind us on the upper deck are empty. When I turn back to Kerr, he's holding a knife.

I back up carefully, keeping my eye on Kerr. He's an old man, but I'm sure he's very comfortable using that knife; it's probably the same one he was using to gut fish.

"What are you doing Mr. Kerr?" I say, holding up my hands, trying to placate him. "There's no need for that. I'm only here for Jay." Kerr's eyes narrow and he steps toward me.

"He's not here," he says.

"Jay!" I shout, into the lower deck. "Jay, are you all right?" There's no response.

Suddenly there's a crack of lighting and it starts to rain, fat drops that start pounding the hardtop of the boat and bouncing off the hull. Then the boat is swept into the breakwall by the waves and I hear the hull grind against the rocks. I lose my balance and stumble as Kerr lunges for me. I feel him push against my side, hard, as if I've been punched and I know he's stabbed me.

Then he runs down the steps to the lower deck and I hear a door slam. I look down and see blood soaking my t-shirt, seeping from the wound. I can't tell how deep it is, but I know I need to get help. But my phone is back in Vogel's boat and I don't want to leave Jay. The pain isn't too bad, probably due to adrenaline pumping through me, so I press my left hand hard against the wound to staunch the flow and run after Kerr, who has shut himself in the bathroom.

Jay is standing at the foot of the steps. His face goes white when he sees the blood and he has a strange light in his eyes, as if he's excited or almost ecstatic. I know instantly he's off his meds again. The boat bumps up against the breakwall again and we lurch to one side. Jay barely notices.

"Jay," I say grabbing for his hand. "We need to leave, now." He smiles at me serenely, and doesn't seem to understand what I'm saying. "You're in danger, Jay."

I shove him toward the steps. "Get off the boat! Now!"

Another crack of lightning hits the lighthouse, just a few feet away on the breakwall and the flash of light illuminates the entire cabin in a phosphorescent eerie glow. Jay laughs in delight. Then he looks down at my bloody hand clutching his arm, and his eye travels to my blood-covered shirt. His eyes roll up into his head and he passes out, his body lying halfway up the steps.

The door to the locked room opens and Kerr springs out, wildly waving his knife and I kick him hard in the balls. He's down, at least for the moment and I resist the urge to run. It's Gauthier Self Defense 101: If your opponent is down, make sure he stays down, otherwise you'll just have pissed him off. He'll just come after you, so make sure he's not able to.

While Kerr is swearing and moaning and clutching his scrotum I pick up a full beer bottle from the case on the table and hit him on the head, hard enough to knock him out. He slumps to the ground.

I'm safe for the moment, so I look around for a towel to press against my wound to stop the bleeding.

Great. Now I've got two unconscious men on a boat, adrift on the lake in a thunderstorm and a stab wound to the abdomen. I don't know how to use the boat's radio, but it can't be much different than a police radio, can it? Or maybe Kerr's got a cell phone somewhere around here. I'm not feeling strong enough to climb over to Vogel's boat and retrieve mine, so I decide to go for Kerr's.

I'm about to reach into Kerr's pocket to look for a cell phone when I see his eyelids flicker. He's waking up. I recoil and scramble to my feet when I'm hit from behind, so hard I see stars, but I don't black out. Instinctively I roll to my side, evading the second blow that I hear hit the deck. It's getting dark in the cabin and I can't see if Jay's still lying on the steps. I have no idea who I'm fighting now.

I scramble into the room Kerr was hiding in and lock the door behind me as whoever it is starts pounding against the other side, trying to break through. Who is it? It's not Kerr, he was lying on the floor, barely conscious. Is it Jay?

I'm unarmed and the door is just flimsy wood and fiberglass. I can see it's already giving way, splintering as he's kicking and punching it from the other side, trying to get in and finish me off. I know he'll be through it in minutes and I look around for anything I can use as a weapon. Then I see a white plastic bucket, some rope and a tub of quickset cement mix. This is the kill room. There's no question Jay is Kerr's next victim.

He's now broken through the door and I can see Kerr's fishing knife coming through the hole, helping him smash his way through. But it can't be Kerr. I saw him lying on the deck. So who is it?

I press my back tight against the wall, bracing myself for when he gets through. Then as he sticks his arm in through hole and reaches around to unlock the door I kick it, hard. I can hear the bone snap as his arm breaks and he screams in pain and rage. But it doesn't stop him. It only slows him down and he continues to smash the door down. He still has a knife, but now only has one good arm he can use to fight me, but I feel myself getting weaker and I don't know how long I can remain conscious.

I'm now bleeding heavily. I'm feeling detached, calm, as if I'm floating above the room. I see myself slumped against the wall and there's a pool of blood on the floor—and I understand it's my blood. Is this how it all ends? I feel no panic, no fear. How long do I have before I lose consciousness?

Then I resist. I fight to live… .to come back. I focus and grasp the last threads of my inner strength. I scrabble around, looking for something to use to defend myself. In the cabinet under the sink I find an old metal box, full of old hinges and screws, and a rusty screwdriver.

I grab it and slump to the floor, holding it in front of my chest, unable to stand any longer… I feel myself slipping away as the door gives way. He's inside now, coming for me and I still can't see who it is.

Then he slips on my blood. He falls right onto me, landing on his broken arm. He yells in pain and rolls off as I raise the screwdriver and stab him, turning away as the warm spray of his blood covers me. I pass out with him lying on top of me, washed in his blood, mixing with mine as I'm bleeding out. So this is how it ends. It feels right. It feels like what I deserve.

I feel someone shaking me, dragging me up to a sitting position.

"C'mon, get up," a voice says. "Get up." I recoil and try to get away, afraid he's going to finish me off. Then through my half-open eyes I can see it's Jay but I'm afraid to trust him. Maybe he wasn't Kerr's victim after all. Maybe he's the one who hit me from behind. Maybe he's the accomplice.

Jay starts half-dragging me, forcing me to walk up the stairs to the upper deck, and I'm too weak to fight him off.

"Can you swim?" The rain is lashing down as the wind whips away his words.

I don't answer and he gives my arm a shake. I'm confused. Why is he doing this? Does he plan to drown me? "Can you swim?" he demands again, then he pushes me overboard, into the black water.

The cold water shocks me alert and I surface, gasping for air. It's so dark if it weren't for the marina lights in the distance, barely visible through the pelting rain, I wouldn't even know which way was shore. I know the lighthouse is somewhere nearby, but I'm so weak I don't think I can make it. Then I hear a splash as Jay jumps into the lake near me. He grabs hold of my shirt and starts swimming toward the breakwall, towing me along.

I stop struggling and allow myself to trust him. Within a few minutes we're safely at the breakwall and he helps me climb up the rocks to the base of the lighthouse. I tell him to get my phone out of Vogel's boat and call for help. He sits next to me in the darkness and applies pressure to my wound as we watch Kerr's boat head out into the lake, its running lights disappearing in the distance.

FORTY THREE

Kerr's boat was found near the Central Basin of Lake Erie this morning, empty. Both the cement and the bucket are missing. So is the dinghy, but it may have been swept away in the storm. We're assuming Kerr is somewhere at the bottom of Lake Erie, but who knows where he went over.

FSU found a lot of blood in the lower cabin—mostly mine, but also some from a different blood group. I guess it's Kerr's, from when I stabbed him with the screwdriver, assuming it was Kerr. They'll be working the crime scene for a while, pulling trace evidence, fingerprints and whatever navigation data they can retrieve from the Marine GPS. Tracking where the boat has been might help locate his body.

I don't remember being rescued off the breakwall. It didn't take me long to lose consciousness once Jay had called for help. I woke up in hospital, where they'd given me a couple of pints of blood, something for the pain, and stitched up the gaping hole in my side. They insisted I remain here for a couple of days and I haven't argued. It's not like there's anyone to go home to.

I didn't tell Maja anything about what happened in our call this morning. She's been gone less than a week and this happens, so I'll just add it to the growing list of things I'm keeping from her. I did call Doreen though—and made her promise not to come to visit me. We'll catch up when I'm released and she comes to stay at my place for a while. She'll look after me and I can use the company.

Of course, the minute Vogel learned what had happened he had himself wheeled down the hall to my room.

"We should become roomies," he'd said when I woke up to find him next to my bed. I didn't think he was joking, so I had a quiet word with the nurse to make sure that couldn't happen. So now he's spent most of the day visiting me, apart from when we need our dressings changed. It's very comfortable; we watch tv together and complain about the food, just like an old married couple.

"We're like the Odd Couple," he laughs and I don't argue.

He's in my room when DS Agu arrives for a debrief. I'm surprised to see him carrying two coffees from The Green Bean, my favourite coffee shop. I'm touched he's even aware of it.

"How are you feeling DC Gauthier?" I can feel his deep, rumbling voice in my chest. Agu nods to Vogel, who rolls his wheelchair back to allow for Agu to pull up a chair. "I see you've got company to help you pass the time," he smiles at Vogel.

"I'm fine, Sir," I say, grabbing for the coffee. "I'll be out of here in a day or so."

"No rush," he says. "You'll both be on leave for six weeks at least."

"Whatever will you do with both of us off work?" I laugh. "Who's going to catch all the bad guys?"

"Ignore her, Sir," Vogel laughs. "It's the meds." Vogel may be right. Agu gives us both a look and we stop laughing.

"I thought I'd stop by and update you on the situation," Agu says. "We've searched Kerr's apartment. Found his computer. The trophy shots are on it, so we're sure he's our guy. Not that there's much doubt after what happened to you on his boat."

"What's his motive?"

Agu shrugs. "To get the Kerr Residence closed down."

"Ironic how he said it was dangerous to the community," I say, thinking of his photo in the paper protesting against it. "Given what he did."

"It looks like Joshua Logan was killed after he tried to blackmail Kerr. Probably the trophy shots were found after his computer was serviced at Logan's shop. Logan must have figured Kerr had lots of money, being from one of the founding families in the area." Something isn't sitting right with me…

"Sir? How do you explain the difference in the murders? Kerr killed the parolees in such a specific, controlled manner—but the way Logan's store was trashed. It feels like someone else did it. Someone who worked with Kerr."

"There's no evidence that anyone worked with Warren Kerr." Agu's tone makes it clear that is not open for discussion.

"We found several sets of car keys, not belonging to Kerr," Agu continues. "We're sure they'll fit some of the cars that were used to dump the bodies. Kudos to you DC Gauthier for your theory— Warren Kerr must have copied them when the vehicles were in for service at his dealership."

"I've also spoken with Jay Reynolds, the young man who you saved from Kerr."

"I'd say he's the one who saved me… ." A look from Agu silences my interruption.

"Unfortunately, he has no coherent explanation for the events on the boat. His mental health is not good, and he's now receiving psychiatric care. Perhaps when he's stabilized and on his medication he'll have more to tell us, but I'm not hopeful.

"All he said was that Warren Kerr was a nice old man, who used to take him fishing, and who offered to take him out on the boat. He had no idea he was in danger.

Agu smirks. "However, he did tell us in great detail about the angel who'd come to him on the boat, the angel with the halo and shining eyes. The angel who flew with him off the boat. Does that tally with your recollection of events, DC Gauthier?"

"Where was the boat?" Vogel asks, saving me from Agu's teasing.

"It was found adrift about forty kilometres offshore, south west of the canal."

"And Kerr's body? Are we going to search for it?"

Agu shakes his head. "It's a big lake, and I'm not sure we have the resources to mount a search. We're not even sure where to look, given the wind direction and the wave action during the storm. Since the boat wasn't at anchor, we can't be sure how far it drifted. It's probably miles from where Kerr went overboard."

"Lake Erie's pretty shallow, isn't it, Sir?" I don't know why, but it's important to me that Kerr's body is found. "Isn't there some sonar technology that can help?"

"There is," Agu nods. "But as I said, it's a big lake. In that area the depth drops off a lot, from around thirty feet to an average of sixty feet, and there are deep trenches, some over two hundred feet deep. If he ended up in one of those…"

"But, on the bright side," Agu changes the subject before I can object. "FSU found fingerprints all over the boat. Every one of the missing parolees, including Nick Melnyk."

My heart skips a beat.

"Our thinking is that Melnyk is probably dead," Agu continues. "His body could be anywhere—most likely at bottom of the lake. We'll have someone inform his parents later today." He gets up to leave.

"Sir?" I stop him on his way out. "It just doesn't add up. Then who hit me on the head, when I was on the boat? Someone else was there, I know it." Agu gives me a patronizing smile. "Gauthier, you probably aren't remembering correctly. Below deck was poorly lit, in the middle of a big storm. You'd been stabbed and were bleeding out. Maybe you just got confused…"

"Or maybe you bumped it yourself in the fight," Vogel chimes in. "Those boats don't have a lot of headroom. And you were in a fight, in the dark. Maybe you just hit the low ceiling…"

I shake my head, rejecting what they're saying. I may have a concussion and blood loss and my memory is a bit fuzzy, but I clearly remember someone hitting me from behind when I was looking for Kerr's cell phone. I wasn't standing at the time, I was crouching over him, on the floor. And it wasn't Jay, I can clearly recall seeing him lying on the steps before Kerr attacked me. He was in front of me, not behind, so it couldn't have been him. Someone else was on the boat. But who?

"But, Sir," I push back. "Someone piloted that boat out into the lake. It wasn't drifting! Someone was driving it. What if it was the person who hit me?"

"Ok," Agu is getting impatient. "So maybe it was Kerr. He woke up after you'd left, got up, took the wheel and piloted the boat out into the storm."

"Then he killed himself?"

"Sure, why not?" He shrugs, dismissing my concerns.

Everything in me resists those explanations, but I don't have the strength to argue. I drop my head back onto the pillow, frustrated and exhausted. I catch Vogel and Agu studying me.

"Not convinced?"

"Someone else drove the boat out," I say obstinately. "And someone else dumped Kerr into the lake. And that someone else then left the boat using Kerr's dinghy. We need to look for that… it'll be scuppered somewhere in shallow water nearby."

"And who's that someone else?"

"Nick Melnyk. It would explain his prints on the boat."

"*Melnyk!?*" They exchange a look that clearly says they think I've lost it.

"Melnyk is clever enough to have hidden when I first came aboard, probably in the kill room. Maybe he's even been living on the boat the entire time since he left the halfway house. Or at Kerr's house on Canal Bank Road."

"So, you think he killed Kerr because he figured out what was going on—that he was the next victim?"

"No. Jay was the next victim. Melnyk is the accomplice."

Agu and Vogel both stare at me in disbelief.

"It makes complete sense. He charmed these guys, made friends with them, got them onto Kerr's boat, made them feel comfortable—more than just some old retired guy would have managed. Let's face it—how many convicted criminals would want to spend their time fishing with some old guy—-unless one of their peers convinced them and went along with it? Melnyk is a sociopath—his own mother said so."

"That's not a lot to go on Gauthier," Agu says. "It makes more sense that he's a victim."

"Sir, I know how we can prove it," I say. "FSU needs to do a blood trace analysis of the scene. Is there a blood trail leading back up to the top deck and the captain's chair? I stabbed someone with that screwdriver and I don't think it was Kerr. Someone else is involved and I'm sure it's Melnyk." Agu nods in reluctant agreement—he and Vogel leave together.

I know in my gut, in every fibre of my being, that Nick Melnyk is involved. But I can't tell them how I know it. It's because he shares my blood—and that, as far as I'm concerned, proves he's guilty. Because I know what I'm capable of.

FORTY FOUR

DOREEN AND I sit in with our coffees, parked down the street from Melnyk's house.

"I've never been on a stakeout before," Doreen chuckles. "What happens if I need to go pee?"

"You hold it. And this isn't a stakeout. We're just… observing."

Doreen laughs then takes a bite of her cinnamon bun. "You're sure it was him?" she finally asks.

I nod. "I'm as sure as I can be. It's him."

"Do you think he'd be stupid enough to come here? To his family home when everyone thinks he's dead?" Melnyk is presumed dead, one of the Kerr Killer's victims. Despite there being no body, the rest of the facts of his disappearance from the residence fit the pattern. But I know he's alive.

"Melynk worked with Kerr, I'm sure of it."

"And now the apprentice becomes the master?" Doreen shakes her head.

"He's going to keep killing. Maybe not here, not right away, but he'll be back. Melnyk is the bad seed. Like my uncles, and maybe like me."

"What are you going to do about it?"

"Nothing I can do at the moment. I can keep watch."

"A vigil?"

"Yeah, exactly. That's what vigilantes do, isn't it?" Then we take the law into our own hands.

ABOUT THE AUTHOR

Liza Drozdov is the author of the Niagara Noir series, including Blood Relative, Dark Water, The One That Got Away, A Life Spent Looking and In the Weeds. She worked as a bookseller and book publicist, as a garden designer and a college professor, and as a producer of lifestyle television, before settling down to writing full-time. She lives in Oakville, Ontario.

www.lizadrozdov.com